THE TIN BOAT

A Novel

Written and Illustrated

by

James Denison-Pender

Author's Note

This is a work of fiction, but Lake Baringo where it is set is a unique and very specific location, so that place names, apart from the name of the Camp, have not been altered. My sons, Jamie and Nicholas, have allowed me to use their names for the characters which are partly based on them. The names of all the other wazungu characters are my own invention. I have given those who may recognise themselves as models for these characters the chance to read the novel before publication. However they are intended as fictional characters. The character of Sion is also my fiction. He has the characteristics of of several Njemps boys, although I have used the name of one of them. Lemeriai and his family are totally fictitious, though I have borrowed the name. The other African characters associated with the camp are closely modelled on real people, and I have retained many of their names. All the military characters and their actions around Baringo are totally fictitious. The least fictional part of the book is the description of the Njemps wedding, which I have set down as accurately as I can remember it in case it's a way of life which doesn't survive Kenya's progress into the modern world.

Historical Note

There was a coup attempt against the Kenyan President in 1982. Most of the fighting was around Nanyuki and Nairobi, where there were some fatalities which included a foreign tourist. The fighting never reached Baringo. That is my invention. The tourists at the lake were prevented from leaving the area for a day or two because road blocks were set up, but that was all.

© 2014 by the author of this book. The author retains sole copyright to his contribution to this book.

ISBN 10 1495376249
ISBN 13 978149536245

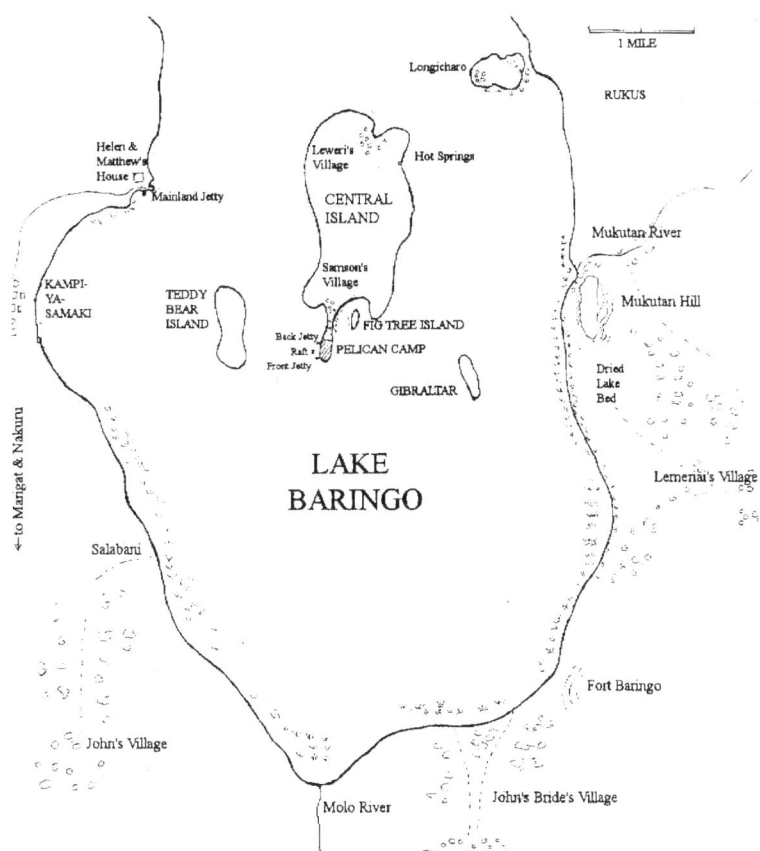

MAP OF THE SOUTHERN PART OF LAKE BARINGO

showing the principle places mentioned in the story.

THE TIN BOAT

Contents

PART 1   THE BRIDE PRICE
Chapter 1	1
Chapter 2	9
Chapter 3	16
Chapter 4	21
Chapter 5	30
Chapter 6	39
Chapter 7	46
Chapter 8	55
Chapter 9	61
Chapter 10	74
Chapter 11	80
Chapter 12	87
Chapter 13	93

PART 2   THE COUP
Chapter 14	101
Chapter 15	114
Chapter 16	120
Chapter 17	134
Chapter 18	143
Chapter 19	152
Chapter 20	163
Chapter 21	172
Chapter 22	179
Chapter 23	188
Chapter 24	199
Chapter 25	206
Chapter 26	214
Chapter 27	226
Chapter 28	235
Chapter 29	249
Chapter 30	256
Chapter 31	263
Chapter 32	274
Swahili Glossary	284
Swahili Phrases	287

THE TIN BOAT

PART ONE – THE BRIDE PRICE

CHAPTER 1

In the peaceful first light before sunrise, when the pelicans and cormorants started to leave their roosts and head out over the water, Matthew stood on the edge of the mainland jetty watching a big wooden boat coming across the lake from Central Island. He was slim, and tall for his eleven years. His very blond hair was slightly stirred by the warm gentle breeze.

All the occupants of the boat were Africans. The driver stopped the outboard engine some way before the jetty and let the heavy boat drift in. He had judged it so well that Matthew only had to lean down and touch the bow to bring the boat to a halt alongside the jetty. He secured the bow while the driver disembarked and made the stern fast.

The passengers, some dozen of them, climbed up onto the jetty. The driver gave a helping hand, not to any of the women, but to a tall elderly man. All the passengers were old except two, a strong young moran, or warrior, and a slim girl in her early teens of great poise and beauty. The boat driver stood aside to let them pass up the steps and along the path which led inland. He kept his eyes on the girl until she was out of sight. He too was an elegant figure, young, tall and strong. Only when the passengers had gone did Matthew approach him.

"Jambo, John. Habari yaku?" he said, using the traditional Swahili greeting.

"Nzuri, Matthew." They shook hands.

"What's been going on with all that lot on the island? I saw you take them over last night."

"The moran there, he wants that girl for a bride. The wazee were meeting at Chief Leweri's on the island with her father. They agree to this marriage. They fix the bride price. It is very high."

"Oh, really?" said Matthew. "Can he pay?"

"I think he needs time, but he will pay."

"Well she's a lovely girl O.K. I suppose that's why she's so expensive," said Matthew smiling, but John was clearly not in the mood for joking.

"Ndiyo, lovely girl," he agreed. "Very good family. I like her. I want to marry that girl."

"You?" exclaimed Matthew. "But I thought her father and the rest of the wazee had agreed to that other man marrying her."

"I am a better man than he," said John confidently. "I have a job at Pelican Camp. I am a big man in my age-group. I think they will agree to me too." Matthew laughed.

"But you can't both marry her, and once he's paid the bride price. . . ?"

"Ah! Then it is too late. I must pay first."

"Can you?"

"I ask the manager, get advance. But I need more. You lend me?"

"Oh, John. You're my rafiki, my friend. I'd like to help, man, really I would, but I'm saving all my money for a boat. I only want an old one, just something my sister and I can run around the lake in. Still, it takes a long time to save out of my pocket money."

"Boat? I find you boat, you lend me money? I repay you. Every month."

"A boat? Where can you get a boat?"

2

"Kuja!" said John, and led him down towards the reeds at the edge of the lake.

Once the first rays of sunlight streamed in through Helen's window she couldn't stay in bed any longer. She and her brother had arrived home the night before from Nairobi where their school term had just ended. She was fourteen. During the term she and Matthew lived with their mother, and they went back to her for part of the holidays too. However they both looked on their father's house at Lake Baringo as their real home. It had been their only home for most of their childhood.

Helen was thrilled to be back, to feel the warm air and hear the sounds of the water birds. Hurriedly she put on her bikini and wrapped a kikoi around her. Then she ran out of the house and down to the jetty to watch the sun come up. She never felt lonely at Baringo, though there were very few European children in that part of Kenya and none of her age for miles around. She and her brother were very close, and relied on each other for company, even if she did have to keep him in order sometimes.

"Hey! Helen! Come and check this out!" Matthew was calling from down among the reeds in the bay behind the jetty. She found him examining an old aluminium boat which must have been under the water for some time before it was exposed by the falling level of the lake.

"How did you find that?" asked Helen.

"Oh, just came across it," said Matthew with his mischievous smile. Helen had a feeling he was keeping something from her. She looked at him inquiringly.

"Yeh, well, John Boat showed it to me. Reckon it'll float?" he asked quickly, not wanting to go into any more detail.

"Let's try it," said Helen enthusiastically. "All we've got to do is bail it and see."

"Better get a bailer then," said Matthew, sitting down on the bow of the boat.

"Oh, no!" said Helen, who sometimes worried that Matthew

took life a little too easily. "You get the bailer."

"But Helen, man...."

She fixed him with her big sisterly stare. He slunk off towards the jetty. She should have known him better. He went only as far as the car park and stopped.

"Eh! Askari! Kuja!" he shouted in his high treble. Hopeless, thought Helen. She knew he could charm his African friends by telling them ghastly schoolboy stories in Swahili. They'd do anything he asked them.

Sure enough the night watchman, an old tribesman in a ragged army greatcoat, emerged from a little hut beside the jetty, carrying a stick and a torch. They greeted each other and had a good laugh over some joke of Matthew's before the old man set off towards the house. Matthew hung around throwing stones into the water and watching a huge goliath heron which was searching in the reeds for frogs.

Helen relaxed and started daydreaming about the fun they might have with a boat of their own. In particular they would be free to visit Pelican Camp whenever they liked. Pelican Camp was the real centre of their world, a place of such magic in their eyes that they couldn't imagine there being anywhere in the world to match it. The camp was built on the big Central Island two miles out across the lake. Helen could see the island now, dark against the rising sun, a single high hill with a low promontory where the camp stood. Her father owned the camp. It was his business, and the reason why they lived in this beautiful place.

The camp consisted of twenty-five fixed tents, accommodating some fifty tourists. There was a bar, a dining room and a small swimming pool. People came to stay there to see the amazing variety of birds on the lake, to sail or water-ski, or just to enjoy the sun and the beauty and peace of the place.

All the tourists, as well as the supplies for the camp, were taken across the lake by boat from the jetty in front of her father's house. As part of the agreement he had made with the chief of the local Njemps tribe, he also gave free transport to the Njemps people when there was space in the boats.

The askari returned and handed Matthew a bailer made out of an old tin can. They had another joke together before Matthew rejoined Helen who was still waiting by the tin boat.

"You are idle," she said. "Couldn't you have got it yourself?"

"Well, it was time for him to check the house out anyway so I thought he could come back with a bailer."

"Oh, Matthew, you must get on their wick sometimes," said Helen.

"Well then," said Matthew, "I got the bailer, how about you bail?"

The boat floated all right, though it had a slow leak in the bows. It was not much more than a tin shell now, but in its heyday it must have had a steering wheel, an instrument panel and various other trimmings.

"We wouldn't need to do much to it," said Matthew, "just put on a mounting board for the engine and get some paddles and a bow painter."

"We'll have to ask Dad if we can use it, but I'm sure he'll agree. He's probably forgotten all about it," said Helen.

"Why? Who does it belong to?"

"Don't you recognise it? It was the very first water-skiing boat for Pelican Camp. Looks a bit different now with all its bits and pieces taken off."

"Yeh, I remember it now," said Matthew. "Let's see if we can put the Seagull engine on it and use it as our own boat."

"It would be great," Helen agreed. "We could go to Pelican Camp whenever we wanted. What a bore we have to spend two whole weeks of the holidays in Nairobi."

A few days later Pam Bartlett, the manager of Pelican Camp, was sitting in the office which was attached to her house on the island. She was coming to the end of her monthly session of paying wages to the staff. They were all Africans except for her assistant manager Joan, who was away on leave. Both Pam and Joan had been brought up on farms in the White Highlands, so they spoke Swahili, the common language of East Africa, which was used by people from different tribes to communicate with each other.

All but ten of the thirty-two Africans who worked at the camp were from the local Njemps tribe. In origin they were Maasai, part of the great tribe of semi-nomadic warriors who herded their cattle over vast stretches of southern Kenya and northern Tanzania, but they had been forced to break away at the beginning of the twentieth century and form their own tribe. Cut off from the rest of the Maasai to the south by the expanding Tugen tribe, the Njemps had settled on the shores of Lake Baringo where they had become fishermen, though they still herded their cattle and goats. The Maasai believed that eating fish made a man effeminate, and for this reason they had disowned them.

Their language and customs were still closely related to those of the Maasai, and their way of life had changed little since they first arrived at the lake. But one of the new skills they had developed was the building of little coracles or 'ngadiches', made from the balsa-like wood of the ambach plant which grew around the edges of the lake. These little boats were light enough to be carried easily by one man. They were paddled from a sitting position with shaft-less hand-held wooden paddles called 'ngalaus'. The Njemps people knew the lake, its weather and all its moods.

When Pelican Camp was first set up the boat drivers were recruited from amongst the Njemps. They proved to be good at the job, and friendly and cheerful with the guests. So gradually, as the camp expanded, more of them were taken on to do other jobs. They had no formal training, but they learnt quickly and Pam enjoyed working with them. She now recruited entirely from the Njemps, so that the presence of the camp would bring benefits to the local people.

There were six boat drivers who took turns to drive the six camp boats. The old clinker-built 'Islander' had an inboard diesel engine. All the other boats had outboard motors. There were two big wooden boats, 'Freji' and 'Mandeleo' which had been brought from Lake Victoria where they had been used for coffee smuggling, and two faster fibre-glass canoes, 'Blue Banana' and 'Krumus'. There was also a little Fletcher speedboat for water-skiing.

It was one of the boat drivers, John Ulesiyanki, known by everybody at the camp as John Boat, who was next in line to collect his wages.

"Jambo John," said Pam. "Hapa pesa yaku," and handed him his money.

"Asante," he said, counting it. "Memsahib Pam?"

"Ndiyo John."

"Nataka...for my wedding. . ."

"Yes, what do you want?" She took a keen interest in the lives of her staff and their families, and became more involved than the job really required. "Not another advance? You had one last week to buy cattle for your bride price."

"Not advance," he assured her, smiling. "I need one more ngombe kidogo, a calf. I heard of one, a good one, but it needs feeding."

"So?"

"Please Memsahib, can I bring the calf from Longicharo to Pelican Camp? It is very important. There is another man wants this bride. The wazee say O.K. to him too. I only need this one more good calf before this man can pay his bride price. It must be well and strong in two weeks. Then I must take it to the bride's father."

"But why do you want it here?" asked Pam, although she thought she could guess.

"This calf needs grazing. The camp lawns, they are watered, they are green..."

"I see," said Pam, "and you think your ngombe can be my lawn mower. It's a problem, John. You know I have somebody in here almost every week asking the same thing. I can't have the camp overrun with cattle and goats. If I say yes to you, what do I say to the others? You understand." John's face fell. "I'd like to help. I don't know. Let me think about it. Now, I have some news for you. Tomorrow I go to Nairobi to collect your old friends Jamie and Nicholas. I expect they will be very pleased to see you. My sister Sue and her husband David are bringing them here from England for six weeks. She will help me run the camp while the assistant manager is on leave, like she did two years ago."

"Oh that is good," said John with a broad grin. He had become very friendly with Pam's two nephews who had spent three months at Pelican Camp on their last visit to Kenya. "How old those boys now?"

"Well, Jamie is ten and Nicholas is eight," said Pam. "And this time I have another nephew coming to stay with me, son of my other sister. His name is William. He is fourteen. It will be his first time in Africa. Now, you know that Helen and Matthew have been using that little tin boat?"

"Ndiyo," said John, without letting on now much he really knew about it.

"They've gone to Nairobi and will be back in two weeks. They said the boys could borrow the tin boat until they return, which will be fun for them. But I don't want to risk using their Seagull engine. I think Morris has an old fifteen horsepower outboard. Can you see if it works and if it is O.K. for the tin boat?"

"O.K." said John. "I do that. I very happy to see Jamie and Nicholas. Maybe they come to my wedding."

"Oh, yes, they'd be most excited to be asked," said Pam.

"But I must get my calf fattened for the mzee."

"Yes. Yes. Kwenda now. Work to do."

CHAPTER 2

William was woken by hilarious laughter from his two cousins. When he opened his eyes he instinctively grabbed the seat in front of him. He thought his aunt Pam was going to crash her car into the army lorry they were following. They seemed so close to it. But once he was fully awake he saw how slowly they were moving and he relaxed.

"Go on, William!" said Nicholas. "Wave to them!" The back of the lorry was filled with African soldiers in army greatcoats, some of them wearing balaclava helmets. The boys had caught their attention and had started a waving game. When a wave was returned with a broad grin they thought it was a tremendous joke.

"Come on Pam. Let's try the next one," said Jamie. Pam overtook, but there was another army lorry only a hundred yards ahead. The waving and laughter started again.

"How many have we passed?" asked William. He'd been in a bad mood when they set off from Nairobi after the long night flight from London. He hadn't slept much on the plane, his mind going round and round the events which had led to him being included at the last minute in this holiday with his cousins. Now, after his sleep, he was feeling a little less sulky, though he wasn't prepared to join in the waving game.

"Oh, lots," said Sue. "At least a dozen."

"And there have been army land rovers with guns behind them," said Jamie. "I wonder where they're heading."

"Must be a big military exercise," said David.

After stopping for lunch at the club in Nakuru, they left the main road and headed north. Though the road was newly tarmacked there seemed to be more cattle and goats on it than cars. Many of the animals were tended by very young raggedly dressed boys who chased them out of the way of the car with long sticks. Soon they were passing fields of dry red soil planted with what looked like giant pineapples with long poles growing out of them.

"Sisal," explained Pam. "The fibres of the leaves are used to make ropes, and those long poles are used by the Africans to build their huts."

Still further on they went through miles of low bush, and the ground became drier and drier, and the air noticeably warmer. From time to time William saw some of the little round thatched African huts which Pam had mentioned.

"Is that where they live?" he asked.

"That's right," said Pam. "A whole family will live in one of those. When we get to Baringo you'll be able to have a look inside one." William didn't like the idea much, but he kept quiet.

"I can see the lake!" shouted Jamie. The road in front of them descended sharply, and they could see for miles across the lower ground ahead of them. In the far distance William could see the pale flat expanse of water.

"Can you see the hill in the middle of the lake?" asked Jamie.

"Yes," said William.

"That's the island. That's where we're going."

Down at the level of the lake the country was even drier and rockier. They passed the town of Marigat, just a collection of tin huts with a police station. An escarpment of dark brown rock rose above the road to the left. On the right there was a view of the lake over the flat tops of the trees. The hills of the islands were caught by the evening sun, making the soil look even redder.

"Look, William," said Jamie. "There's Teddy Bear Island." From the side William could see why it had acquired its nickname. It consisted of two hills, the taller southern one shaped like a cone and the northern one was a long shallow dome. The effect was that of a teddy bear floating on its back. Beyond it was the large Central Island on which Pelican Camp stood.

"You can see the camp lights now," said Pam. "They must have started the generator." Some ten miles from Marigat they turned off the main road towards the lake. From here they caught a glimpse of the jetty and the house where Helen and Matthew lived.

"Are they here?" asked Jamie.

"Who's that?" asked Pam.

"Matthew and Helen." Jamie and Nicholas had met them during their last stay and were longing to see them again.

"No. They've gone to their mother in Nairobi for a couple of weeks," said Pam. Inwardly William greeted this piece of information with relief. He had no idea who Helen and Matthew were. Nobody had even mentioned them to him before, but he instinctively felt threatened by the presence of other children on the lake who might be buddies of Jamie and Nicholas, and who might leave him as the outsider of the group as usual. His difficult upbringing had left him with little confidence when meeting new people, particularly people of his own age.

"I'll tell you one bit of news that'll please you," Pam went on. "They've got an old tin boat which the two of them use to get around the lake. They've left it at the island for you to use till they get back."

"Fantastic!" said Jamie. "Has it got an engine?"

"Well they've been using a little Seagull of their father's, but I think it would be best not to use theirs. I've got one at Pelican Camp. It's old, but it works. You can use that."

"How powerful is it?" asked Nicholas. He was the boat engine enthusiast.

"Fifteen horsepower I think," said Pam.

"Hey," said Jamie. "That'll be fine. Can I be driver?"

"I hope you'll all learn," said Pam, "but nobody's going to drive until you've had some lessons from one of the boat drivers and he thinks you're safe. William will be in charge. He's the oldest."

"But he's never driven a boat," said Jamie.

"He soon will," said Pam. "I'm not letting you have somebody else's boat unless you are sensible. The oldest is the one who takes responsibility. O.K. William?"

"Yes, of course," said William, surprising even himself with his own enthusiasm. Suddenly it all seemed to suit him rather well - a boat just for the three of them, with him, far from tagging on as the outsider, actually being put in charge.

"Look," said Pam. "We've reached Kampi-ya-Samaki. There should be a boat driver around somewhere." She gave two blasts of the horn, but nobody took any notice.

They had stopped between two rows of dukas, or shops, and bars which made up the only street. All the little shacks looked much the same in the dwindling light, though the pillars along the street side were painted different colours. There were no cars in the street, just one old bus. A few bicycles leant against the dukas. Most people travelled by foot.

Pam hooted again. The Africans around the bar opposite looked up with detached interest. She leant out of the window and called to them.

"Wapi driver ya meli ya Pelican Camp?"

One of the Africans detached himself from the group and strolled over to the car.

"Wapi mutu ya Pelican Camp?" Pam asked again more quietly. "Jackson? Singh? John?"

"Ndiyo. Iku hapa," he replied. He strolled over to another duka and disappeared into the dark inside. After a minute or two a tall young man appeared out of the same door. He saw the car, gave a broad grin, and hurried over.

"Oh, boys! You're in luck," said Pam. "It's your friend John."

"Oh good!" said Jamie, and Nicholas started bouncing up and down on his father's knee on which he had been sitting all the way from Nakuru. John bent down and looked through the front window.

"Jambo, John!" said Sue.

"Jambo, Memsahib! Jambo. Bwana!" said John. "Habari yaku? Habari yote?"

"Nzuri! Nzuri!"

"Jambo!" piped up two little voices from the back.

"Jambo Jamie! Jambo Nicholas! Habari Nicholas?" John leant through the window past Pam and shook both boys' hands. "Nicholas, wewe kbwa sasa!" Jamie had probably grown more noticeably, but Nicholas was the baby and everybody seemed surprised that he should grow at all.

"Huyu kijana naitwa William," said Sue.

"Jambo, William," said John, and shook his hand. William grunted. He had never taken part in a conversation in a foreign language before. He understood not a word and was not sure he cared for it.

"Which boat have you got here?" asked Jamie.

"Islander," said John. He spoke a good deal of English although he never used it with people who spoke Swahili.

"Can one of us drive, John?" Jamie went on.

"Come on," Pam interrupted. "Let's get going before the wind blows up. The lake can get quite rough at this time of year. Tayari John?"

John said that he was ready and set off on foot along the shortest route to the jetty. By car the last mile was twisty and extremely rough. When they reached the car park they found it full of mini-buses and cars.

"Looks like a full camp," said Sue.

"Always is these days," said Pam, "especially at weekends. Exhausting!"

Two Africans seemed to materialise from nowhere and helped them unload the luggage into the boat. They all clambered down into Islander, except Pam who was having an animated conversation with one of the Africans about a box of laundry. That too was loaded into the boat. There was a further delay when some headlights were seen coming down the road. It was almost dark now. Pam insisted they wait in case it turned out to be more camp guests. While they were waiting an old Njemps man, with an even older woman and a young woman with a baby slung on her front, arrived on foot and boarded the boat, sitting in the stern without a word. The late arrivals, two young couples, were finally settled into the boat with their luggage.

While all this was going on John lifted the wooden cover off the inboard diesel engine. He and Nicholas squatted on their haunches looking lovingly at the oily, black machine.

"The oldest engine but the best," said John. "This one it keep working all the time. Now, I think we ready to start."

"Can I do it?" Nicholas asked excitedly.

"No me!" shouted Jamie from up in the bow, where he had been sitting with William.

"Nicholas try first," laughed John, but Nicholas was not strong enough to turn the handle more than half a turn.

"Leave it to me, weakling," said Jamie. Although he was less than two years older, he was very strongly built. He managed a couple of turns. The engine spluttered but would not start.

"Kwenda!" said Pam, growing impatient. The wind had become a stiff breeze now, and there was only a faint glow left in the sky. John took the handle and started the engine with no more than a flick of the wrist. The night watchman cast them off. John tacked away from the jetty, and turned the bows into the narrow channel which led through the reeds to the open lake.

The journey took half an hour. They carried no lights. The nights at Baringo were never pitch black, and the boat drivers could see better without the glare of artificial light. The lights of the camp were visible across the water, and even at night the white wash of another boat could be seen almost as if it gave out its own light.

Beyond the reeds the water was rougher, but John wasn't worried. He asked Nicholas if he wanted to drive.

"Yes, please!" said Nicholas, and took over the little steering wheel which was mounted sideways along the gunwale near the stern.

"You drive to Teddy Bear Island, then I'll have a go," said Jamie.

William sat silently up in the bow. His black mood evaporated in the warm night air, and he felt relaxed and happy. The sound and movement of the boat going through the water was soothing. The sky was clear and filled with stars, more and brighter than he had ever seen.

He watched Pam talking energetically with the four new Pelican Camp guests, already back in her role as manager. Sue looked equally at home talking to the African woman about her baby. As for the boys, they were back with their old friend John and their beloved boats. 'I'm the outsider as usual,' he thought, but it was a pleasant place to be, on a lake beneath the African night sky.

A flock of birds, dark shadows in a hurry, flew very low over the water across the bows. William leant over to see what they were, but they were quickly gone. David saw him alone and went to sit with him. A light spray was blowing into their faces.

"Did you see the ducks?" he asked.

"Yes," said William.

"White-faced tree ducks, going to the east side of the lake for the night. One day we will go on an early morning trip and see them and all the other fabulous birds. You O.K.?"

"Yes," said William. "I'm glad I came now. It's lovely. I think I'm going to like it."

THE TIN BOAT

CHAPTER 3

"Cm'on William! Get up! We're all waiting for you!"

"Jamie! For goodness sake! I was fast asleep!" complained William. "What on earth time is it?"

"It's seven thirty," said Jamie. "We all get up at six here when the sun comes up. I'm surprised the generator didn't wake you." William could hear it now, throbbing away behind the house. He pulled his mosquito net aside and looked out across the lake. His room only had three walls. The fourth side was completely open.

"Get dressed quickly and come and have breakfast," said Jamie. "We're waiting to go and try out the tin boat."

William found some shorts and a T shirt. As he followed Jamie up the path to the dining room some memories of their arrival the night before came back to him. The camp staff had greeted them at the jetty with torches and had led them up past the bar to the manager's house which was to be their home for the next six weeks. There they had been given a quick meal before he had tumbled into bed and gone straight to sleep. The only other thing he remembered, though it might have been a dream, was looking across the lake in the middle of the night and watching an endless succession of vehicle headlights go by on the far shore, little specks of light travelling north at a constant speed.

William was served a large cooked breakfast which he ate as fast as he could with Jamie hovering over him impatiently.

"Where's Nicholas?" he asked.

THE TIN BOAT

Nicholas was down by the back jetty with Morris the engineer in the little workshop where the boat engines were stored and maintained. It was a noisy place when both the generator and the water pump were working right next door, but Nicholas was happy there, helping Morris and learning about outboard motors.

They were inspecting the fifteen horsepower Yamaha which Pam had told them they could use for the tin boat. Morris had taken the propeller off to look at the sheer pin.

"You see! It is bent again," he said. Nicholas looked hard at it and nodded. "But I think it is O.K. This pin was new one week ago. If the propeller hit something it bends. It should stay straight, or it should break, but it bends. I only have one spare sheer pin for this engine. Spares very difficult to get now. Mbaya sana. So we must leave the bent one in."

He replaced the two large washers which were supposed to separate the sheer pin from the propeller and keep it in its groove. It was clearly a makeshift arrangement to replace some lost or broken part. He replaced the propeller and fixed it with a rusty old split pin.

"Now we fix it on the boat," he said.

Jamie and William appeared.

"We're going to take the engine down to the tin boat," said Nicholas. "Give us a hand."

William and Jamie carried the engine onto the jetty, while Morris climbed down into the tin boat to receive it. They all helped lower it gently to Morris before going aboard. He produced a short piece of rope.

"We must tie the engine onto the boat," he explained, "then if we drop it we can pull it up again." This done, they started lifting the engine over the stern. Nicholas stayed up in the bow, but Jamie rocked the boat by clambering back to help.

"Keep still!" shouted William. He and Morris lowered the engine over the stern until the screw clasps fitted over the mounting board. When it was centred they tightened the clamps.

"Where's the cover?" asked Jamie.

"No cover. It is at the bottom of the lake," laughed Morris. "Not matter." Certainly it didn't look too promising with the knobs and leads exposed instead of being under a streamlined cover, but then the whole boat had seen better days. The seats were just metal thwarts which became very hot in the sun.

Morris searched around in the bottom of the boat and found the starting rope. He attached the rubber pipe from the petrol tank onto the engine and squeezed the pump to push the petrol through.

"You watching?" he asked William. "Squeeze petrol through first until you feel the pressure. Now. Make sure is in neutral. Take the clutch and try." He pointed to a blue lever at the side of the engine. "Up is neutral. When it clicks. Towards you for forwards. Away for reverse. But never reverse fast. The engine will jump out of the water. You try."

William moved the clutch lever backwards and forwards until he was familiar with its three positions.

"Now. This one here, it is the throttle," Morris went on, taking hold of the black end of the tiller. He twisted it one way and then the other. "Slow. Fast," he explained. "To start, have it like this." He lined the arrow up with a faded letter "S" which was all that was left of the word "START". "O.K. In neutral." William checked. Morris checked again.

He fitted the knot of the rope into a slot in the starting wheel, wound it round twice, and prepared to pull.

"Mind your faces," he said. The boys ducked and he pulled. After a couple of phutts the engine popped and roared happily into life. There was a loud cheer from the three boys.

"Now slow a little," Morris said to William. "That is good. Nicholas, let go." Nicholas let go of the jetty. "Now forward gear." William realised that he was being given the controls straight away. He wasn't used to being trusted like this, but there was too much to think about to be nervous.

"Push off a bit, Jamie," he said. He wanted the bows pointing out towards open water before he set off. He eased the engine into gear. They moved forward but the engine slowed right down with the effort.

"Little bit more throttle," said Morris.

At first William turned it the wrong way. The engine almost died. Then he overdid it the other way. The boat lurched forward leaving everybody grabbing onto the side to stop themselves falling over

THE TIN BOAT

backwards.

"Slowly, slowly," said Morris gently. William eased off the throttle a little and regained control. Cautiously he tried the steering, first one way, and then the other way. The boat reacted rather sluggishly. He increased the speed a little more and tried again. He was able to turn the boat more sharply now, but not alarmingly so. He decided to try just a little faster when he realised that he was already going full speed.

"Nzuri sana," said Morris. "So now you are fundi boat-boy. You take me back now. I must do more work."

William took the boat in a wide circle so that he could come alongside the jetty without too much manoeuvring. He came in very smoothly indeed and everybody clapped. He felt really proud of himself.

He left the engine running. When Morris had clambered out they pushed off again. Jamie and Nicholas were much too pleased that the three of them were going to be allowed to go by themselves to argue about who drove. They were excited with their new toy and both moved down into the stern with William.

This proved to be a mistake. Without Morris's weight the tin boat behaved very differently. As William put the engine into gear, and confidently opened the throttle, the boat shot forward at much greater speed, and the bow rose up out of the water. They were very close to the rocky shore. William turned the boat away too sharply, and they all felt that they must surely go over. But he had the presence of mind to shut the throttle right down and this had the effect of lowering the bow gently into the water again.

"You're useless!" said Jamie unsympathetically.

"No I'm not. It's the weight," insisted William. "Without Morris we are much lighter and we can go much faster. I think you've got to sit nearer the front." The two boys obeyed and they set off again, this time with perfect control, towards the raft.

The raft was moored about two hundred yards off the main jetty. It was roughly made out of planks wired to empty oil drums, with a ladder going down into the water at one corner. It was there primarily for water-skiers, so that they could make deep water starts well away from the comings and goings of the boats at the jetty.

THE TIN BOAT

Other people would swim out there to sunbathe.

"Let's go and tie the boat to the raft and swim," said Nicholas. "I'm hot." So they tied up, and Jamie and Nicholas climbed out onto the raft. In no time they had taken off their shirts and flip-flops and dived into the water. But William was having a problem. Morris had not told him how to switch the engine off. He hoped that if he turned the throttle right down it might stall, but it didn't. It just kept chugging away.

At that moment Nicholas bobbed up beside the boat.

"Turn it off and come and swim, William," he said.

"But I don't know how," said William irritably.

"Oh," said Nicholas, "let me look." He swam round to where the raft was lowest in the water and pulled himself out. He came over and examined the engine.

"Try that black button," he said. William pushed the rubber covered button and the engine stopped.

"See," said Nicholas, in a friendly way, and with a shout and a huge splash he jumped back into the water.

William stood at the edge of the raft and took off his shirt He enjoyed swimming, but feeling the hot sun on his back for the first time he was in no particular hurry to dive into the muddy brown water. It was wonderful to stand there surrounded by water, with the sun already so high in the sky that it looked as if the day might go on for ever. The hills beyond the lake looked infinitely distant. They had all tried to describe to him how beautiful it was, but he had not been able to imagine it.

'Six weeks,' he thought. 'Six weeks in this paradise, and to think I didn't even want to come.'

Over at the jetty one of the old grey wooden boats was being loaded up with departing tourists and their luggage. There must have been at least twenty of them. Soon they would be back in their minibuses, driven from place to place for a day at a time, never having long enough to be aware of where they were. It made six weeks look like a lifetime. William dived into the deliciously warm water.

CHAPTER 4

After lunch they all went down to the house to rest for an hour during the hottest part of the day. Even Pam managed to snatch a little time away from the problems of the camp. They were lounging around reading books when Jamie broke the silence.

"Pam," he said, "why won't you let John bring his calf here? Surely one little calf can't do any harm."

"Oh, he's been talking to you about it, has he?" she said.

"I saw him outside the kitchen just before lunch," Jamie went on. "He looked a bit sad, so I asked him why and he told me."

"It's so difficult," Pam explained. "They're always asking me if they can graze sick calves or goats or something. Once you start, it's never ending. I know John is your friend and I'd like to help him too, if only I could find a way without everybody else wanting to do the same. Anyway," she went on, deliberately changing the subject, "did you all have a good time in the tin boat?"

"Brilliant," said Jamie. "It goes really fast."

"Don't know when I've enjoyed myself so much," said William.

"William is a really good driver," said Nicholas generously.

"Yes, but I'm going to drive this afternoon," Jamie insisted.

"No," David intervened. "You and Nicolas aren't going to

drive until you've had a lesson from Morris or one of the boat drivers."

"But I know how ..." Pam interrupted Jamie.

"Do what your father says. Tomorrow afternoon I've asked John to take you over to collect the ambach boats which I've ordered for you from Longicharo. He can give you a lesson on the way. If he is happy with you, then you can all drive." So for the next twenty-four hours William enjoyed the position of sole driver of the tin boat.

Next afternoon, when the worst of the heat was over, they set off with John to Longicharo, an island in the north-east part of the lake where the 'ngadiches', or ambach coracles, were made.

"Go straight there and don't hang around too long when you get there," Pam had told John firmly. "The evening winds are blowing up pretty strongly at the moment. I don't want you caught in a storm in the tin boat. We've no idea yet how it would behave in rough water. Do you understand?"

"Ndiyo, Memsahib. We come straight back. I take care of these boys. You not worry," John had answered with a reassuring smile.

As promised he let the two younger boys drive. Jamie managed well, but Nicholas was always looking at the engine instead of watching where he was going. John wasn't worried. He just laughed and altered course from time to time.

Suddenly he said, quite quietly,

"Pole, pole kidogo. Slow down," and pointing over the starboard side, "Look! Mamba!"

"Crocodile?" said Jamie.

"Ndiyo." They all had a good view of it before it vanished below the surface.

"Should we be swimming in this lake?" William asked nervously.

"No mambas near jetty," John reassured him.

"Everybody swims here," Jamie added, "and nobody has been

eaten yet. It's not like Lake Turkana where they are really dangerous. Here you've got to be more careful of the hippos."

Later they slowed down again so that William could see the steam rising from the hot springs at the north end of the island. They watched a fish eagle throwing its head back and making its beautiful clear-throated call. On they went until they came to where an Njemps fisherman was sitting in his little ngadich pulling up his nets.

"See these nets?" said John. "Chunga howa sana. Watch for the floats on the water and go round them."

Jamie appointed himself lookout man because he liked lying along the bow watching where they were going. He could see the line of floats ahead of them. He stuck his right arm out but Nicholas carried straight on.

"Right, Nicholas! Quickly!" Nicholas swung the boat sharply to the left so that they were heading straight for the fishing boat. John only laughed. He put his hand over Nicholas's on the tiller and took the boat in a wide circle until they were going parallel with the floats and away from the fishing boat.

"You're clear now!" shouted Jamie. John made sure they were past the end of the net and headed once more for Longicharo.

"I drive now," he said a little while later. They were approaching the island and there was a very difficult channel to negotiate through the reeds. Standing up as far as he could without letting go of the tiller, he found his way along a zig-zag route which eventually brought them out into the open shallow water before the shore.

He stopped the engine and tilted it, and Jamie and William paddled the boat to the beach. There was a jetty but it had been left high and dry by the receding level of the lake. It was crowded with little boys dressed only in dirty loin cloths. They started waving and shouting excited "Jambos" as they rushed down to the water line to help pull in the boat. They all greeted John like an old friend and everyone wanted to shake William, Jamie and Nicholas by the hand. Without the grown-ups of his family watching William felt much less inhibited and enjoyed warm welcome.

"Chunga howa sana!" said John, pointing to the boat, and some of the totos stayed behind to look after it. Turning to the boys he said, "Now come," and led them, followed by the rest of the totos, along a path through the thorn bushes to another beach. There they found the old man who made the ambach boats.

He was sitting under a tree near the edge of the lake with ten tapered branches of the cork-like ambach tree spreading fan-wise in front of him. The branches were tied together with nylon twine only at the thinnest end. This end was to be the bow of an ngadich.

John greeted the old man and introduced the boys.

"Watch this man. You will see how ngadich is made," he said. "I must go see a man. I be very quick. Ngoja hapa kidogo."

"O.K." said Jamie.

"Where's he gone?" asked William.

"Well I don't know, but I bet it's got something to do with this calf he needs for the last bit of his bride price. He's really bothered about the whole thing." They watched in silence as the old man began to draw the fan of branches together, weaving the twine between them and binding them into the shape of a boat. His misshapen old hands worked the twine surprisingly nimbly.

"You know," said William to Jamie as they watched him, "I was listening to what Pam said about the calf. I think she'd turn a blind eye to John grazing his calf at the camp if the other Africans thought she didn't know about it."

"You could be right," Jamie admitted hopefully. "Perhaps if he kept it outside the fence we could slip it in at night or something."

"There's that new lawn up by the swimming pool," said Nicholas. "We could get it in there without Pam even seeing. She doesn't often have time to go up there."

"Great idea," said Jamie. "We'd probably have to get Eleru in on it, but nobody else. Eleru looks after the swimming pool, William. I know he is a friend of John's because they come from the same village."

By this time the old man had worked his way along half the length of the little boat, and it had taken on a very recognisable shape. William and Jamie watched for a while before they became restless and wandered down to the water's edge. Nicholas was far more interested in watching the ngadich take shape, so the old man invited him to help tie some of the knots.

They waited and waited until at last William heard John's voice behind them. Turning round he saw John coming down to the shore with another African smartly dressed in some sort of military uniform. John was leading a beautiful little white bull calf by a rope around its neck.

"You were dead right," William whispered to Jamie. John said something to his military friend who shook his hand warmly and left.

"Is that for your bride price?" asked Jamie when John rejoined them.

"It is," said John, a little shamefaced. "The last one I need. I think maybe if we take it with us I….."

"It's O.K." said Jamie. "We've got an idea about it, haven't we?" He gave a conspiratorial glance at the other two who nodded. "We won't say a word."

"Asante sana," said John seriously.

"Who is that man?" asked Nicholas. "He looks like a soldier."

"He my friend, brother of Stephen the barman. He works at the air force base at Nanyuki. He say all the aeroplanes go away to big exercise up north with the army. You see the army go past, night before this last one?"

"Yes," said William. "I thought I had dreamt it, but I did see all the lights go past. In fact we got stuck in that convoy on the way here, didn't we?"

"Yes, we waved at all the soldiers," said Nicholas, smiling.

"This man, he bring the ngombe for me from Nanyuki. Very good calf, but too thin. Now he is here on leave. He say he very happy man to get away. He say bad things happening in the air force."

"Bad things?" asked Jamie. "What bad things?" But John just shrugged his shoulders. If he knew more he wasn't saying.

"Now we look at these ngadiches," he said more cheerfully. The old man left off his work and took them to the end of the beach where three beautiful new ngadiches were waiting for them. Two were full-sized and one a little smaller. A pair of little wooden paddles lay in each. The 'fundi', or craftsman, looked anxiously at John as he inspected them.

"They're great," said Nicholas. "The little one must be mine."

John took a little longer before he pronounced them 'nzuri' and handed over the money which Sue had given him to pay for them.

The boys wanted to paddle the ngadiches round to where they had left the tin boat, but John knew it was getting late and was worried about the stiff breeze which had started to blow. He offered to bring the tin boat round to them. Jamie volunteered to hold the calf.

John returned in the tin boat, with the small boys running along the shore parallel to him. He tied the three ngadiches in line astern behind the boat. He told William and Nicholas to climb aboard before he and Jamie tried to lead the calf through the shallow water towards the boat.

The animal was scared and wouldn't go. John lifted it and waded out, but he stumbled on a submerged rock and dropped the calf, which ran floundering and splashing back to the shore. It was lucky that so many small boys were there to stop it, or it may not have been seen again for a very long time. In the end the calf was defeated by sheer numbers, and had so many boys sitting on it that it might have been damaged had John not rushed back to rescue it. He took the rope from around its neck and hobbled it by tying all four legs together.

He carried it back to the boat. Jamie helped lift it into the stern and clambered in after it. There he stroked it and pampered it, and the frightened little thing seemed reassured

When John tried to climb on board his weight grounded the boat. He pushed it out into deeper water until he was up to his

THE TIN BOAT

waist. Even then it was difficult for him to take his feet off the bottom because the wind kept blowing the boats towards the shore. He told Jamie to start the engine.

"In gear when I say," he said. "Now!"

Jamie eased it into forward gear. At the same time John leapt on board. The boat rocked violently, and Jamie's attempt to right it by steering made it worse. John took over the tiller and steadied them up.

They were on their way, but their progress was slow. With the extra weight, the ever increasing wind against them, and the drag of the ngadiches, they sometimes appeared to be making no progress at all. The blanched landscape was taking on richer evening colours. Overhead the sky was clear, but huge banks of cumulus clouds were building up over the high part of the Central Island.

The bows beat against the regular pattern of waves. A flight of tree duck, and another of cormorants, passed them at wing tip height above the water, heading for Longicharo with a following wind, making the boys feel that they had chosen to struggle in the wrong direction.

John decided to head for the north end of the Central Island. Their new course gave them a cross wind which caused a good deal of water to splash over the side of the boat, but it did mean that they made faster progress. By now they were in a race against the gathering darkness and the oncoming storm. For the first time he was looking anxious and unhappy. But for the business of the calf they would have been safely home by now. He made the children put on life jackets and start bailing. The wind grew stronger and the waves larger. A mountainous cloud hung over the island.

In the end they were lucky. As the sun dipped behind the western hills they felt the first drops of rain, but at that moment they rounded the north end of the island and came into the lea of the hill. It was a different world. The wind disappeared and the lake was calm.

John pointed up at the cloud above the island. Against the darkest part of it a huge flock of pelicans wheeled up and up, picked out by the setting sun. John began to sing one of the high pitched rhythmic songs of the Njemps people.

But the adventures of the day were not yet ever. On one of the wide beaches along the west coast of the island three women were waving frantically at the tin boat, obviously in distress. John slowed the boat down and drew closer. They could see a fourth person lying on the beach.

Fortunately it was an easy place to run ashore. John and the boys jumped out one by one as the water became shallower. The calf struggled a bit but could not move.

A woman was lying on the beach with a shawl pulled over her face. The other three were all shouting excitedly. One of them pulled the shawl back and showed them the appalling gash which had been inflicted down the young woman's forehead and cheek, all the way to her mouth. William felt sick. He was glad his young cousins were making the boat fast.

The three women screeched explanation to John all at the same time. They were clearly begging him to take the victim back to the camp.

"What happened?" asked William, although he wasn't at all sure he wanted to know.

"I think maybe it was her husband, but they say no. Another man, not from the island. Not Njemps. We carry her."

They lifted her as gently as possible because she was very weak. They laid her down in the boat and set off. Her anxious companions wanted to come too, but there wasn't room, so they set out to walk the two miles overland.

It was almost dark and the speedboat had come out looking for them. Singh was driving with David by his side. Although they found the tin boat only a mile short of the jetty, they decided to speed things up by transferring some of the passengers into the speedboat. The injured woman refused to be moved so Jamie and Nicholas climbed gratefully into the speedboat leaving William to help John.

"What on earth have you been doing?" asked David. Both boys started telling their story, but they were too tired to be coherent.

"That African woman's got an awful cut on her head," said Jamie.

"You haven't seen," commented Nicholas.

"No, but William told me and he says it's ghastly. Really yukky."

Pam was furious with John. The boys, who had their supper down at the house, heard her giving him a formidable dressing down in Swahili in the office next door. She refused to listen to any explanations or excuses, and sent him away looking pretty dejected.

"No way she'll let him keep the calf in the camp now," Jamie whispered to William. "We've got to try and help him without her knowing."

Pam came out of the office muttering about people never quite doing as they were told, and asked Sue to go with her to help patch up the injured woman's face. Much later, after he had gone to bed, William heard them return to the house and describe to David how bad the injury was. Pam was obviously very concerned.

"Probably just a family argument," suggested David.

"I hope you're right," said Pam. "I'm not sure. None of those women would talk about it. There's been quite an increase in violence and thefts and so on over on the mainland recently. I just hope it's not going to spread over here. It's one reason why this camp is so popular. Up to now we just haven't had this sort of trouble."

"Go to bed now," said Sue. "You're exhausted. It'll probably all seem less serious in the morning."

Outside the wind had dropped, and it was hard to imagine the peace of the island being disturbed by anything. William lay in bed and let the lapping of the waves below the house lull him to sleep.

THE TIN BOAT

CHAPTER 5

Jamie slipped out of the house very early next morning before Pam was awake. He wanted to talk to John before he went on duty. John lived in the staff quarters on the slope above the back jetty. He wasn't up yet, but Jamie found Rotich the cook setting off to work.

"Wapi John Boat?" he asked.

"John Boat? Ngoja. I fetch him," said Rotich. He knocked on one of the other doors and John emerged still buttoning up his Pelican Camp uniform.

"Jamie!" he said. "Nataka nini?"

"What've you done with the calf?" asked Jamie. "We're all worried about it, and we've got an idea." John laughed gently when he heard this.

"You not worry now. Calf is nzuri sana."

"But I thought...."

"Is O.K. Is with Sion. So no more worry with this calf."

"Sion?" said Jamie. "Who is Sion?"

"You not know Sion? He the kijana, William's age. He look after the gate. He stop goats from the village coming into the camp."

"Oh, yes," said Jamie, wondering what scheme John had

thought up now. "John? What are you up to?" he laughed. John laughed too.

"Now you forget the calf. Tonight I go on leave. Two weeks. Till my wedding."

"Are you sure you'll have one?" Jamie asked.

"I think so. Ndiyo. And you all come."

"Yeh, that'd be great," said Jamie. "But what about this other man who wants your bride?"

"I not worried too much," said John. "I have my calf. This man, he does not have one."

"But why don't you take your calf now and make sure?"

"He not big enough yet. If I take him now, so little, I need two like him."

"Oh, I see," said Jamie. "Why are you going on leave now?"

"I must build a house for my wife. It is not finished. Then there is a big ngoma for her circumcision." Jamie absorbed this last information in silence. "Now I must go. Winge wageni to take to the mainland."

Over breakfast in the dining room Jamie reported his conversation with John to the other two boys.

"He's got something planned. I bet he's got Sion to let the calf in through the gate when he thinks it is safe."

"Pam won't be pleased if she finds out," said Nicholas. "I wonder if Eleru knows. He's bound to see it."

"I think he's being a bit silly," said William. "I'm sure Pam would eventually come round to letting him graze it here."

"Pam's not very pleased with him at the moment," said Jamie, "and he goes on leave today."

"Why?" asked Nicholas. "How long for?" Pelican Camp wouldn't seem the same to him without John there.

"About two weeks, till his wedding," said Jamie. "He's got to finish building his house. Then there's his bride's, well, there's this ceremony, not very nice, which girls have to go through before they can be married." He leaned over and whispered something to

William so that Nicholas couldn't hear.

"WHAT?" gasped William.

"Yes, I promise you," said Jamie showing off his knowledge.

"Sounds awful," said William. "What happens?"

"What are you talking about. I want to know too," squeaked Nicholas.

"No, you're too young," said Jamie. "You wouldn't understand."

"Yes I would," Nicholas insisted. His mother had just come into the dining room. She joined them carrying her orange juice and a plate of paw-paw.

"Mum," said Nicholas loud enough for all the other guests in the dining room to hear, "Jamie and William are whispering things and they won't tell me about it." Sue looked enquiringly at Jamie.

"There's going to be an ngoma for John's bride. You know..." The room had suddenly gone quiet. Sue looked round at the other guests with an embarrassed smile.

"Not now!" she whispered to the boys, and changed the subject as quickly as she could. "Now listen," she said, "Pam says she might let you water-ski before lunch. The camp will be nice and quiet. Most of the weekend guests are leaving this morning, and the new ones don't usually come in till later in the afternoon."

"Brilliant!" enthused Jamie.

"I'm going to have a go this time," said Nicholas confidently.

"Yes, of course," said his mother. "Pam says she will give you and William a lesson. She's taught lots of people while she's been working here. Keep yourselves amused until about half-past twelve, then she should be free."

As they wandered out of the dining room Nicholas said,

"Come on, let's try out our new ambaches. I'll show you how to paddle, William."

"O.K." said William. "You coming, Jamie?"

"I'll catch you up," said Jamie. "I think I'm just going to have a look for this chap Sion."

He walked up to the swimming pool, the highest part of the

camp, and down across the lawn to the gate in the bamboo fence. He looked around quickly, half expecting the calf to be grazing there, but he couldn't see it.

He opened the gate and passed through into the dustier, noisier world of the African village. Last night's rain had already been dried out by the morning sun. Chickens and goats wandered amongst the huts on the bare earth.

"Jambo!" said a friendly voice from behind him. He turned round to see a boy rather older than himself sitting in the shade of the fence through which he had just passed. He was wearing a green Pelican Camp T-shirt and a pair of shorts, rather than the usual African dress.

"Jambo!" said Jamie. "Are you Sion?"

"Yes, I am Sion. And you are Jammie," he said with a warm smile. He was obviously happy to speak English. Jamie went and sat with him, feeling straight away that they were going to be friends.

"John says you're looking after his calf," said Jamie. "Is it all right?"

"It is very good," Sion assured him.

"But where is it?" Jamie asked. "Has it got any grazing?"

"Is O.K." Sion repeated. He seemed reluctant to pursue the subject further. "How is that boat? Is it very good?" he asked.

"It's great," said Jamie. "Have you seen it?"

"Yes, I seen it." said Sion. "You go fishing in it?"

"Not yet," admitted Jamie, "but we'd like to."

"Me, I show you where. I very good at fishing."

"You mean you want to come fishing in the tin boat with us?" Jamie asked.

"You take me. I show you how to catch winge samaki."

"Right. You show me where John's calf is, and I'll take you," he said.

"Why you want the calf?" Sion was suspicious.

"John says it needs fattening. We've got an idea. We could let it in to graze in the camp, but we'd have to have Eleru on our side because he'd see it from the swimming pool for sure."

"You not tell the manager?" Sion asked anxiously.

"No, no," Jamie explained. "Anyway, I don't think she'd really mind. It is just that she doesn't want everyone doing it. We certainly won't tell."

"Come," said Sion. He led Jamie down along the line of the fence towards the eastern shore. The fence ended at a big rocky outcrop which rose and then fell steeply into the lake. In the side of the rock was a cave, in front of which was a small patch of land enclosed by a boma. The calf was lying in the shade of the cave.

"Here it is," said Sion proudly. "At night I take it through the gate to eat grass in the camp. I bring him back before the wageni wake up."

"Does Eleru know?" asked Jamie.

"Ndiyo," said Sion. "When we go fishing?"

"This afternoon?" Jamie suggested. "You off duty then?"

"Ndiyo," said Sion.

"O.K. I'll come and find you."

William was well advanced in his first lesson at paddling his ambach boat when Jamie joined them. He found it uncomfortable at first, sitting with his legs stretched out in front of him and working the little shell-like paddles through the water with alternating strokes of his arms, like a swimmer trying to do the crawl sitting upright. He tried to follow Nicholas but his boat had a tendency to go round in circles until he learned to sit nearer the stern. After that he got the hang of it, and the three boys had a happy morning boating and swimming around the raft.

Pam joined them as she had promised just before lunch, with Samson, the most experienced boat driver, in the speed boat for their water-skiing lesson. Jamie was already a competent skier so he was allowed to go first. He made his deep water start and completed his circuit with no trouble, finishing by skiing perilously close to the raft and splashing the others who were sunbathing.

THE TIN BOAT

When it was William's turn Pam went into the water with him to hold him in the right position. After two failed attempts to get up he became discouraged, and Pam had to persuade him not to give up. He considered himself to be no good at sports and felt that this sort thing was not for him. So it was a great surprise to him when, at the third attempt, he managed to keep his skis together for long enough to pull himself out of the water. He nearly lost his balance straight away, but recovered and skied for at least two minutes before he finally fell. He swam back to the raft to warm congratulations from Pam and the other boys, feeling delighted with himself.

Nicholas had more difficulty, but he went on and on trying. He did get up once, which gave him some hope, but his skis slid forward from under him and he fell again. At last Pam suggested that he stop because he was too tired and had swallowed a great deal of lake water. She promised to try and give them all another chance the next day.

In the afternoon Jamie went to find Sion, and they set off from the back jetty in the tin boat to go fishing. They took hand lines and hooks and Sion brought some pieces of stale bread. He assured them it was by far the most effective bait. He showed them how to moisten it and roll it up into small doughy balls of just the right consistency to stay on the hook. He took them round the southern point of Pelican Camp and past the little island known as Fig Tree Island which stood in the bay to the east of the camp. He told them this was one of the places where Njemps fishermen came with their nets.

They didn't catch much, only a couple of barbel which Sion insists were delicious, but Jamie and Nicholas had tried them before. They told William that they were all bones and tasted horrible. Sion proved to be a delightful companion, full of humour and high spirits.

When on the way home he admitted that much the best fishing was from the back jetty, they realized that all he had wanted was a ride in the boat. But they were pleased that he had come along, and later that evening they all agreed that they would ask him to join them again. He soon became a firm friend.

The subject of the calf hadn't been mentioned again, though it was preying on Jamie's mind. Now that he knew that John had organized its secret grazing in the camp anyway he wished he hadn't tried to interfere. He was worried about being caught up in a row between John and Pam, and was afraid that Eleru and their new friend Sion would be in trouble. He just wished that it could all be done openly. He wondered whether to talk to Pam in a day or two, when she might not be feeling so cross with John.

As things turned out he didn't have to wait that long. Next morning the boys had another water skiing session. Once again Jamie went first. He decided not to wait while Nicholas spent ages trying to get out of the water, so he swam ashore, put on his shorts and T-shirt and went up to the bar for a coke.

Stephen, an Njemps who was head barman and the senior member of the African staff, was struggling to serve a package tour of some twenty Swiss guests who had arrived that morning. Having been shown to their tents to unpack, they had all come up to the bar at the same time and were ordering soft drinks. Jamie offered to help and Stephen gratefully accepted. Pam was happy for the boys to help behind the bar as long as they only served the soft drinks. When all the Swiss guests had been served, and their bar chits filed away under their respective tent numbers, Jamie helped himself to a coke.

Three young Americans, two men and a girl, came in next and sat up at the bar stools. They had arrived the day before, so Jamie had already met them. They were obviously amused to see a small boy behind the bar, and got into conversation with him.

"You being trained as barman?" one of the men asked jokingly.

"I like helping," said Jamie. "I just came in for a coke, really. I had my turn at water skiing, and now my little brother's trying, but he's not as good as me."

"Oh, is that your brother?" said the girl. "We were just

watching him. He sure doesn't give up easily." The sound of the boat engine revving and dying as Nicholas tried to get up and fell could still be heard from the bar.

Pam came in and joined them.

"Hello," she said. "I've had to leave that little chap to it. He won't give up." Turning to the Americans she said, "I hope you are comfortable in tents one and two down there. I'm afraid it's a long way from the bar, but you have a nice view."

"Oh, it's just wonderful," exclaimed the girl. "This has got to be the nicest place we've been to. You know we came out here to see Africa, and there it is right next to us."

"You mean the village just over the fence? I hope it's not too noisy."

"We love it," the girl reassured her. "And do you know, this morning I was woken by something munching away right next to my tent. I looked out and there was the most beautiful little calf you ever saw. It was all white. A real African one with a little hump and this lovely soft dewlap. Do you keep it here to give a bit of African flavour to the camp? I think it's just great." But Pam couldn't answer. She was choking on her drink. Jamie had gone quite scarlet.

"Oh, did I say something?" asked the girl.

"No, no," said Pam recovering, but not before she had shot an accusing glance at Jamie. "It's just that they're not supposed to be in the camp."

"Oh, but it's so lovely," said the girl. "I think you should let it stay."

"Well, perhaps," said Pam, and whispered to Jamie, "I'll talk to you later." The tension was broken by a cheer from the Swiss tourists. They had been watching Nicholas from the far end of the bar which commanded a good view of the lake. He had just managed a full circuit on his skis.

So the business of the calf came out into the open, though Jamie shielded his African friends by saying that it was all his idea. Sue intervened and said that Pam had only been angry with John because they had all been anxious about the boys being so late back in the boat from Longicharo.

Finally Pam relented, but she told Jamie to make it absolutely plain to Sion that if any of the other animals came into the camp from the village the calf would have to go.

"I hope John gets his bride after all this," Jamie said to Sion as they watched the calf grazing peacefully on the little lawn beyond the swimming pool that evening. "What if this other man pays his bride price first?"

"It is a problem," Sion admitted. "Let us hope this ngombe fatten quick. It is much too thin. He cannot take it like this. But do not worry. I have friends in Rukus where this other man lives. They watch, and they warn me if this man is ready first."

"Then John would have to get moving," said Jamie seriously. It made Sion laugh to see how much Jamie minded about the whole business.

"You really want John to win," he said.

"We're all in it together, aren't we?" said Jamie. "I can't stand losing."

CHAPTER 6

There were many treats for the boys to enjoy in the days that followed. Once they joined a party of guests on an early morning bird trip to the marsh behind Longicharo. They sailed, water skied, and spent many hours playing around in their little ambach boats or swimming off the raft.

Above all they were determined to make the most of the time left to them with the tin boat. Now that they were all competent drivers it was considered safe for them to go off on their own. If they planned to go out of sight of the camp they promised to say where they were going and to wear life jackets.

From time to time Jamie and Nicholas would make friends with children staying at the camp. Few families stayed for more than two or three nights, so the friendships were short-lived, but they enjoyed having a temporary new member of the tin boat crew. Occasionally there would be somebody of William's age staying, but he found it difficult to make friends quickly and preferred the company of the adults when he was not with Jamie and Nicholas.

They had a favourite trip which always impressed any new

member of the crew. Instead of having breakfast at the camp, they would collect some eggs from the kitchen and take the tin boat up to the hot springs on the north west coast of the island. Here they would boil their eggs in one of the hot bubbling pools.

Sometimes they managed to make themselves useful by crossing to the mainland taking messages, members of staff, and on one occasion even some guests when none of the camp boats were available. They also performed a fairly frequent service towing becalmed sailors and windsurfers back to the camp. The wind, which always seemed so promising in the morning, invariably died during the hottest part of the day. Many a guest, grateful for being rescued from the scorching heat, ended up buying the boys a round of sodas before lunch. During this time Sion became friendly with all of them, and frequently came out in the tin boat when he was off duty.

John's calf grew bolder and wandered all over the camp in search or the tastiest grazing, to the delight of the guests. It was noticeably putting on weight and the boys wondered how long it would be before John returned to collect it.

All this time Pam grew more and more concerned about the case of the woman who had been so badly injured. The night she had been brought in to the camp in the tin boat Pam and Sue had done their best to patch her up, and had given her antibiotics to try to prevent infection. However, the wounds were deep and she clearly needed proper treatment, so the next morning they had put her into the first boat with one of her co-wives and sent her to the clinic at Kampi-ya-Samaki. Even there the facilities were very limited, and they heard later that she had ended up in the Nakuru hospital for a few days.

About ten days after the incident the three grown-ups were down at the house enjoying an evening drink and watching the sun go down. The camp was full of Germans on a package tour who ate punctually and never spent money at the bar, so for once there wasn't much to do. The boys were in the house having their supper. Pam had put on a tape of gentle guitar music on her cassette player, and they watched the guinea fowl jostling for roosting positions in the big thorn tree outside the house.

In the fading light the nightjars arrived, giving an amazing display of aerobatics as they plucked insects out of the air. Other birds were off to find their roosting places, small groups of pelicans, cormorants, egrets and tree duck flying low across the lake in formation. They watched for a while in silence, except for the sound of the guitar, the lapping of the water and the clunking of the children's knives and forks. It was all very peaceful, but Pam couldn't forget the problem of the woman who had been attacked. She started discussing it again with Sue and David.

"She seemed so frightened, didn't she? And the other two women with her. It bothers me that they wouldn't tell us what had happened. I can't help wishing I had asked John Boat. They may have talked to him."

"Yes they did," mumbled William between mouthfuls of moussaka. This made Pam sit up.

"What was that, William?"

"They did."

"Did what?"

"Talk to John. Those women. He told me." Jamie and Nicholas looked expectantly at William.

"What did he say, William?" asked Sue.

"Well," said William, "he said he had asked the other women if her husband had done it, but they said no, it was another man from some other part of the lake. They seemed sure he wasn't an Njemps"

"And....?" said Pam. William paused for a long time before admitting,

"That's all. That's all he said."

"Well thank you William, and well remembered," said Pam. She thought for a bit and went on. "I think I must have a chat with the Njemps chiefs about this. I'm sure they don't want trouble makers on the island, and nor do we."

Early next morning she set off in the speed boat to the other end of the island to see James Leweri, the most influential mzee of the island community. She took Stephen the head barman with her, and on the way he told her of other incidents he had heard of in which people had been attacked by men from outside the tribe. He thought the new road had encouraged bad people to come to Kampi-ya-Samaki.

They went on with Leweri to Longicharo to talk to Chief Rapili, and were away for the entire morning. Though the two wazee were as worried as Pam and Stephen by the incidents, they said that before bringing in the police they wanted to make absolutely certain that nobody from within the tribe was involved. They had their own ways of dealing with trouble within the tribe, whatever the law of the land might be.

So for that morning Sue was left to run the camp with Jackson, the second barman. It was the first time during that visit that she had been left in charge, and it was a day full of problems.

She saw the German tourists on their way by nine o'clock. That left the camp nice and empty. Apart from the three Americans there remained only a young couple in tent fifteen right out on the point of the island, and they had booked a boat for departure at ten-thirty. Soon new guests would arrive, but the bulk of them were not expected until the afternoon so it should have been a peaceful morning.

Meanwhile the boys were out in the tin boat.

"We're just going round the bay behind the camp to see if we can see George," William had told her. George was the only hippo regularly seen near the island, most of them preferring to stay down the south west corner of the lake.

"O.K. But don't get too close to him," Sue had said.

To reach the bay they passed round the southern point of the camp on which tent fifteen stood. Near the tent they were surprised to see a young African whom they did not recognize, crouching in the shade of a tree. Instead of the usual pink shuka he wore a green and yellow printed kikoi. Near him an ambach boat was pulled up onto the rocks. He looked displeased to see the boys. There was no smile, no wave and no 'jambo'.

They went on round the corner, past the east facing tents spread out on different levels along the slope and the assistant manager's house down on the water's edge which David was using as a studio. He looked up and waved as the tin boat went by. They passed the camp boundary fence and entered the narrow channel between the main island and the little Fig Tree Island which stood in the bay. This was where they were expecting to find George.

They were opposite the Njemps village now and several girls were down on the shore doing their washing. Further round the bay some of the humped cattle were standing knee deep in the water, watched over by a little boy who looked no older than Nicholas. They hunted around for George but without success. After a while they lost interest and drove round to the far side of Fig Tree Island. There they found a little beach which looked like a suitably shady place to stop and drink the cokes which they had collected from the bar before they set off.

They pulled the boat up on to the shore and settled themselves under a tree whose branches spread right down until they almost touched the water. As they sat and swigged their drinks a pied kingfisher landed on one of the branches in front of them. They sat very still and watched as it took off again and hovered over the water. Suddenly it dived and came up with a fish in its bill. It returned to the same branch and softened up the fish by beating it against a branch before swallowing it whole.

"What an amazing sight," said William.

"More interesting than anything George the hippo might have done for us," Jamie agreed.

It was a pleasant place to sit. There was nobody to bother them, though they could hear the occasional raised voice from the camp or the village behind them. They sat for a while discussing whether they could use the tin boat for water skiing.

"Not powerful enough to get any of us out of the water, I don't think," said Jamie.

"Except me perhaps," said Nicholas hopefully. Jamie was about to protest at this idea when William diverted their attention.

"Someone's waving at us from the other shore," he said. They all got up and went down to the water's edge.

"It's Sion, isn't it?" said Jamie. "Let's go and see what he wants." They launched the boat and crossed to the shore of the bay where they were greeted by their friend.

"Will you take me to Gibraltar?" he asked.

"What do you want over there?" asked Jamie,

"My uncle Samson is mending the roof of his house. The best grass for this is on Gibraltar. He not need much, but I think too much for my ngadich." It sounded like another interesting little excursion and they all readily agreed.

Gibraltar was like an island cut in half. The whole of the west side consisted of a high cliff. This was the side visible from the camp. The east side slope gently down from the cliff top to the lake. In between the bushes and low trees the rocky slope was covered with clumps of thick dry grass up to three feet high. It was obvious why it was so suitable for thatch.

They soon discovered that the grass was too tough to pull up by hand. Sion had brought a panga with him, so the boys let him do the cutting while they bundled up the grass and carried it down to the boat. By the time they had each made three journeys up and down the slope in the blazing sun they were feeling pretty hot and tired.

"Not sure where we'll sit if we put any more in the boat," said William, hoping that would be a good enough excuse to call it a day.

"Yeh, reckon we've done enough," agreed Jamie. "HEY! SION! THE BOAT'S ABOUT FULL," he shouted. They were relieved to see Sion collect up the rest of the grass he had cut and set off down the slope towards them. Suddenly they heard a man's voice shouting angrily in Swahili from somewhere in the bush up to their right. From where they stood they couldn't see who it was, but Sion obviously could because he stopped as if he was waiting for the man to approach him. However the shouting was renewed and Sion seemed to take fright and hasten down the slope.

"A man is there," he gasped when he reached the boys. "He very angry we here. He tell us go away or we get hit. I think we go now."

"Who was he?" asked Jamie as they pushed the boat out. "I didn't think any one lived on Gibraltar."

"I not know this man," said Sion, "but he not live here. Nobody live here."

"What's he look like?" asked Jamie.

"See for yourself," said William, pointing back up the slope. The inhospitable stranger was standing watching them from a large rock above the shore, as if making sure they were going.

"I recognize him," said Jamie.

"We saw him at the camp this morning, didn't we?" asked Nicholas. "Wasn't he by tent fifteen?"

"C'mon", said William. "We know when we're not wanted. Let's get out of here." He started the engine and they left Gibraltar behind with a sense of considerable relief.

CHAPTER 7

The boys were very late for lunch by the time they had delivered Sion to his uncle's village and helped unload the grass. However, they realized as soon as they reached the jetty that Sue and Jackson had far too many problems to have had time to worry about them. Two policemen, in their grey uniforms with shorts and long stockings were being driven away by the boat driver Singh in Blue Banana. With them were Moses and Matteus, two of the tent staff. Everyone looked sullen and anxious, and even Singh didn't wave or smile when saw the tin boat. Sue stood dejectedly on the jetty. Many of the camp staff watched soberly as Blue Banana headed towards the mainland.

"What's happened?" shouted Jamie from the tin boat. The engine was still running so they couldn't hear his mother's reply, but they saw her point towards the house and set off up the hill in that direction followed by Jackson. They took the tin boat round to the back jetty and tied it up.

"What on earth is going on?" asked William when they reached the house.

"Have Moses and Matteus been arrested?" asked Nicholas.

"What have they done?" Jamie asked.

Sue put up her hand to silence their questions. She would obviously have preferred not to say anything to the boys at that moment, but knew that she was going to have to give them some explanation as they had seen too much for themselves.

"I'm sure they haven't done anything," she said, trying to make light of it all but not succeeding.

"But why……?"

"Some money was stolen from tent fifteen. That young couple wouldn't let me try to sort it out and went to the police at Marigat on their way out. Moses and Matteus are the tent staff for number fifteen, so the police decided to question them."

Everyone was quiet for a while, then Sue continued, almost to herself.

"I'm sure none of our people would do it. We've never had that kind of trouble here." Then after another silence, "God! I wish Pam would come back." Pulling herself together, and regretting that she had let her anxiety show in front of the children, she smiled reassuringly and said,

"Anyway, what have you all been up to this morning?" She looked at her watch and, surprised to see how late it was, added, "you've been gone ages."

"We've been to Gibraltar with Sion to help him collect grass.'" said Nicholas.

"Grass? What for?" asked Sue.

"It's for Samson to mend his roof with," Jamie explained. "It was quite fun really except it was rather hot, but then this man came and……"

"Well it all sounds most exciting," said Sue, still too preoccupied to take in much of what they were saying. "Now I must have a word with Jackson. He's waiting in the office. So why don't you all get yourselves a bit tidier for lunch and go and find Dad in the bar. He's being barman for me at the moment and I expect he's a bit bored as there's hardly anybody here. I'll come up in a minute and we'll have lunch."

The boys did as they were told, leaving Sue to have an urgent and animated discussion in Swahili with Jackson. The three young American guests were sitting up at the bar talking to David.

The gentle thudding of a boat engine was heard and, looking down at the lake, they saw Mandeleo arriving full of tourists with broad-brimmed hats and sunglasses. As there was no-one else around to check then in, David grabbed the bookings book and set off down to the jetty.

"Excuse me a minute," he said to the Americans, and turning to the boys he said, "William and Jamie, perhaps you could watch the bar for me for a few minutes. Nicholas, just pop into the kitchen and see what Rotich is up to. It's after one and lunch should be ready. I expect our guests are getting hungry." And off he went.

Jamie and William went behind the bar feeling most important, although there wasn't much to do except collect up a few dirty glasses and empty bottles and pile them on a tray for old Lekejos who came to take them away.

Nicholas disappeared into the kitchen and emerged again with the news that lunch was ready.

"Oh, great!" said the American girl with a friendly smile. "I'm starving. We had a kinda early breakfast. Let's go eat."

"O.K." said Bill, one of her companions, "we'll see you guys later."

The bar was now empty. The three boys helped themselves to sodas, remembering to jot them down in the family's bar book, and settled themselves on the bar stools. They had realized that the subject of the theft and the police was not to be mentioned in front of guests, but now they were free to talk.

"Do you think Matteus or Moses could have done it?" asked Jamie.

"I don't know," said William, "you know them better than I do. Your mother didn't think so, but she'd say that to us anyway."

"I know they didn't," said Nicholas, for whom the camp staff could do no wrong.

"God we're being thick," said William.

"I've just clicked as well," said Jamie. "The man we saw on

Gibraltar."

"He was hanging around by tent fifteen when we first saw him, wasn't he?" said William.

"I bet he did it," said Nicholas.

"It seems extremely likely, doesn't it?" said William. "We'd better tell your mother."

It was some time before Sue or anybody else wound listen to them. David, who didn't often get involved with greeting new guests and allocating tent numbers, had his hands full with a difficult party of package tourists. Their courier was complaining about the tents which he allocated them, and one humourless lady was making an hysterical fuss because she had met a spider in her tent.

In the meantime Sue had finished her discussion with Jackson. Apart from her anxiety about the fate of the two tent boys - she knew the local police might not be too gentle with suspects who didn't confess - she had the practical problem of reorganizing the staff to fill the gap. When she was half way up the path on her way to the bar she heard to her relief the sound of the speedboat returning. Pam was driving and Stephen was sitting beside her. Sue turned and went down to the jetty. She wanted to talk to her sister and explain the whole situation before she heard garbled versions from other people.

Pam must have known instinctively that all was not well, because she jumped out onto the jetty before the speedboat was properly alongside, leaving Stephen to make it fast. Sue met her on the steps. She was miserable at having to tell Pam that things had gone so wrong while she was in charge.

"There's been a theft from number fifteen." She wasted no time in telling Pam the essential facts of the story. "The Osbornes, that young couple. They claim they've lost six thousand shillings."

"Oh, God!" said Pam.

"The stupid people," Sue went on. "I told them not to go to the police until we had had a thorough search and asked some questions around the camp. But they wouldn't wait and went rushing off back to Nairobi, obviously stopping off at Marigat police station."

"Well they can't be that anxious to see their money again if they wouldn't wait," said Pam.

"Oh yes they are," explained Sue. "They've left their address in Nairobi and I'm sure we haven't heard the last of them." While Pam was absorbing all this Sue said, "I'm sure it's not one of our chaps."

"I hope you're right," said Pam, who had been in Africa long enough to learn to take nothing for granted. "You can never be quite sure, can you? I mean we've never had this sort of problem here, but I'm always terrified that one day it will start." She paused again, and relaxed a little. "No," she said firmly. "I'm sure you're right. There is a bad lot of outsiders around at the moment. I've been hearing one or two disturbing stories this morning. Much more likely to be connected with them." Sue was about to continue with her story when Pam said, "Are you sure they've gone to the police?"

"Oh yes! They've been."

"Who?"

"The police. From Marigat. Two of them came."

"Are they still here?"

"No. They left nearly an hour ago. The worst thing is they've taken Moses and Matteus with them for questioning."

"Oh, God!" said Pam in genuine alarm, and then "Damn! Just because they are the tent staff for number fifteen I suppose?"

"Yes," said Sue.

"They can be pretty rough, these policemen out here. Oh dear. What can I do?" It didn't take her long to make up her mind. "I'd better go to Marigat right now," she said.

"Oh, Pam, for goodness sake," said Sue. "At least have some lunch before you go. You missed out on breakfast as it is."

"No," said Pam, and then "yes, O.K. I'll run up and grab a quick bite and then go."

"Mum, come here quickly! We've got to tell you something!

THE TIN BOAT

It's very important!" Jamie shouted down from the bar.

"I'm coming in a minute," Sue answered.

"But it's important!" Jamie repeated as insistently as he could.

"All right!" snapped Sue, now feeling irritable with anxiety. "I said I'm coming. You three go and start lunch."

Jamie gave up. He knew it was no use trying to say anything to anybody when they were all as preoccupied as this. So they went in to lunch, still whispering to each other about their important piece of evidence.

At last Sue and Pam did arrive. Pam ate very quickly, and prattled away in a nervous state, deliberately preventing anybody from getting on to the subject of the theft. Whether she wanted to keep the children out of it or whether she was just worried about the guests overhearing was difficult to tell. William kept on trying to interrupt - they had agreed that he should be the one to speak - but Pam went on talking and made it impossible for him to say what he had to.

Then William saw David coming up the steps. Quickly he got to his feet and rushed out without explanation. He stopped David before he reached the top of the steps.

"David!" he said in an urgent whisper. "There's something we've get to tell you but nobody will listen."

"Oh, all right," said David, at least prepared to make a show of taking William seriously.

"It's about the theft," said William. This did pull David up short.

"You know about it then?" he asked.

"Oh, yes. And about Moses and Matteus," he said. "But we know it wasn't them."

"Well, we're all hoping and praying you're right about that," said David reassuringly.

"But we KNOW!" exclaimed William impatiently. "At least we're almost certain." Now David really was listening. "We saw this man from the tin boat, on our way out this morning. He was lurking in the shadows by tent fifteen, and he didn't look at all pleased to see us."

"Who was he?" asked David.

"I don't know. Not one of the camp staff. Not even an Njemps I don't think, although he did have an ambach with him. He had a green and yellow kikoi. These people all wear those pink shukas, don't they?"

"Yes, you're right. They do. How old was he?"

"Oh, I can never tell," admitted William. "About John Boat's age, perhaps a bit older. Not as tall as John, though, but darker skinned and very muscular."

"Did you talk to him?"

"No. As I say he wasn't friendly so we let him alone. He was even more unfriendly next time we saw him."

"You saw him again? Where was that?"

"On Gibraltar when we went with Sion. We were collecting grass for Samson's roof when the same guy appeared and threatened poor Sion and told us to clear off, so we did."

"Really," said David, taking in the full significance of what he had been told. "Well, if he was enough of a fundi at paddling an ambach to get himself to Gibraltar he must have some connection with the lake. Good. Well done, all of you." He paused to think. "What time did you see him first?"

"It was just after we set off. What time would that have been? Eight? Eight-thirty? Soon after breakfast, anyway."

"That fits," said David. "These people reckoned their money was stolen while they were having breakfast. Now. Not a word to anybody. Not even the staff. And especially not the wagenis. O.K?"

"Oh, yes. We all realize that," said William.

"Good. Well done. Now I must talk to Pam. Actually, William, do you mind waiting here. It's probably best if you repeat all this to her yourself."

David went into the dining room and, inclining his head so that he could whisper to Sue and Pam at the same time, said,

"I think you had better come and hear what William has to say."

"Oh, what's he on about now?" said Pam. "I've got to get to Marigat."

"That's what it's about," explained David. "It's very important, I promise you." Jamie and Nicholas overheard and smiled at each other. They were being taken seriously at last.

"O.K." said Pam, and she and Sue left the dining room with David.

"Now tell Pam everything you've just told me," he said to William, who repeated the whole story.

"It sounds to me like our friends who have been making mischief up the other end of the island, or at least one of them," said Pam seriously. "Leweri and Rapili seem to know who they are but haven't been able to discover where they operate from. There are two or three of them and by all accounts they're quite a violent lot. Well thank you William. At least that clears our chaps, or seems to. Maybe these ruffians are camped out on Gibraltar. Now, I must get to Marigat and rescue those two."

Pam did not return until late into the evening. The boys were already in bed and didn't see Matteus and Moses, but they heard enough of the conversation from the office to know that the poor tent boys had been given a rough time before Pam had arrived and, after a long argument, secured their release. She had only succeeded in the end by insisting that she talk to the chief of the Marigat police, who was not at the station and had to be sent for from his house. Once she explained the whole story to him, together with the information she had gleaned from Rapili and Leweri, the police chief was satisfied that he knew who the culprits were and allowed the tent boys to go.

Two days later a message came with one of the boat drivers from the Marigat police. They had arrested their three suspects. To the boys' disappointment there had been no great stakeout of Gibraltar, nor a race and chase across the lake. The police knew from the descriptions whom they were after, and knew they were drinkers.

Kampi-ya-Samaki was the only place accessible to them where they could buy drink, and it was no great problem to watch the bars for a couple of days. Inevitably they showed up with their newly acquired wealth, and were finally bundled into the police land rover in the middle of the night, blind drunk and offering no resistance.

There was no actual apology for what had happened to Matteus and Moses, but there was an acknowledgement that there should be more consultation with the camp management if a similar incident occurred.

THE TIN BOAT

CHAPTER 8

One morning towards the end of the second week Pam said to the boys,

"You know Matthew and Helen are coming back tonight. That means we will have to take the tin boat over to their house this afternoon and leave it for them." The boys groaned. They had almost forgotten that they would have to give the boat back. It had become so much part of their lives.

They started planning hopelessly ambitious trips to make the best use of their last day with the boat, but Pam begged them not to run any risks.

"It really was very generous of them to lend it to you," she reminded them. "They love that boat just as you do. They probably can't wait to be home and have it for themselves again. It would be too awful if you damaged it now." She insisted that they stay within sight of the camp. In the end they settled for taking a picnic lunch to Teddy Bear Island.

They waited around for their packed lunches to be ready, and set off when the sun was already too hot for comfort. They pulled the boat ashore, but they found the island to be rocky and steep, without shade and most unfriendly. They walked up a stony path towards the centre of the island. It was terribly hot and dry, and the insects were appalling. They ate their picnic as fast as they could, standing up for fear of being bitten, and returned to camp without having enjoyed their expedition at all.

They fooled around in the area of the raft for most of the afternoon, trying to enjoy the tin boat while they could, but not able to forget that they were about to lose it. At about four o'clock Pam came down to the jetty and beckoned them to bring the boat in. They spent a sad half hour cleaning it out.

They had all been invited to visit friends on the mainland later that afternoon. Pam asked the boys to set off in the tin boat, saying that she would catch them up with Sue and David in the speedboat. Nicholas decided not to prolong his farewell to the tin boat and said he would wait for the grown-ups, so William and Jamie set off by themselves. They didn't talk much, but were both thinking the same thought. They knew they still had another wonderful month ahead of them, but from now on they would have to depend on the grown-ups for any boating other than fooling around in their little ambaches. Before they arrived they had never expected to enjoy the sort of freedom which the tin boat had given them. Now they wondered what they would do without it.

About a mile from the mainland jetty the speedboat caught them up and shot past them, making a wash which splashed over their bows. Nicholas found this very amusing. He seemed to have said goodbye to the tin boat in his mind already, so he had cheered up and was enjoying himself.

He and the grown-ups waited on the jetty while William and Jamie tied up the tin boat and walked up to the house. There was nobody around so they left a note of thanks for the loan of the boat, saying where they had left it. They all set off in the speedboat to call on friends further along the shore. As they pulled away they saw a car coming along the road from Kampi-ya-Samaki. They knew it was Helen and Matthew returning with their father.

THE TIN BOAT

The grown-ups talked on and on with the friends they were visiting. The sun was setting by the time they were back in the speedboat, heading for the island. In the distance, out beyond the mainland jetty, they could see the tin boat being driven round and round in circles. Helen and Matthew were already having a good time.

The boys were in a hopeless mood next morning, moping around the house and driving the grown-ups mad because they wouldn't make up their minds to do anything. They were kicked out and wandered up to the swimming pool. There they came to life for a short time, making a good deal of noise jumping into the water and chasing each other.

There was only one guest in the pool, a round, middle-aged lady apparently bent on swimming an infinite number of lengths at a very sedate pace. She regarded the boys as a definite nuisance, but she was not to be deterred, and this rather took the edge off the boys' enjoyment. Soon they were lounging around again with no enthusiasm to do anything, waiting for something to happen.

Eleru came over to talk to them. He was responsible for keeping the swimming pool clean. He had been given this humble job because he could not write or cook, and spoke little English. However he was an important figure within the Njemps tribe. He belonged to the dominant age group of young wazee, and had been chosen as one of the leaders of that group. This meant that in due course he would become one of the most respected elders. He had a natural elegance and good manners. Like many of the staff he understood a good deal more English than he spoke.

"You not swim?" he asked the boys sympathetically, sensing their mood. They shook their heads. "Ndiyo," he said, "hakuna boat. Mbaya sana." Perhaps, thought William, the whole camp knows why we are sad.

Eleru went over and sat on the stone wall from where he could see down to the part of the lake where boats passed on their way to the jetty. The boys felt they should be friendly and talk to him, but they were not in the mood to be cheered up. Presently Eleru said, quite casually,

"Helen nakuja. Nzuri," but they all knew about Helen's arrival and it wasn't nzuri at all.

"Kuja!" he said, beckoning them and sailing. "Helen yupo hapa!" It took them a few seconds to realize what he was saying. Suddenly they all cottoned on at the same moment and rushed over to the wall. There below them, approaching the island, was the tin boat, driven by a teenage girl with long fair hair and a slightly younger, even blonder boy.

Without waiting to say more than "Kwaheri Eleru, and asante sana," Jamie and Nicholas rushed out of the swimming pool and down towards the jetty. William followed them more slowly, pleased to see the tin boat return but nervous that the arrival of two old friends of his cousins, whom he had never met, was going to break up their happy little group and leave him once again as the outsider.

At the top level of the jetty Jamie and Nicholas stopped and watched Helen bring the boat in. The possibility only occurred to them then that the two children might not have come to see them, but they needn't have worried. Helen brought the boat alongside the jetty, Matthew tied up, and they both leaped out. It was all done in one smooth, well practiced movement.

"Hi, you guys!" called out Matthew in his high-pitched voice. Jamie and Nicholas rushed down the steep wooden steps to meet him and his sister. William waited at the top. He watched them greet each other with mounting apprehension.

'How lovely it would be to have the confidence just to go down and introduce myself and join the gang,' he thought miserably. 'But I can't. What will they want with me now? They're all buddies together and I don't belong at all. Oh, leave them to it. I'll go and see if I can help in the bar.' He turned his back on them and started walking dejectedly up the path.

"Hey! Wait!" he heard a friendly unfamiliar voice call out behind him. Turning round he saw that Helen was following him.

THE TIN BOAT

The warmth of her smile persuaded him that he should at least stop and talk to her.

His first impression of her was that she was not one of those teenage girls who was in a great hurry to become sophisticated and leave her childhood behind. She was dressed in a striped rugby shirt and running shorts, and moved and spoke with a complete lack of teenage self-consciousness. She went straight up to William and introduced herself,

"Hi! I'm Helen," she said, offering her hand. "I guess you must be William."

"Yes," said William. "How did you......?"

"Oh, everybody knows who's around in a little place like this," she said with a reassuring smile. "Listen, I've just got to go up to the office with a message from my Dad. How about after that we all go skiing in the tin boat, eh? See you in a minute." Without waiting for an answer she rushed off up the path as if she couldn't get back fast enough.

William was left wondering whether she could be serious. He remembered the discussion with Jamie and Nicholas when they decided that skiing behind the tin boat would be impossible.

Matthew was still on the jetty with the two boys. They were already sharing some big joke. Matthew was a clown. William could see that in his face. Encouraged now by Helen's friendliness he came down to join them.

"This is William," said Jamie.

"Yeh, jambo man, I'm Matthew," he said, giving William an African style slap on the palm of his outstretched hand.

"Hello Matthew," said William. "Listen, Helen's just said something about skiing behind the tin boat." Jamie and Nicholas looked at him in disbelief, but Matthew said,

"Yeh man, great. Let's go!" and ran over towards the hut where the skis were kept.

"But you can't, surely," said Nicholas, hoping you could, but not wanting to be proved wrong on a technical matter.

"Yeh, man, sure thing. With this engine, no problem," said

Matthew confidently, "We can ski all we want."

And so they did. It was no good with more than one person in the boat, and getting William out of the water was heavy going. But it did work, and they could ski without being dependent on anyone else.

Helen was tireless. She seemed happy to drive for them all morning. Eventually she persuaded William to try to drive for her. At first he lacked confidence and didn't dare go fast enough, but she made him persevere though he let her down again and again. Eventually he took the boat back to the raft.

"Sorry, I'm no use at this," he said to her, all his confidence draining away. "Let one of the others try. You'll do better without me. I'll let you get on with it and go and see if I can help Pam."

"What rubbish!" said Helen laughing. "Come on, we nearly made it. Just start at full throttle and we're away. Don't go slinking off to the grown-ups. This is fun."

'You're very persistent,' he thought. "O.K. If you're really not totally fed up with me I'll try once more," he said.

This time he succeeded, and gave her a good ski all the way to Gibraltar and back.

CHAPTER 9

It was nearly two o'clock when they decided to have a break for lunch. By that time the sun was very hot indeed and they were all in need of long cool drinks. They treated themselves to club specials, pint glasses of mixed fruit juices and chopped fresh fruit. They took their drinks to the dining room, where they talked excitedly while they ate their lunch.

"Want to go on after lunch?" asked Helen.

"Yeh! Fantastic!" answered Matthew.

"Really great." said Jamie. "I could go on all day."

"Me too!" piped up Nicholas.

"You're not fed up with driving us?" asked William.

"Hell, no," said Helen. "Anyway, you can do it just as well as me now, so we can share. It's fun. I enjoy it."

"Yes it is," William agreed, glowing.

"Jammie!" Jamie recognized his name as pronounced by Sion, but couldn't tell straight away where the voice was coming from. "Nataka Jammie," the voice repeated. Jamie looked over the low wall along the open side of the dining room. Sion was standing on the path below, looking up. "Kuja!" he beckoned.

"Sion's got some sort of problem I think," said Jamie. "He looks worried. I'll go down and see." He returned five minutes later to tell them what it was all about.

"There seems to be a great mneno over John's wedding," he said. "You know Sion's been fattening up his calf for him here. Well Kilima, you know, who does the generator, he's just come back from Rukus. He told Sion that this man who wants to marry the same girl as John has his bride price together. He's setting off now on foot to take all these cattle and goats to the bride's father. If he gets there before John he might get the bride."

"Well what does Sion want us to do?" asked Nicholas.

"He wants a boat so that he can take the calf to John and tell him to take it to the bride's father. But he'd have to do it right now. It wouldn't take more than three or four hours for the other man to get from Rukus to the Molo River."

"Is that where the bride lives?" asked Helen.

"Yes, somewhere between Fort Baringo and the Molo River, then inland about a mile. Sion knows how to find it."

"Right. Let's go!" said Matthew. "We'll take them in the tin boat, what d'you reckon?" It sounded like a good adventure, and they all wanted to help John. Only William, who was still rather nervous about the unfamiliar world of the Africans, was less than enthusiastic.

"You all go," he said. "I'll stay here. You'll be quicker with less weight."

"But you can't miss out on this," Helen insisted. "It could be exciting." William still wasn't convinced. "Hey, don't be a dampener," she said in a perfectly friendly way. "It'll be much more fun if we all go."

"Yes, come on!" Jamie joined in.

"O.K." said William, cheering up. "I'll go and fill up the fuel tank."

"I knew we couldn't do without you," said Helen. "Jamie, tell Sion we'll take him. Get him to bring the calf round to the back jetty." So lunch was gobbled hastily or simply abandoned, and

THE TIN BOAT

they hurried away to find the one or two items, such as hats and gym shoes, which they needed to take. In the rush nobody remembered to tell the grown-ups where they were going.

They met Sion by the back jetty. He was leading the little white calf by a rope round its neck.

"Not much to pay for a bride," quipped Matthew, who hadn't seen it before.

"Oh, I think this is just the last instalment," said William. Helen was having an earnest conversation with Sion in Swahili.

"Listen," she said eventually. "I think Sion has got a point. He thinks we should drop him off at Salabani, which is the nearest place on the lake to John's home. He can run inland from there to tell John what's happened, and get him to meet us further round the lake. He's explained where. He wants us to take the calf so that it doesn't have to run so far."

"Yeh, see what you mean, Sion," Matthew agreed. Jamie was stroking the calf.

"He's lovely," he said. "Feel how soft his dewlap is. He looks really well now." William was already in the tin boat, reconnecting the fuel tank which he had refilled. Sion climbed down to join him.

"Lift the calf down to me," he said to Jamie, who was very pleased to be trusted with the precious burden again.

The boat was rather heavily laden by the time they were all on board. They agreed that Helen should drive because she was the most experienced. It was slow going.

"I wish we knew how much time we had," said Jamie. "Do you think this other guy will beat us to it, Sion?"

"It is a long way from Rukus," Sion reassured him. "He walk. We are in the boat. And he has wengi ngombe and goats. I think he not go too fast."

"Anyway, he doesn't know he's in a race," Helen pointed out.

"Still, you'd better run to John's house," said Nicholas.

"Oh, yes. I run. I very fast man!" joked Sion. They landed him near Salabani, in the south west corner of the lake. Before he went he made sure they knew where to meet John.

"Take the boat to that bay between Fort Baringo and the river," he said. "Leave it there. Take the path straight, straight pande ile," he indicated a due south direction by chopping the air with his hand. "I tell John he meet you on this path by the first house. I go now. Wait for John if he not there. He must change to wear the right clothes, but I tell him be very quick. Kwaheri yote. Asante sana."

"You not coming with John?" asked Jamie.

"Hapana. He run too quick for me," laughed Sion, and trotted off with a final wave.

They pushed off and Helen restarted the engine. She steered out through the reeds into the middle of the lake, following the same channel through which they had come into the shore.

"I'd love to know where the other man has got to," said Jamie. His competitive blood was up.

"We could go and have a look see," suggested Matthew. "He'll be coming down the far side past Mukutan. We might spot him."

"Be worth knowing if we're in a hurry," said William, who dreaded being made to break into a run.

"O.K." Helen agreed, "but we won't spend too long looking. We mustn't keep John waiting." She opened the throttle and headed east across the southern end of the lake, making for the wide flat part of the shore between Fort Baringo and the Mukutan Hill. As usual they had to slow down to negotiate the reeds which guarded the shoreline. Beyond them was a barrier of ambach bushes through which they found a very narrow gap. Unfortunately the water was too shallow to take the boat right through to where they could see.

"Why don't you and William hop out and have a look," Helen suggested to Matthew. "We'll turn the boat round." The two older boys climbed out. The calf became restless and Jamie had to cling to it to stop it jumping overboard.

Helen and Nicholas used the paddles to turn the boat round, but they only just had it pointing in the right direction when Matthew

THE TIN BOAT

and William returned breathless.

"Quick! He's there! In fact he's past us," William gasped.

"What? You're sure it's him?" asked Helen.

"Got to be!" said Matthew, climbing is over the stern. "All dressed up in a new shuka with a white feather in his hair, and driving a herd of ngombes and goats. There's a mass of totos helping him. They're going at a trot."

"Push off, William," said Helen. "Lets slip out without them seeing us if we can." William pushed the boat clear of the ambaches and clambered in with the help of Jamie and Matthew. Helen lowered the engine and started it.

"We can get a start on him," said Jamie, "but how long will John be?"

"It's touch and go. It really is," agreed Helen.

"They're bound to see us," said Nicholas.

"Well as long as they can't stop us!" shouted Helen over the noise of the engine as she opened the throttle having cleared the reeds. She made for the next bay. John's rival had passed the ambaches by the time the boat entered the reeds again. They could see him with his followers bringing the cattle into single file to pass along the little beach which ran below Fort Baringo hill.

"We must have four hundred yards on him if we go straight in," said Jamie,

"Go on!" shouted Matthew from the bows. "I'll show you the way in. Don't slow down." Helen throttled back as little as she dared and followed Matthew's hand signals through the channel. There was about a hundred yards between them and the shore.

"He's past Fort Baringo," said Jamie.

"Wow! He's going quickly," said Nicholas. Suddenly there was a snort and a tremendous splash behind them.

"Hell!" said Helen. "How did we miss that hippo?" She was about to throttle down when William screamed.

"It's after us!" he shouted. There was no doubt about it. The hippo was coming straight for the boat, and it was gaining on them. Helen had to slow down. The water was shallow and the

THE TIN BOAT

reeds were thick all along the shore. The hippo wouldn't leave them alone so she had to speed up again.

"No!" shouted Matthew. They were about to go aground in the reeds. She swerved to the right to run parallel with the shore. The hippo wasn't put off. It cut the corner and was still closing on them. Suddenly Helen saw a gap in the reeds and a clear channel to the shore, but they were going too fast to turn into it.

Without warning Matthew jumped for it. Nicholas followed. William, taking this for a general 'abandon ship', did the same. The boat tilted so violently that Helen, who was sitting up on the gunwale, simply fell out. She screamed, thinking the hippo must get her, but it kept on after the boat which had swung away from the shore.

Jamie had been thrown into the bottom of the boat and was all tangled up with the rope and the calf's legs. He'd hit his shoulder on the thwart and was cursing and swearing. He pulled himself up and grabbed the tiller. The hippo was still behind him, but with its greatly lightened load the tin boat was going too fast for it. He slowed a little, brought the boat under control and, to the cheers from his companions, took it in a wide circle and back to the shore.

"You bloody fools! What the hell were you doing?" he shouted at them as they helped him pull the boat up. They all tried to justify themselves and there was a heated argument about what they should or shouldn't have done. Most of them were more frightened than angry, but William seemed genuinely upset by the whole episode.

"I think it's all bloody stupid," he said. "We shouldn't have come."

"Oh, belt up!" said Jamie. "Come on! Forget about that now! Is the calf O.K? And where's the other guy got to?" The rival had reached the east end of the bay.

"Quick!" said Helen. "Get the calf on its feet." The poor little thing was thrashing around in the boat, but Jamie grabbed it round the middle and with Helen's help he lifted it out.

"Keep hold of the rope!" shouted Matthew. It was apparently

THE TIN BOAT

unharmed, but eager to make a bid for freedom.

"C'mon," urged Jamie, "we'll have to run. Where's the path?"

"Over here. I've found it!" called Nicholas.

"We're still a couple of hundred yards ahead," said Helen. "We should be O.K., but we mustn't stop. I hope John's there."

"We're not you know," said Matthew. "Look! He's gone up off the beach towards the bush. There must be a parallel path. We're only just ahead, if at all."

"O.K. Run!" shouted Jamie, as they too left the rocky shore and felt the smooth hard earth of the path under their feet. They were glad of their wet clothes for, though the hottest part of the day was over, it was still very warm for running. They set off at a pace which seemed to suit the calf and which, to start with, allowed them all to keep up. But William and Nicholas soon fell behind. Nicholas tried hard but his little legs were too short. William simply hated running, especially in that heat. He was in a bad mood anyway by now.

"You all go on!" he shouted. "I'll go back and look after the boat."

"No, c'mon man," said Helen. "It'll be fun."

"Oh, leave him," said Jamie. So William turned back. Helen said to Jamie and Matthew,

"Keep going. I'll wait for Nicholas." When he caught up with her she took his hand and they trotted along together. The bush was too thick for them to have any idea how their rival was doing. After half a mile or so the two boys with the calf were some hundred metres ahead of Helen and Nicholas, When the first little thatched roof came into sight she was most relieved to see John, looking splendid in his new shuka and white feather, standing in the middle of the path. Before they reached him Matthew shouted,

"Kwenda, man! Take the calf and go! The other guy's right in there somewhere!" He pointed towards the bush on his left. Jamie handed over the rope as if it was the baton in a relay race, and John was off. Jamie and Matthew waited for Helen and Nicholas to catch up.

THE TIN BOAT

"What d'you reckon?" said Matthew. "Shall we go on?"

"We've got to see who wins," insisted Jamie.

"What about you?" Helen asked Nicholas. "I'll take you back to the boat if you like."

"No way!" squeaked Nicholas, and they all set off laughing to follow John. Inevitably they picked up a gang of African children as they went along, all shouting and chanting and joining in the excitement.

After a while they could see John ahead of them having difficulty with the calf. It was obviously fed up with the whole exercise and wanted to go its own way. It was pulling and struggling and slowing John down alarmingly. The children were catching him up. At the same time they became aware that the bush to their left was alive with the bellowing of cows, the bleating of goats and the goading shouts of the drovers. The sounds seemed virtually level with them.

"Go! Go! Go! John!" shouted Jamie. John looked up and must have heard what they could hear. He put his long arms round the calf's four legs and lifted it. "Wow!" said Jamie. The children had caught up with John. He set off at a trot. The effort must have been stupendous. They were all feeling the heat without that weight to carry. Jamie remembered his rugby training sessions and decided to give John some practical encouragement:

"One! Two! One! Two!"

"Moja! Mbili! Moja! Mbili!" Matthew chanted in Swahili. The measured pace certainly made them feel less tired and kept them moving. Even Nicholas, still clutching Helen's hand, managed to keep up. "Moja! Mbili! Moja! Mbili!"

"Moja! Mbili! Tatu! Nne!" They all joined in the chanting. The thick bush suddenly came to an end, and they were in the wide open space of a typical Njemps village, with huts and bomas spread out all round them. John didn't stop, but he nodded towards a boma ahead of them across the open space and slightly to the right.

"This one there," he said breathlessly and headed towards it. It was fortunate for John that the boma was on the right, because to the left his rival's cattle and goats were emerging from the bush in clouds of dust. The position of the boma just gave John the advantage he needed.

"Go, John!" urged Jamie. "You've made it!" They were horrified to see John put the calf down and lead it at a very slow and dignified pace towards the entrance of the boma.

"What the hell's he doing?" exclaimed Jamie, watching the rival's cattle and goats almost stampeding across the open space.

"See that tall old man standing just inside the boma?" said Matthew. "That's the girl's father."

"How do you know that?" asked Helen a little surprised.

"Never mind," said Matthew, "but I reckon John thinks he's being watched and he's got to do this properly."

"You're right, Matthew," said Helen. "Solemn business, buying a wife."

"If these leading cattle beat him to the boma there's no way he'll ever get through," said Jamie. By now a huge crowd had gathered to watch the spectacle. Most of them were smiling and enjoying themselves, but Helen sensed that she and the boys were getting some disapproving looks from one or two of the older women.

"Hey, you guys!" she said as discreetly as possible. "I think we've interfered enough. Better let things take their course." She encouraged them to withdraw to the back of the crowd. But the first of the cattle were almost level with them and were about to push past John who still hadn't reached the boma. Matthew wasn't going to let victory slip away at the last minute. He had a pocket full of sweets. Shouting "Kwaheri" to the crowd in general he threw the sweets up in the air so that they just happened to land a few yards in front of the advancing cattle. All the little children who were watching made a mad scramble for the sweets. The adults grabbed them and pulled then back, but the cows had stopped in their tracks.

"Hey! Matthew! Enough!" Helen hissed, pulling him away, but

THE TIN BOAT

the trick had worked. John was passing through the gate without a backwards glance. The rival drove his herd forward and entered the boma just behind him. The thorn branches were pulled across the entrance.

Some of the crowd dispersed. Others hung around. The lucky totos who had sweets ran off pursued by those who had missed out. Helen and the boys were trying to get their breath back.

"A fanta would be good," said Matthew.

"Yeh!" gasped Jamie. They were all rather subdued and not feeling like joking.

"I hope we haven't mucked it up for John," said Helen.

"But he did win," Jamie insisted.

"Yeh, but we were rather over the top."

"I think John will get her," piped up Nicholas. "The other man didn't look nearly as nice. I'm sure she'll prefer John."

"It's not up to her, you idiot!" said Jamie.

"One never knows," said Helen. "If she really likes John best I bet the old ladies pull a few strings behind the scenes."

"Complicated rules this game has," commented Matthew.

"We haven't got all that long if we're going to get back before dark," said Helen.

"But we must see what happens," said Jamie. "Can't we go and ask?"

"Absolutely not," she insisted. "I'm terrified we've interfered too much already."

They were too breathless to think of setting off anyway at that moment so they waited around in silence, pouring with sweat, their faces burning. After a while a little voice piped up behind them:

"Memsahib!" Helen turned round. A toto with a dirty old shuka was holding out two opened bottles of coke to them.

"Am I glad to see you!" said Matthew. The little boy handed over the cokes and recited his message.

"John na sema asante sana. Yeye na sema hapana ngoja. Yeye hapana kuja sasa."

"What's he say?" asked Nicholas.

"He says that John says thank you very much, but he can't come now so we mustn't wait."

"But has he won?" worried Jamie.

Helen put the question to the little boy. He nodded with a bashful smile.

"Ndiyo," he said. The children cheered and punched the air.

"Asanti sana," said Helen. Matthew found one more sweet in his pocket and gave it to the little messenger

"O.K." said Helen, "we must get going. You all right, Nicholas?"

"Yes," said Nicholas, refreshed by his coke. "But I'm not running."

"Nor me," said Matthew.

"Right, but brisk walk," Helen insisted. Their departure didn't go unnoticed and they were followed by the usual gang of totos.

"Hey, what a race!" said Jamie.

"Yeh, close finish, eh?" laughed Matthew. "That hippo nearly did for John though."

"Nearly did for me and all," Jamie joked. "I don't know what you all thought you were doing. Still, we won. That's the great thing."

"Wouldn't like to bump into that other guy right now," said Matthew. "He must be feeling pretty choked. He went in with John though. I'd love to know what happened."

"Yeh, poor chap," said Helen. "Never mind, perhaps she's got a sister."

"Sister for sale, eh?" said Matthew. "Good idea. How many cows does Dad want for you?"

"She'd fetch a good price," said Jamie. "I bet there'd be lots of rivals."

"D'you reckon?" quipped Matthew. "Regular Olympic Games to compete for her, you reckon?"

"All right you guys!" laughed Helen. "Joke flogged to death."

"I'm tired," squeaked Nicholas. He was clutching one coke bottle. Helen let him have most of it. Matthew and Jamie were sharing the other one.

"Must keep going, I'm afraid," Helen said. Jamie started his chanting again.

"Moja! Mbili! Moja Mbili!"

"Moja! Mbili! Tatu! Nne!" Nicholas joined in and felt better immediately. They all sang out the numbers and strode along in high spirits. Then Matthew started, up a bouncier rhythm.

"Mtu moja na kwenda,
 Na kwenda lima shamba.
 Mtu moja na mbwa yake
 Na kwenda lima shamba."

It was "One Man Went to Mow" in Swahili. Jamie and Nicholas had been taught it by their mother so they all joined in, linking arms and bouncing down the path.

"Watu wawili na kwenda
 Na kwenda lima shamba
 Watu wawili
 Mtu moja na mbwa yake
 Na kwenda lima shamba."

Clutching their coke bottles they looked like any old bunch of drunks turned out of the pub at closing time on a Saturday night. Their toto followers soon got the hang of it and sang along too. William heard them from a long way off and went up the path to meet them.

"We won!" shouted Jamie when he saw him. "You should have seen it!"

"Amazing!" said Matthew as they met up with him, and they all four tried to tell him the story at once.

"Yeh, you really should have been there," said Helen. "Why didn't you come?"

"I'm sorry," said William. "Can't bear running. Never was any good at it."

"Well, never mind," said Helen. "Perhaps it was a good idea for somebody to stay and watch the boat. You want to drive home?"

THE TIN BOAT

'Why doesn't she just tell me I'm a drag and a pain in the backside?' thought William.

"I'm always a dampener," he said.

"Ah, rubbish!" said Helen. "C'mon. We must get moving."

THE TIN BOAT

CHAPTER 10

There was a bit of a row when they got back just before dark because they hadn't said where they were going. However Pam, Sue and David were soon caught up in their infectious high spirits as they told them their story. They were all delighted for John, particularly Pam who felt she had been a bit hard or him.

The children skied endlessly for the next three days without a care in the world. By the end of the fourth day they were beginning to tire. It had been exceptionally hot, and the sun had burnt the skin off their noses and made their eyes sleepy and heavy. At around five o'clock Helen, having just given Jamie a long circuit round Gibraltar and back, came in to the raft and said,

"Call it a day, eh?"

"Yeh, man!" said Matthew without stirring from his sunbathing position.

"What you say we go up to the bar?" Helen went on.

"But I want another turn!" insisted Jamie as he climbed the ladder onto the raft .

"We've had enough, man," said Matthew, and they all shouted Jamie down.

They brought the tin boat to the jetty, unloaded the skis and, pulling T-shirts over their bathers, wandered lazily up to the bar. Tea had been cleared away and it was too early for guests to start their evening drinking, so the bar was deserted. There wasn't even a barman on duty.

Helen opened up the bar as if she owned the place.

"Cokes all you guys?" she asked, opening one.

"Fanta please," said Nicholas.

"Sprite please," said William.

"Beer please," said Jamie laughing.

"Oh, so you're a big boy are you?" teased Matthew.

"I've tasted beer lots of times," insisted Jamie defensively.

"And whisky too, I suppose," taunted Matthew. Jamie was about to lie and say yes, and whisky too, but Matthew was staring him hard in the eye and he reckoned he wouldn't get away with it.

"Well, I haven't actually......."

"Hey, Helen, give him a taste," said Matthew quickly with his high pitched giggle.

She hesitated for a moment but couldn't resist the fun. Taking a small tumbler from under the counter she poured some whisky into it from a bottle which wasn't attached to a tot measure. Jamie took rather a large sip and, for a moment, pretended to enjoy it, but soon turned bright red and started coughing and spluttering.

"No, man, not like that," shouted Matthew, taking the glass and having a sip himself. But almost immediately he too was choking and coughing.

"Man that's a strong one," he cried. Nicholas tried, but spat it straight out.

"Yuk! Disgusting!" he shouted.

Helen took a gulp, and they all waited for the reaction. But with no more than the faintest clearing of the throat and a slight reddening of the face and watering of the eyes it was gone. She smiled triumphantly and they all clapped.

"Go on William. Now you," said Jamie.

"No, thanks," said William, hoping the subject would be dropped, but of course it wasn't.

"Oh, come on, man!" said Helen encouragingly.

"Yeh, we've all done it," shouted the others.

"Oh, O.K." William conceded. He took the tumbler and let the smallest possible sip pass his lips. He pretended to swallow, and put the glass down.

"Not very nice," he said smiling uncertainly and wondering if he had got away with it.

"That wasn't even enough to taste," protested Jamie. "Go on. Have a proper sip."

"Oh, hell," said William under his breath, and took much too large a gulp. He jumped off the bar stool and ran around the floor doubled up, unable to stop coughing. Matthew slapped him on the back until last he caught his breath and straightened up.

"God! It's like fire!" he gasped

"Let's have some more," suggested Jamie.

"No," said Helen. "We'll try something else this time."

"This is bloody stupid!" shouted William.

"Oh come on William!" said Helen. "It's just a bit of fun. Don't spoil it all."

"No it's not," said William. "It's idiotic. The grown-ups trust us, and now look how we're behaving. I'm off!" He was close to tears as he stormed off towards the far end of the room. Helen came round from behind the bar as if to follow him.

"Oh, leave him be," said Jamie. She looked over at William uncertainly and went back behind the bar. William sat on a seat looking out across the lake with his back to the other children, who were laughing and joking, their voices getting steadily louder. Helen wiped the glass and poured in some gin.

"Bet you won't like this. It's revolting by itself." They all agreed. Nicholas didn't get further than smelling it. They rather preferred the Kenya cane. The brandy had them all coughing again.

"They're all disgusting," said Nicholas,

"Here's one you'd like," said Helen, pouring out some Bristol Cream.

"Yum. It's delicious!" agreed Nicholas. They were all about to try when Sue walked in.

"Quiet!" she shouted. "The whole camp can hear you! What

on earth are you up to?"

The children tried to be quiet but they were all very giggly. Sue was not about to see the funny side of it. She had got as far as saying to Helen,

"What would your father say?" when Pam appeared.

"Come on, you lot," she said when she realized what was going on, "down to the house before the guests stumble on this appalling orgy."

"O.K.," said Helen trying to pull herself together. "My fault. I shouldn't have encouraged this. Sorry sana."

"We'll talk about it down at the house," said Pam. "Come on."

Helen turned to look at William who was still sitting way over the other end of the room.

"You coming," she called out.

"Oh, leave me alone!" he said, without even looking round at her

Once they were down at Pam's house and out of hearing of the rest of the camp Pam confronted Helen.

"What on earth are you thinking of?" she asked. "It's up to your father what you and Matthew are allowed to get up to, but it's not happening here while I'm running this camp, and certainly not when you've been trusted to look after children as young as Jamie and Nicholas. First of all you go off for the whole day without telling any of us where you're going, and now this. You've given them a wonderful time in the tin boat, but if you and William can't be trusted to look after the younger ones then sadly it's going to have to come to an end."

"William did his best to stop it," said Helen, looking down to avoid Pam's gaze. "Please don't blame him. It was my fault." Raising her eyes and looking first at Pam and then at Sue she said, "I promise we won't do anything stupid like that again. Please trust me!"

"Yeh, me too," added Matthew. "Please don't tell Dad."

Pam looked at Sue.

"It's up to you," she said. "It's your children." At that moment

David walked in. Sue took him into the office and the children waited nervously until they came out again.

"Look," David said to Helen, "I'm sure you understand. You can't behave like irresponsible teenagers when you're looking after younger children, and you certainly can't start pouring alcohol down their throats."

"Of course," she said. "I know I should have been sensible and responsible like William. It's just that I want him to enjoy himself while he's here."

"I know you do," said David. "We all appreciate that."

In the end they were forgiven. The four drinkers were given an early supper to sober them up, but even after they had eaten Jamie and Nicholas were very drowsy and were happy to tumble into bed. By seven o'clock they were asleep.

"Are you O.K. to get home?" Sue asked Helen. "You can't be feeling your best and you'll be going back in the dark."

"Oh, we'll manage," said Helen confidently, but spoiled it all by yawning uncontrollably.

"I think I'd better drive you," said David. "I can come back on the next boat. There'll be lots of guests coming over late on a Friday night." Helen had to agree that it was a good idea. David found a torch and they set off for the jetty. "Look," he said to her on the way down, "Of course we know we can trust you. Just be careful not to spoil it."

"Thanks," said Helen. She saw William sitting in the garden under the big thorn tree, watching the very last glow of daylight disappearing beyond the lake.

"I'll catch you up," she said to David and Matthew, and went to sit with William for a minute. He looked round briefly as she approached, and resumed his gloomy contemplation of the lake.

"I'm sorry, William," she said. "You're right. That was stupid of me."

"I'm just a drag on everyone," murmured William.

"That's rubbish," said Helen. "You were the responsible one. I'm the one who's at fault."

"Yes, yes," said William, "but I'm the one who spoils everybody's fun. I'd much rather be like you."

"But you can be. Of course you can," she said sympathetically. "Life doesn't come much better than this, you know. What is it? Something's bothering you. Please tell me."

"I don't really want to talk about it," he said, "but the drinking thing's always been a big problem at home, specially with my step dad. It makes it hard for me to see the funny side of it."

"I'd no idea," said Helen. "I really am sorry. But hey, I'm your rafiki now, your friend. If you ever want to talk about it..."

"Thanks," said William, his mood beginning to lift.

"Yeh, well, from now on you're going to enjoy yourself," said Helen. "I think it's great you being here. It's years since anybody of my age came to the lake for more than a few days. Tell you what," she went on, "Dad wants us home over the weekend, and the camp'll be full anyway. But early next week we'll come over here and stay a night if there's a spare tent. We'll get up very early and go fishing at the Mukutan in the tin boat, just the five of us. We'll have a good time, eh?"

William nodded and smiled. David was calling from the jetty. Helen got up to leave.

"See ya," she said, "and you cheer up now. That's a deal."

"I promise," said William.

Much later, with Nicholas sound asleep and Jamie snoring away beside him under his mosquito net, William lay awake listening to the evening wind dying away. There were distant flashes of lightening beyond the hills. They were there almost every night now, but never seemed to come near the lake. The last of the clouds hurried away leaving the water bathed in moonlight.

He thought back over the last four wonderful days of endless sunlight and skiing and fun, and wondered what drove him to go and spoil it by being so moody. He remembered Helen's voice saying softly "Life doesn't come any better than this." Dead right, he thought, and resolved to pull himself together.

CHAPTER 11

Next morning Eleru appeared early at the house to tell them that John's wedding was to be that day and they were all invited. Pam felt that she couldn't leave an overbooked camp on a Saturday, but suggested that Eleru and Singh took Sue, David and the three boys to the wedding in Blue Banana. She insisted that they were back by five or the camp would be short of boats and drivers.

They left with plenty of time to spare because Eleru had told them that they would have to walk a mile or two from the boat to John's village. As they crossed the lake they were surprised by the roar of two jet fighters flying low overhead from north to south. Eleru took the boat in close to where they had dropped Sion off four days earlier.

He led them along a raised track which had been made by the road builders when they were pumping water from the lake. At the end of the track they turned off along a goat path through the bush. Away from the lake breeze they began to feel the heat.

"Is it far?" asked William.

"Eleru says a mile or two," Sue told him.

"Sion ran all this way," Jamie pointed out.

Singh asked if he might go on ahead so as to be ready with the rest of his age-group when the bride arrived, but Eleru stayed with them. One by one the boys took off their shirts. They were all a

THE TIN BOAT

rich brown colour and could take much more sun now as long as they kept their heads covered.

Gradually the relatively open ground broken by low bushes and wide thorn trees gave way to much denser bush. The path narrowed so that they had to walk in single file, Eleru at their head. Even at this green time of the year the ground was hard and dusty. There was little grass to be seen. Cattle crossed their path from time to time in search of grazing. Eleru proudly pointed out one beast in a group of six which was his.

William was enjoying the experience. The call of the namaqua doves, the hot dry air, the involvement with everyday African life suddenly seemed quite normal to him. He was beginning to feel that he belonged here.

His thoughts were disturbed by the sound of an aeroplane engine.

"Somebody must be taking off from the airstrip," said Sue.

"Sounds like a helicopter to me," said Nicholas confidently. Sure enough two air force helicopters passed straight over them at about a thousand feet, heading south like the jets had earlier on.

"Lot of air force activity," remarked David.

"John said something about trouble in the air force," William remembered. "He's got a friend in the air force somewhere or other."

"Nanyuki," Jamie prompted him.

"Yes, that's it. He was on leave at Longicharo that day we went to collect the ambaches. He seemed to be relieved to have got away."

They passed a deserted hut with a tin roof. Nicholas felt sure they must have arrived, but Eleru explained that it was just an old duka which was no longer used. On they walked. Another aeroplane droned overhead, much higher this time. It looked like some sort of military transport. Their hopes rose when they saw the familiar round thatched roof of an African hut.

"This must be it," said Nicholas.

The dense bush gave way to a wide flat area of open ground

with a few spreading acacia trees and bushes. Huts enclosed in bomas were widely spaced out, most of the enclosures containing two or three huts. People were gathered in groups under the trees. Some twenty cows were being herded through the village by a man with a spear and a little boy with a long stick. Goats and chickens wandered about at will

Eleru pointed out a large boma to their right which enclosed three huts. He told them this was his home, and invited them all to go in and meet his mother, his two wives and his children.

"Ndiyo. Asante sana," said Sue.

"But we won't miss John's wedding, will we?" asked Jamie. Sue checked with Eleru who said that there was plenty of time before the bride's arrival.

Inside Eleru's boma they were greeted by five children aged from one to about thirteen. The oldest girl was carrying the baby. They came running from the furthest hut, which Eleru explained belonged to his older wife. The nearest hut was his mother's. He went in to find her, and reappeared with a grey-haired, wrinkled old woman.

"Jambo, mama," said Sue, and shook her by the hand.

"Jambo sana," said the old woman in a high screeching voice. They all shook her horny old hand. She led them to the door of her hut. Eleru took Sue aside and said something quietly and seriously to her in Swahili.

"What's he say?" asked Jamie.

"He says his mother would like us to have tea with her. We are invited to be her guests."

The hut was dark and smoky inside, although the smoke wasn't enough to drive away the flies. In fact it was so dark that at first none of them could see the bench on which the old lady was asking them to sit. She went ahead to the far side of the hut where her tea was brewing in a suferia over a smouldering fire.

'I really am involved in African life now,' thought William, his eyes growing accustomed to the darkness but still smarting from the smoke.

THE TIN BOAT

The old lady ladled tea into tin mugs and passed each one to Eleru who in turn handed it to each of his guests. The tea had been stewed up with milk and sugar, and was very strong and sweet. Nicholas thought it was delicious and asked for more, to Eleru's mother's obvious delight. The others found it refreshing after their long walk, but hoped that they could get away with one cup without causing offense.

Sue tried to translate the old lady's Swahili but she found much of it hard to understand. Eleru hovered over them, always the perfect host, helping with translations and keeping the conversation going. By the time Sue had translated the replies a few topics were stretched a long way.

From time to time, very deferentially and apparently in some sort of prearranged pecking order, other relations of Eleru's came into the hut out of the dazzling sunlight to meet the wazungu guests. They smiled warmly, said little and withdrew.

Eventually Eleru suggested most politely that they finish their tea because the bride would soon be arriving in the village. So after more smiles, handshakes and profuse thanks they filed out into the blinding glare and followed Eleru into the centre of the village.

They were greeted by a tall young man in tribal dress. Eleru introduced him as John's brother.

"This one here," said the man, pointing to one of the bomas, "is the home of my mother." Eleru explained that John would bring his bride to his mother's house, where the ceremony would take place. Jamie wanted to know more.

"Is it anything like an English wedding?" he asked. So Sue asked Eleru exactly what would happen.

"He says that a man marries a girl by getting the agreement of the wazee and by paying the bride price to her father."

"That's that calf," giggled Nicholas.

"Yes," said Sue. "Then the man must go to the bride's house carrying the branch of a certain tree instead of a spear to show that he comes in peace. He brings the bride back to his family's house.

She also carries one of these branches to show there is peace between the families. Her family usually comes with her. The bride and groom have to sit down four times between the two houses. I can't quite make out why, but I think it may be to help the bride. She has to go through quite a lot before the wedding and isn't probably feeling very strong by this stage."

'Good Lord,' thought William, 'it's dreadful how these girls are treated.' Sue went on.

"Apparently they all go into the bridegroom's mother's house, where the bride and groom sit together. Two babies are brought in, a boy and a girl. The boy is put on the bride's knee, and the girl on the bridegroom's, and they are pinched to make them cry. That's supposed to bring the couple luck and make sure they have children. There are speeches by the two fathers and that's it. They are married."

'And all this time the poor girl is in agony,' thought William. 'They don't seem like cruel people. I wonder if the girls ever rebel.'

"Don't they mind?" he asked David. "I mean being sold off like that and treated so cruelly?"

"I've often wondered that," David agreed. "Stephen Bar says he hopes female circumcision will stop one day. He reckons it's the old women who keep it going. It's illegal now you know, but these people follow their own laws. Stephen admits that he wouldn't marry a girl who hasn't been through it, and yet he hopes his daughters won't have to. Odd that, isn't it?"

"Very odd," said William. "I think it's awful. I don't understand why everybody doesn't get angry about it and put a stop to it."

There was no time to continue the conversation. The open space was rapidly filling up with people. Morans and young wazee were arriving from every direction, dressed in clean pink shukas and carrying spears. The women, many of whom carried children, were much more colourfully dressed in reds and yellows and rich blues. They were laden with beaded jewelry in loops round their necks, bracelets, anklets and dangling earrings. The young unmarried girls wore little straw headbands.

"Wanwakuja sasa," said Eleru. The crowd had drifted towards a gap in the bushes to the south of the village. Presently they parted to allow through two beautifully dressed young men.

"Don't they look fantastic!" said Sue.

"Is that John? I don't recognize him," said Nicholas.

"Yes, it's John and Kilima. Kilima is John's best man." They all knew Kilima. He was the man who worked the generator and the water pump. They were both dressed the same, though John looked the more impressive because he was so tall and elegant. He wore a long cowhide of rich reddish brown, fastened over the right shoulder and falling to just below his knees. It was elaborately decorated with beads sown on in V-shaped patterns. His hair was dyed with ochre, giving it much the same colour as his cloak. What gave his appearance a real splendour was a strip of cowhide worn round his temples the way a victor ludorum would wear his laurels at a classical games.

They walked solemnly, their heads bowed, Kilima behind John, who carried the peace branch at the horizontal. The sight of their solemn bearing brought silence to the crowd. William watched in admiration as John passed him and stopped just short of the entrance to his mother's boma. He hadn't often seen John without a smile on his face and laughter in his eyes. It was easy to imagine him becoming a great chief of his tribe. He was even more moved by the sight of the bride.

She walked alone, some ten paces behind Kilima. Her two attendants, both older women, were just behind her, followed by the other members of her family. Her head had also been dyed red, but it had been shaved. She wore a thin band around it. She had a full calf-length dress of rich dark blue, fastened with a wide black belt. She too carried the peace branch.

She walked very stiffly, as if each step was an effort of will. Her head was bowed, but in her case it was a posture of humility. She stopped when John and Kilima stopped, keeping the distance between them. She was directly opposite William. He stared at her in disbelief.

'She's just a little girl,' he thought, 'surely no older than Helen.' She was small, thin and frail. She looked so beautiful, her ochred head giving the impression that she had been sculptured in terracotta with great sensitivity and delicacy. 'How miserable she looks,' William thought. She seemed to have to stand there far too long under the midday sun with no covering, not even any hair, on her head. He could see that she was fighting against pain. Her eyes closed, and she swayed almost imperceptibly. 'Surely she's going to faint,' he thought. 'Why don't they get a move on?'

At last they moved off into the boma. Eleru told his guests that they could follow to see the bride being received into her mother-in-law's house. Outside the hut she stopped again, although John and Kilima had already entered. John's mother placed on the bride's shoulders a cloak similar to John's. Then walking backwards she led the bride in through the door of her house. Two women with babies followed them in.

CHAPTER 12

Eleru explained that there wasn't space in the hut to be able to invite them in. However there was plenty to watch outside. The tension of the solemn procession was broken by the singing of the women, who formed a circle and began to dance.

Jamie and Nicholas were far more intrigued by three little boys who were carrying bows with curious arrows. The points had been covered with blobs of hard gum.

"What are they for?" asked Jamie. Sue translated. One of the little boys answered by pointing an arrow at Jamie's feet and firing. He saw it coming in the nick of time and jumped out of the way. Another boy aimed at Nicholas's feet. His reactions weren't so quick.

"OW!" he squealed, but treated it as a joke.

"Is it a game, or what?" asked William. Sue again asked for an explanation, this time from Eleru. He told them that if a little boy hit the feet of a girl with his arrow she had to give him a piece of her jewelery.

"You want a go, Jammie?" said a familiar voice.

"Sion! Have you been here all the time?" Jamie was pleased to see his new friend again. "Yeh! Let's all have a go!" So Sion persuaded the little boys to lend their bows to the wasungu guests, and everybody joined in the game.

William had been glancing around all the time they'd been there with the hope in the back of his mind that Helen and Matthew might show up. He had no particular reason to expect them. Helen hadn't said anything about it, and in fact none of them had known for sure until that morning that the wedding was to be that day. Now that Sion had joined them he wanted the tin boat gang to be complete. In particular he needed to be seen by Helen to be involved and enjoying himself. He couldn't forget how she was prepared to make an effort with him in spite of having seen him at his moody worst.

John's brother came out of the hut smiling.

"Nataka sodas?" he asked Sue.

"Boys! John's brother has some drinks for you," said Sue. He led them out of the boma to the shade of one of the broad acacia trees, where a table and some benches were set out. Cokes and sodas were brought.

"Asante sana!" said all the children.

"I wonder how long we ought to stay," Sue said to David. "We mustn't impose too much on their hospitality." But they weren't to be allowed to go yet. John joined them, all trace of his former solemnity gone.

"Jambo yote!" he said. Everybody shook his hand and congratulated him.

"Your bride is a lovely girl," said Sue. "What's her name?"

"I don't know," said John to everybody's amazement.

"Where is she? Can we meet her?" Sue went on, not knowing what to make of his reply to her first question.

"Hapana," said John. "She stay now in the house with my mother." She obviously wasn't to take part in the rest of the celebrations. John quickly changed the subject.

"Nyama iku tiari," he said proudly, and explained that they

were invited to share the goat which had been ceremonially killed that morning. A bowl of muddy water was brought to the table for them to wash their hands. This was removed and replaced with a white enamel dish. John was handed a leg of the goat and a dagger-like knife, with which he cut off chunks of the fatty meat into the dish. They were all invited to help themselves with their fingers.

William had never tasted goat before, so he had no idea what to expect. He had gathered that the killing and eating of a goat was reserved for special occasions. He didn't think the taste was all that special though. He decided he wouldn't go out of his way to eat it again, but like the others he put on a good show of enjoying it, which pleased his host. Once again Nicholas excelled himself by asking for more.

"I go to dance now," said John to the boys. "When you finish your food you come and watch."

The young men had gathered in a semi-circle in the shade of another tree on the west side of the clearing.

"I'm going to have a look," said Jamie, getting up from the table.

"Me too!" said Nicholas. They could hear the rhythmic murmur and stamping which marked the beginning of the tribal dance. Gradually the rhythm accelerated and the chanting grew louder. All the dancers carried spears except for John who still held the peace branch. The spears were thrust into the air in time to the rhythm. Suddenly with a joyous whoop from the dancers all the spears were held aloft and the singing stopped. Then the spears were stuck in the ground behind the dancers and the dance continued without them.

A new song started. William was watching with Sion. He noticed that two more little boys with bows and gummed arrows were standing next to them.

"What's the point of that game they play?" William asked Sion, pointing to one of the bows.

"This one is just fun for the little watotos," said Sion. "This way they practice. Become fundis."

"Practice for what?" asked Jamie, overhearing the conversation.

"You want I show you?" asked Sion and beckoned the three boys to follow him.

"What are we going to see now?" asked Nicholas.

"I take you to see this boy. He just come back from the bush. He has been circumcised. Then he must live in the bush one month by himself. With these arrows he shoot birds. He hang the skins from his head. You see. If he has minge birds he has done well."

"Must be a bit smelly after a month," said William, which made Sion laugh.

Soon they saw what they were looking for. A boy of about sixteen was standing by himself. He was wearing a cow skin like John's, but black and without ornamentation. His head must have been shaved recently although a short stubble had begun to grow again. He wore a band around it which supported two big black ostrich feathers, Red Indian fashion. All round his head dangled the little dried up bodies of beautiful birds. Even from his limited experience of bird-watching William could recognize the spectacular shining blue and lilac of the roller bird and the black and white speckles of a cardinal woodpecker. There were doves and weavers and others he didn't recognize. The boy must have done well. In his left hand he held the bow and gummed arrows which had done the damage.

William noticed that the boy's heavy skin cloak was held away from his body in front by some sort of frame. 'He's obviously walking around in pain as well,' thought William. He found it hard to accept this cruel side of the Njemps people's lives when their nature was so friendly and cheerful.

The dancing behind them had become noisier. The throb of the singing and stamping of feet was now punctuated by frequent high-pitched yelps.

"Thanks, Sion," said William. "That was really interesting. Shall we go and see what's happening with the dancers?" They ran off back to join the crowd of spectators. John saw them from his position in the centre of the dancers' semi-circle.

"Hey! Jamie! Kuja!" he called cut.

"I think he wants you to join in the dancing," said David who had joined the audience with Sue. "Go on! I'll take a picture of you." There was nothing self-conscious about Jamie. He didn't need any more persuading.

The young men were singing in a rhythmic drone as an accompaniment to a lead singer who gabbled out his words in an excited recitative. The men took turns to come out from the circle and perform the jumping dance, achieving incredible heights from a standing start. At the end of their jumps they hopped one pace forward and leaned back with a triumphant yelp before returning to their place in the circle.

Jamie took up a position next to John, grinning from ear to ear. He was given a dancing stick, which he held like a spear. Whenever John went out to jump Jamie went with him and tried to do it too. The other dancers were delighted with his efforts.

John saw William and Nicholas enjoying Jamie's performance and persuaded them to join in too. William was really exhilarated by now and did his best when it was his turn to jump. He couldn't see how the dancers were able to get so high off the ground. The jarring pressure on his knees was tremendous. More than ever he wished that Helen was there so that he could show her that he was able to take part and enjoy himself. All this time the women had continued their dance outside John's mother's house, and their songs and shouts could be heard across the open space. At last it seemed that it was time for the two groups of dancers to join together. The women advanced, still singing and bouncing in rhythm, towards the men in two ranks, like a wave. The men's dance grew more and more animated as the women approached. Sue, who was watching from the side, was swept up by the wave of advancing women and found herself in the middle of the front rank.

David was having a field day with his camera, photographing

the dancers and his own family's part in the celebrations, but he wasn't going to be allowed to miss out on the dancing. Eleru's old mother, now looking as sprightly as many of the younger women, grabbed him and pulled him into the middle of the dwindling space between the men and the women, and made him dance with her. The wave of women closed in on them. The ranks broke, and the men took partners. So that part of the great wedding ngoma ended with men and women dancing together, hands on each other's hips.

A huge yelp from everybody brought the dancing to a temporary halt. The men and women separated into their own groups.

Eleru, quiet and dignified as ever, approached Sue and asked if she would like him to escort them back to the boat. The boys were reluctant to leave, but Sue said to David,

"I think we should say our kwaheris and go now. Eleru's probably suggesting that we shouldn't outstay our welcome."

"Yes, I'm sure you're right," said David. "We've got to get Singh back with the boat anyway. It was amazing to be included, but they must want some of it to themselves."

John had slipped away at the end of the dance. He reappeared with a piece of goat.

"For Memsahib Pam," he said. "I sorry sana she is not here."

"But can't we stay longer?" begged Jamie. "It's getting fun."

"I think it will be very noisy for you now," said John, glancing over at one of the bomas. Under a little shelter of poles with a reed roof the old wazee were gathering round a huge pot talking very loudly.

"They're brewing the pombe," Sue explained.

"What's that?" asked Jamie.

"It's their beer. That's why it might get a bit noisy. Come on. Best leave them to it." Turning to John she said, "It has been a wonderful day. Asante sana. You are very kind to ask us here."

"And I very happy you come, all my friends," said John. They found Singh, who had already had a little taste of the pombe, and set off on the long walk back to the boat.

CHAPTER 13

"I'm really glad to see you all back," said Pam. She was waiting for them on the jetty with a party of tourists who had booked a boat trip round the island. She told Singh to refuel straight away ready to take them.

"I expect they'll be told all sorts of unlikely things on their guided tour," Sue confided to her sister. "The pombe was already flowing when we left."

"Oh, lore! Is he safe?" asked Pam anxiously.

"Yes, I'm sure he is," said Sue. "Just a bit happy and very chatty. They'll probably have a lovely time."

"Have you had fun?" asked Pam. All the boys began to tell her at once. "Well I'll have to hear all about it later," she interrupted. "It's been frantic here all day - overbooked camp and half the staff away at the wedding. I need some help." Turning to the tour leader for the boat trip group she said, "The boat will be back in five minutes to take you. O.K.?" The leader accepted the small further delay with less than good grace.

"What a day!" Pam gasped as they walked back up the hill. "Sue, could you possibly take over in the kitchen. They're very short of people. They're behind hand with dinner as it is and somebody's got to start thinking about tomorrow's Sunday lunch."

"Why don't I get William to help?" suggested Sue. "You know how he enjoys cooking. If he really wants to go into catering eventually it would be excellent experience for him."

"Good idea," said Pam. "Would you like to do that, William?"

"Yes I certainly would," said William enthusiastically,

"Can't we help too?" asked Jamie.

"I'm taking over the bar now. Jackson's been doing it alone all day. I must let him off for a couple of hours. You can both come and help me there," said Pam. "David, I've got a nice little job for you, too. The big German group has ordered tribal dancing at six. I went and said 'yes' without realizing quite how many of the usual dancers were at the wedding. Anyway, they say they can get some sort of a scratch team together. It'll probably be ghastly, but can you get the wagenis down to the village and make sure they see something? Try and convince them they're seeing quality stuff. Hopefully they won't know the difference."

"We could put on a show ourselves after today's performance," said David, "but yes. Don't worry. I'll jolly them along."

So everybody had a busy evening. There were several small children in the camp, and by the time they were given their early supper Nicholas was tired enough to be persuaded to join them and go to bed early. Jamie put up more resistance, but by eight-thirty he too was ready to pack it in.

David had returned from the village with twenty-two happy tourists who felt that they had been steeped in African culture.

"Not quite up to the standard of this afternoon," David told Sue. "Most of them were very young, and didn't always know what to do next. Still, they tried hard. The wagenis thought it was wonderful."

"Well that's great," said Sue, who was chopping up mushrooms for a sauce to go with the tilapia fish course. William had been given the task of making pizza dough for the next day's buffet lunch, and was up to his elbows in flour. He seemed to be happy and to know exactly what he was doing. "Can you take over the bar?" Sue said to David. "It's going to be a hard working night."

THE TIN BOAT

It was nearly midnight when the four of them finally sat down to eat.

"William, you've done an amazing job," said Pam. "You must be exhausted."

"I've enjoyed it," said William.

"And what about the wedding? I haven't heard all about it yet."

"It was fascinating," said William. "You know we all had to join in the dancing."

"Really?" said Pam. "I've seen it done endless times, but I've never tried to do it."

"I felt very earthbound," said William. "They all jump so high. But it was fun trying." Although she was very tired Pam was enjoying her first chance that day to relax and unwind. She sat and listened to William's detailed account of the wedding ngoma. She was interested to know what a young man with no previous experience of Africa would make of it all. Sue and David slipped away down to the house leaving the two of them to talk.

"I couldn't help wondering what feelings that poor little bride had," William confided to his aunt. "She was so young. I mean it must be so awful for John. Presumably he loves her if he wanted to marry her. How can he stand to watch her suffer like that? I find it very hard to understand. They're such kind and gentle people. They were incredibly kind to us today - really made us feel welcome."

"You've certainly had a fascinating insight into their lives," said Pam.

"The strangest thing of all," William went on, "was that when Sue asked John what his wife's name was, he said he didn't know. We weren't even allowed to meet her." Pam smiled.

"I should have warned you about all that," she said. "What happens is that she will have had a childhood name which she stops using when a man buys her as a wife. She is then given a new name, presumably by the wazee. Before the wedding only the best man is told what the new name is. You must have seen John with his best man."

"Yes, it was Kilima," said William.

"That's right," said Pam. "His function is to announce the bride's new name, I assume at the ceremony, so before that even John won't have known it."

"I wonder why he wouldn't tell us even after that, though," said William. "Is it some sort of secret?"

"No. That's the odd thing. A husband is never allowed to speak his wife's name, to her or anyone else. Once she has had a child he can call her 'mother of so-and-so', but before that he really doesn't call her anything. It's almost as if she has no identity in his eyes until she gives him a child."

"Gosh, it seems to be a really bad deal to born a girl into a tribe like this. I mean, being bought and sold instead of choosing who you marry, and then these awful things they do to them. David says that bit's already illegal."

"I know. It's a really thorny problem. It seems appalling to us that these things still goes on, now in 1982. I often have girls brought to me with dreadful infections and needing penicillin. I'd love to see the end of it. But once you start breaking down tribal customs where does it stop? Their tribal life works well. Everybody knows where they belong, and some of these things continue just because it's always been like that. They put up with it because they've never known anything different, and they think any change might be a threat to their way of life. And one has to admit that there is very little conflict in this particular tribe. There isn't even any real struggle for power amongst them. They all seem to think that being chosen as a top mzee is too much hassle."

"Doesn't the government interfere if they are breaking the law?"

"They haven't made any serious attempt over that issue," said Pam. "In the long term they have dreams of detribalisation and turning the whole of Kenya into a modern state, but what have they got to offer? In fact the President put everybody's backs up by coming to Baringo a few weeks ago and making a speech about how everybody ought to come into the modern world and wear

European dress. What do they need modern European dress for here?"

"Isn't the President very popular then?" asked William.

"I don't think these people mind about the government in Nairobi one way or the other as long as it leaves them alone. But generally, yes, I think he's well enough liked. He's done very well. But many people think he's not tough enough, especially with his own ministers, and there are always those from other tribes who want their own man in power."

"You mean somebody might try to overthrow him?"

"There are always rumours and scares around but nothing ever happens."

"Memsahib, ninawesa funga bar?" It was Jackson. Pam looked at her watch.

"Heavens. It's nearly one o'clock. Have all the guests gone to bed?"

"Ndiyo, Memsahib."

"Yes, of course. Start closing the bar. I'm coming to collect the cash box. You must be exhausted. You too, William. Time you were in bed. Thanks for your help. I could probably do with it tomorrow if you felt like it. Even if all those chaps do come back as they should I don't suppose they'll be at their brightest after a big ngoma like that."

In spite of going to bed so late William was up in good time next morning and spent the whole day helping in the kitchen and the bar. Jamie and Nicholas slept late. Everybody was too busy to do anything with them so they had to amuse themselves. Nicholas was delighted to find that Sion had returned to the camp, and spent the morning fishing with him off the back jetty.

Jamie was more difficult to please. He kept pestering William to come and swim with him, and couldn't understand why William wanted to spend all day doing boring work with the grown-ups.

Life improved after lunch when John turned up unexpectedly and reported for duty. Pam was delighted to see him back so soon.

"Didn't you want a day or two with your wife before you came back?" she asked.

"Hapana," said John smiling. "She is mbaya sana. I leave her with my mother till she is nzuri again."

"Well we can certainly use you here," said Pam. "You can take out a boat trip to the hippos at four in Blue Banana. Take Jamie and Nicholas. They need something to do."

"Ndiyo, Mensahib," said John.

"Oh, and thank you for the goat. It was very good," said Pam. In truth she had put it down somewhere and forgotten about it. She had no doubt it would make its presence felt in due course.

"Why's he come back?" asked William when John had left.

"What we were talking about last night," said Pam. "His wife's obviously still not feeling great. He's left her in the care of his mother until she's better."

"He doesn't seem too unhappy about it," observed William.

"I dare say he regards it as a woman's problem. None of his business," said Pam. William shook his head.

"Not a great start to married life," he said.

In the evening exhaustion overtook William, so he had an early supper by himself down at the house and was in bed soon after eight. When their mother suggested that Jamie and Nicholas also went to bed they protested vigorously that they had been to bed early the night before and slept late that morning, so she relented. However they were pretty sleepy by the time they had waited for supper with the grown-ups after the guests had eaten. They were about to go down to the house when a boat was heard approaching the jetty,

"Not more wagenis at this time of night?" complained Sue. "Pam, have we got any more beds?"

"Only tent nineteen. But nobody else is booked to come, and I'm certainly not feeding anyone else tonight. The kitchen staff have had it. I've let them go to bed."

"D'you want me to go and see who it is?" said Jamie.

"Would you?" said Pam. "That would be very kind. Take a torch from the bar."

"I'll come too," said Nicholas.

"No, I'm doing it," Jamie insisted.

"Let him!" said their mother.

"Oh, O.K. Come on," said Jamie.

They reached the jetty as the boat was coming in, and shone a torch towards it.

"Hey man! You're dazzling me!" squealed a familiar voice.

"Matthew!" shouted Jamie. "You're back! Brilliant! It's been dull here without you."

"No it hasn't," Nicholas insisted. "We went to John Boat's wedding. It was great."

"Don't tell me!" said Helen, stepping out of the tin boat and tying it up to the jetty. "I wish we hadn't missed that wedding. I bet it was fun."

"Yeh, it really was," said Jamie. "We joined in the dancing. Amazing." Helen laughed.

"Well, we've had a boring time all right, being polite to Dad's guests. Real drag," said Matthew.

"We're going to make up for lost time," said Helen enthusiastically as the four of them followed the torch beam up to the bar. "We're going to sleep here and get up very early to go fishing at the Mukutan in the tin boat. Leave before dawn."

"Great!" said Nicholas. "Can I come?"

"'Course," said Matthew. "You too Jamie?"

"Jamie thinks fishing's boring, don't you Jamie?" Nicholas couldn't resist getting his own back on his brother who had refused to fish with him that morning.

"I do not, Nicholas. Not this sort of fishing."

"Come then," said Helen. "What about William? Where's he?" They'd reached the bar.

"Helen and Matthew! What a surprise!" said Pam warmly. "What are you doing here? I thought you were meant to be at home."

"Well we were," said Helen rather sheepishly, "but we were bored so we asked if we could come over. Dad didn't seem to

THE TIN BOAT

mind too much. Can we stay?"

"There's tent nineteen. You sound as if you've got something planned."

"Sure thing man," said Matthew. "Up before dawn. Fishing at Mukutan. Can the boys come?"

"Of course," said Sue after a pause for thought. "I'm sure you'll be responsible. No more silly pranks. But look after them, especially Nicholas. He is only eight, remember."

"Oh, sure," said Helen reassuringly. "Where's William?"

"Asleep," said Jamie disparagingly. "He's been a real pain all day, hanging around the grown-ups. Wouldn't do anything fun. Anyway you'll never get William up before dawn."

"You are unfair," Sue rebuked him. "William's worked incredibly hard. I don't know what we'd have done without him. But I do agree it's no fun waking him up in the morning."

"Leave him to me," said Helen. "I'll fix him. We can't let him miss this. It's a real paradise over there."

"We were hoping for a bit of a lie in tomorrow," said David. "We're all whacked. So I expect you'll be gone before we're up. What time do you want rescuing if you don't reappear?"

"We'll be fine, don't worry," said Helen. "But I suppose if we're not back by about eleven..."

"O.K. We won't worry about you before that," said David. "Have a good time"

"We will," said Matthew.

PART 2 – THE COUP

CHAPTER 14

They did set off before breakfast. Helen had asked Pam's houseboy Joseph to wake them before he made the tea. He went to the house first to wake the boys, and then to tent nineteen where Helen and Matthew were sleeping. The sky was still dark enough for a few stars to be visible. The early morning clatter in the kitchen had only just begun.

Jamie was ready when Helen and Matthew arrived at the house. Nicholas was searching for a lost flip-flop. They had failed to persuade William to get out of bed.

"Leave him!" whispered Matthew. "Let's go, man!" But Helen had slipped upstairs.

"C'mon, you said you'd come," she whispered, not wanting to wake the adults.

"In a minute. It's too early," groaned Willliam, incapable of shaking off his sleep. She left him and went downstairs.

"Lazy creature!" she said. "We must think of something."

"Oh, leave him, man," repeated Matthew.

THE TIN BOAT

"Throw some cold water over him," giggled Nicholas. "I'll get some." He disappeared into the bathroom. 'Oh, good,' he thought, 'there's my other flip-flop.' Then he noticed a long thin green grass-snake, sliding out from behind the cistern. He ran back to tell the others.

A mischievous look came over Helen's face which Matthew was quick to notice.

"Hey, you wouldn't, man, would you?" But Helen was already in the bathroom. The snake was climbing up the wall. The three boys followed her in time to see her hand flash out and grab the snake just below the head. It was very impressive.

"Dad taught her that," said Matthew.

"Won't it bite her?" asked Nicholas.

"They're not poisonous, you wally." said Jamie, though secretly he thought she'd been immensely brave. The snake thrashed its tail around but its head could do nothing.

"Mind out," said Helen, pushing past them towards the stairs. They followed her up and saw her go over to William's bed. "Your early morning call, sir!" she said in breezy, air hostess sort of voice. As William looked up she dropped the snake on his bed. He was out of it in a flash, his face like thunder.

Helen suddenly panicked that she had gone too far. William was so touchy. The boys were doubled up with laughter. There was an anxious moment when it could have gone either way. Then William managed to raise a smile, to everybody's relief.

"I'm not getting back into that bed!" he said with all the good humour he could muster. "Go ahead. I'm just coming." So the fishing party was complete. A few minutes later the five of them were whispering excitedly to each other on their way down to the jetty.

It had rained overnight and there was a certain amount of water in the bottom of the boat, but the children decided to set off and bail as they went along. They were impatient to get going. The sky was lightening. They knew it would be broad daylight by the time they'd crossed the lake to the Mukutan.

THE TIN BOAT

They'd already pushed of from the jetty when Nicholas piped up,

"Have we got the spare sheer pin?"

"Oh, it doesn't matter," said Matthew, but for once Jamie supported his brother.

"If it goes we're stuck," he said. They paddled back to the jetty. Jamie volunteered to run up to the house. He found the last spare sheer pin in a tin in the office. As he left he saw Joseph running anxiously from the kitchen towards the house, but he didn't stop to ask what the problem was.

If the children had been wide enough awake they might also have remembered to take some food and drink with them, but it never crossed their minds as they rounded the point of the island and followed three low flying pelicans towards the sunrise. No little worries like that were going to be allowed to spoil their excitement. The sun was not yet up and they were on their way.

Sue and David had heard the children leave, but they were allowing themselves the luxury of waiting for tea to arrive before getting out of bed. They waited and waited but no tea came. They could hear Joseph's voice talking excitedly to Pam in the office. Then they heard the whining and crackling of the radio being tuned. They both got out of bed to see what was going on.

"Ssh!" said Pam, her ear close to the speaker and her fingers on the tuning knob. They listened in silence until she had found the BBC World Service. The newsreader was reporting on the progress of the Israeli invasion of Lebanon.

"The watu say there's been a coup in Nairobi," said Pam. "They heard it on the radio in the kitchen." David tried to ask her more but she held up her hand for silence. The reception on the radio was not good. The news came to an end.

"They obviously haven't picked it up yet," she said, and began twiddling the knob again. A high pitched whistle and a crack gave way to some imperfectly played martial music. Pam left it there and explained what she had been told.

"It looks as if the President has been kicked out by a group of military people and students. Apparently they made a broadcast in Swahili saying they had taken over."

"What about the President," asked Sue.

"He's out of the country, isn't he?" said David. "He's at the O.A.U. Summit in Cairo."

"That's right," said Pam. "They've picked their moment."

"Is that all we know?" asked Sue.

"Yes," answered Pam, and then reflected, "I suppose somebody was bound to have a go sooner or later." At that moment the martial music was interrupted by a voice speaking in English,

"Ah," said Pam. The three of them fell silent.

"The corrupt regime of the President is at an end," said the voice. "The revolutionary committee of the students and the air force is in control. Plis stay calm. Do not liv your homes. Listen for furda instructions." The music continued.

Pam quickly realized that she would have to take some sort of responsibility for the guests in the camp in an unpredictable situation.

"We have no idea what's going on beyond the shores of this island," she said, wishing she had a radio link with her boss on the mainland which she had repeatedly asked for. "I assume there won't be any trouble yet at Kampi-ya-Samaaki, but there are police and army at Marigat. We have no way of knowing where their loyalties will lie."

"What about the Njemps?" asked Sue.

"Oh, I'm sure they'll avoid taking sides if they possibly can. They are not political animals. We are fortunate here. I've no doubt we are among friends, but I will discuss it all with Stephen." Her mind was racing on to the problems which might arise. "I don't think we should allow any of the wagenis to leave at the moment," she said.

"I don't think you can really stop them if they insist," said David.

"Fair enough," said Pam, "but it would have to be entirely at their own risk. We ought to be advising very strongly against it."

THE TIN BOAT

"I can't believe anyone would want to," said Sue.

"No. This is obviously as safe a place as any," David agreed. "And that's going to create more problems for us. How many new guests are due in this morning?"

"There are nineteen coming south from Maralal," said Pam. "They usually leave very early. They probably won't have heard the news."

"I bet they'd rather be here anyway," said Sue. "They are bound to come, and there'll be more as well. We could have a very full camp, and no more food coming in for all we know. Lucky this week's orders arrived yesterday."

"Still, we need to be careful," said Pam. "Sue, can you go to the kitchen. Send Stephen down to me, and Samson Boat. We'd better not let any boats go out at present. Johnson is on the mainland with Mandeleo. He might come over with some news. Tell Rotich to cut down the size of the meals. The wagenis needn't starve, but no more four course meals. I'll leave it to you."

"We'd better use the fresh food first," said Sue. She was extremely practical when it came to catering. "We'll keep the frozen and tinned stuff in reserve."

"How much fuel have we got for generators, pumps, etc?" asked David.

"Oh, goodness! That's a point," said Pam. "Sue, you'd better get Kilima down here too. We must work out priorities for fuel. There are ways we can cut down our use of water and electricity if everybody cooperates. Water can even be brought up in buckets if necessary."

"That'll be a lot of hard work," said David. "You're counting on the loyalty of the staff?"

"Absolutely," Pam assured him. "I'm sure we're all on the same side in this. They don't want this sort of upheaval any more than we do. They will want to know their families are O.K. though. I'll send somebody in a boat to the south end of the lake as soon as I dare. In the meantime, I'm sure we can rely on them to do all they can to help."

"What about the guests? They can help too if needs be," David suggested.

"I expect most of them will," said Pam, "but they're a more unpredictable lot. Perhaps you could go up to the bar. Tell people what we know and advise them to stay put. Reassure them that they are safe here."

In the days that followed, when the children were all they thought about, it seemed incredible that nobody remembered them at that moment. It was still very early. Perhaps in the confusion they had all forgotten that the children weren't happily asleep in their beds, for once not getting in the way at a time when the grown-ups had other problems on their hands. From then on there wasn't time to think.

For Pam's part, the children weren't her prime responsibility anyway, but the camp was. Stephen and Samson came to the office together to see her. Stephen was clearly worried. He had a brother in the air force, just returned to duty after his leave, who was bound to be involved however much against his will. However, he reassured her that the staff would co-operate in every possible way, and that the Njemps people would want no part in the trouble.

She thanked him and in return promised that Samson could take a boat to see that all was well on the southern side of the lake as soon as any news reached them from the mainland. In the meantime she asked Samson to check on stocks of petrol and diesel for the boats.

By the time Kilima arrived she had worked out her priorities for the engines. She would reduce electricity consumption by leaving only one light bulb in each tent, and by disconnecting the ice-making machine in the bar. She would only put the generator on for the minimum time necessary to keep the freezers cold. She decided to continue to pump water for the present, but the swimming pool would be out of action. She hoped the guests could be persuaded to use their showers sparingly. They could always wash in the lake.

Gas was also going to be a problem. Sue had already thought of that. She revived the oven which had been carved out of a termite hill to cook the turkey at Christmas. The kitchen staff were edgy and had lost much of their usual good humour. They were used to working to a well-tried routine, and Sue realized that she would have to supervise the new sparser menus step by step.

It was David who found himself in the immediate front line.

"What's goin' arn for heavens sakes?" It was a middle-aged American lady who had arrived two days before with her elderly mother. "It's six-thirty and we ain't had our tea yet which was ordered for six."

"I'm sorry," said David. "I'm afraid things aren't quite normal today. Everybody is a little on edge. We've heard on the radio that there's been a coup against the President in Nairobi. . ." Other guests kept arriving in the bar so he had to start the story all over again several times. "We are in no danger here," he assured them. "I strongly recommend that everybody stays put for the time being even if you were planning to leave today. We will keep you informed, as far as we can."

Of course he was bombarded, with questions, most of which he couldn't answer. Pam came in and he took her to one side.

"I think it would be best if we got all or most of the wagenis together in about half an hour and told them the plans," he suggested.

"Yes. O.K." said Pam, obviously distracted by a hundred and one other things. "Yes, that's a good idea."

"Have you heard any more?"

"No. They just keep repeating the same message. The watu are listening in the kitchen."

"O.K." David told everybody. "If you all gather here at seven o'clock we will tell you as far as possible what is going on. I'll have some tea sent in as I know most of you missed out."

The tin boat had reached the first of the reeds which hid the mouth of the Mukutan River. Helen had driven all the way. There had been no arguing. They were all too excited about the adventure they had set out on to fall out with each other or behave irresponsibly.

Helen slowed down so that they could see the cormorants and darters perched on the dead trees drying their wings. Between there and the river they had a new obstacle to negotiate. There was no permanent channel through to the mouth of the river. Floating islands of tangled reeds drifted around making it difficult to find the way in.

"Is this the river?" asked William.

"Yeh, man. It was here last time," said Matthew. Jamie stood up in the bows to try and see over the reeds.

"Sit down!" shouted Nicholas as the boat rocked alarmingly. A cloud of crimson-rumped waxbills burst out of the reeds just beside them.

"I'm trying to see!" insisted Jamie.

"It's O.K." said Helen. "We'll find it. See that low hill with a bit of a cliff? The river comes out just below it."

She slowed the engine right down and weaved her way in and out of the floating islands. The water, which had been stirred up by a strong wind off the lake, became calmer in the shelter of the reeds. At last they left the floating islands behind. They were in a more open stretch of water, beyond which they could see clearly the mouth of the river. There were tall rushes on either side, and behind them the yellow flowering ambach trees. Even at its mouth the river was very narrow, no more than four widths of the boat.

"I think we should cut out the engine and paddle now." said Jamie.

"You're right. It's going to get shallow," Helen agreed. Just then there was an eruption in the water behind them. A hippo's head appeared only a few metres away.

"Not again!" gasped William, genuinely frightened. Helen instinctively revved up the engine. The boat shot forward into the mouth of the river.

THE TIN BOAT

"It's O.K. This one's not after us," shouted Matthew, but it was too late. Another floating island was blocking their way. Helen swerved to avoid it but the boat was going to fast. It swung round so that the propeller was caught in the reeds. The engine slowed right down as if it was going to stall, then suddenly revved violently.

"Damn!" said Helen and stopped the engine. In the silence, even at that moment of crisis, it was impossible not to be struck by all the noises which suddenly became audible; the barking of the herons, the piping of jacanas hopping from lily-pad to lily-pad, the squeal of a flight of whistling teal. The air was still in the enclosed river. The children could feel the warmth of the sun.

"What's happened?" asked William.

"It can only be the sheer pin," said Helen. "The engine was revving but the propeller wasn't moving."

"It wasn't in neutral?" suggested Nicholas.

"No," said Helen. "Look at the lever." They could all see that it was in the forward position.

"Lucky we brought a spare one," said Nicholas, feeling quite pleased with himself.

"Yes, but it's a hell of a place to change it," said Helen. "There's nowhere to land."

"Take the engine off and mend it in the boat," said Matthew.

"Yes, good idea," said William.

"It'll fall in for sure," said Nicholas.

"But it's tied on," said Jamie.

"That'll stop us losing it," Nicholas agreed, "but if it's all wet it won't start again."

"It's not much use as it is," said Matthew.

"Let's row," said William. "I'm worried about that hippo." The others laughed.

"Forget about him, man," said Matthew. "They don't often behave like that one the other day." But Helen could see that William was really frightened

"O.K. We'll have a go at lifting the engine," she announced.

109

THE TIN BOAT

"I think you're mad," said Nicholas, but nobody listened and the four older children crowded into the stern to help lift. As usual this unbalanced the boat.

"Get back, for God's sake!" shouted William. He was getting panicky.

"Matthew, go onto the bows with Nicholas," Helen ordered. "The rest of us will lift. Now keep the boat trimmed. William and Jamie, you take the strain while I loosen the mounting bolts." William and Jamie tried to get a grip of the engine, but they knew they weren't holding it. It was greasy and hot, and the bottom of the boat was too slippery for them to get a foothold.

"We're not ready," shouted William.

"I can't stand properly," said Jamie. "Move over, Helen."

"I'll loosen it and we'll all grab, O.K.?" she said. Without waiting for an answer she loosened the bolts. The engine lurched sideways. They stopped it falling overboard but couldn't lift it. It was too slippery.

"Tighten the bolts quickly," said William, and Helen did so. The engine was safe, but they had achieved nothing.

"I'll get overboard," Jamie volunteered. "I expect I can stand here, and I can help lift from the other end."

"You're crazy!" shouted William. "What about the hippo? I reckon we just wait here till they come and rescue us. They know we are here."

"They think we're happily fishing. They won't come for hours," Matthew pointed out.

Without waiting for further discussion Jamie jumped in. The water was cool below the first foot or so. He could just feel the soft mud under his feet, but it was too deep to stand. The reeds tickled his legs. He hoped it was reeds. They had come to find a river full of fish, but now he rather hoped they were wrong.

"Too deep," he said. "Paddle it nearer the shore." He moved with the boat. The soft mud came further up his legs. He tried not to think about leeches. Soon he found that he was able to stand.

Helen loosened the engine bolts and they tried lifting it again, but the weight of it had Jamie slithering around in the mud, unable to keep his footing. Once more they thought better of risking dropping it and bolted it back on. Nicholas had been right.

"Can you replace the sheer pin from there, Jamie?" he asked. Jamie would much rather have climbed back in the boat, but he said he'd have a go.

"Do you know how?" asked Helen.

"Yes, I've seen it done," said Jamie.

"Gees I'm thirsty," said Matthew. That was when they realized that they had brought nothing to eat or drink. He started chanting, "I want a Fanta! I want a Fanta!" William couldn't see the funny side of the situation.

'Don't they realize what a mess we're in?' he thought, but he made a desperate effort to keep his feelings to himself.

"Didn't we even bring a nice jar of olives or something?" joked Matthew, who was addicted to olives.

"Oh, come on! Do help!" said Jamie.

"Sorry, man," said Matthew.

"I need a pair of pliers." They all rummaged around, but there was no tool box.

"Sorry, no pliers," said Matthew.

"Oh, for heaven's sake!" said Jamie in exasperation. "Is there anything I can bang this split pin out with? It's very rusty." All they could find was an old tin which was used as a baler. Helen handed it to him.

"This do?" she asked. "It's all we've got apart from the fishing reels and the handle of the water-skiing rope."

"I'll try with this," said Jamie. They all watched in anxious silence as he banged away at the end of the split pin. He had to support himself on the shaft of the engine because his footing was still insecure. Millimetre by millimetre the pin shifted. When it was half way out he handed the baler back to Helen. He eased the pin out the rest of the way by hand. When it came away he held it in his teeth while he removed the propeller. Then he passed the propeller and the split pin to William.

"The sheer pin's not broken, it's only bent," he told everybody after he had examined it.

"That's the problem Morris had before," said Nicholas. "Can you move it at all?" Jamie tried but it was wedged tight. The whole mechanism was very worn down. The sheer pin was bent just enough to prevent the transmission engaging the propeller.

"No way I can shift it without any tools," said Jamie.

"Can't you break it?" asked Helen.

"Try with the propeller." William handed it back to him. He tried to bang the sheer pin with the edge of one of the blades, but it was the wrong shape. He couldn't make contact.

"Hopeless," he said.

There was a snort from the hippo at the mouth of the river. It was no real threat but it made them all nervous.

"I think you should come back into the boat," said William, trying to sound unruffled. Jamie was only too pleased to agree. They hauled him back on board with some difficulty, because he was no light weight. The hippo snorted again. It was further off this time.

"Can it be done?" asked Helen. Jamie shook his head.

"It needs a good heavy spike, a big nail or something, and a hammer," he said. "There's no possible way of getting it out with what we've got. The two halves of the casing don't fit properly anyway. That's why it's bent instead of breaking clean. If I bang it with this thing I'll only do more damage."

"Well, they'll come and find us in the end," said Helen.

"How long, though?" asked William.

"I said not to worry unless we weren't back by eleven," Helen confessed.

"You did WHAT?" gasped Matthew. "Hell, man. It's only seven-thirty now."

"Why don't we row out of the river?" suggested Jamie. "They might be able to see us then."

"But we must be two miles from the island," said William.

"With, binoculars, though..." said Jamie.

"If they bother to look," said William.

"Well they might," said Nicholas. They discussed the options. There certainly seemed to be no point in staying where they were, so they agreed that they would paddle the tin boat out of the river. There was even talk of taking turns and rowing all the way back to the island.

The sun was already growing hot.

CHAPTER 15

Pam had her binoculars in use, but not in the direction of the Mukutan. She was in her house watching a boat approaching from the mainland. She was hoping for news.

Down on the jetty a group of Israeli guests were gathered, their rucksacks packed, waiting to leave. At the meeting in the bar a little earlier Pam had explained the situation to all the guests as far as she knew it. However, the Israelis had insisted on leaving as planned in spite of her protestations.

"We live with this sort of thing every day in our country," their leader had told her. "If we let a bit of trouble like this stop us we'd never do anything." The item on the news that morning had reminded Pam only too clearly of that. In the end she agreed that they would be taken across as soon as the boat had returned from the mainland.

"At your own risk and against my advice," she had insisted. The leader had told her that he understood.

Pam was worried about them going, but she had to admit that it gave them less mouths to feed. She could see that the boat now passing her house contained another larger group of tourists, presumably the party from Maralal, so she was going to have a very full camp sitting out the trouble for an indefinite period.

THE TIN BOAT

The endlessly repeated martial music on the radio in the office was interrupted again.

"This is the revolutionary Kenya piples council. Your country has been freed from the repressive regime of a corrupt President. All prisoners are to be released from jail in the next two hours. Plis stay calm. Your country is free. Plis stay in your homes." The martial music resumed.

"God! It's anarchy!" said David.

"There'll be a lot of bad-hats drifting around," said Pam. "I believe those rogues they took away from here the other day are still in police cells in Marigat. I suppose they'll be on the loose again." She thought it wise to warn the Israelis of this latest information before they hit the road. She sent David down to the jetty, but he could not dissuade them. They were quite prepared to face any danger, so he chatted with them until the boat arrived. It was the old wooden Mandeleo with Johnson driving. The boat was dangerously overloaded with some thirty people including ten Njemps.

"I bring as many as I can," said Johnson. "They are frightened."

Sue came down to welcome the guests. She explained the situation to them. They already knew that something was wrong, and were relieved to have reached the relative safety of the island. Johnson took David aside.

"Hapana nzuri," he said. "There is talk of shooting in Marigat."

"Who is it? The army?" David asked.

"Ndiyo, the army, I think so. Maybe also the police," he replied. "That big army convoy came down the road this morning, going south. People say they not know which side they on. Some say they still for the President, but some are scared of these new leaders, so they fight for them. I scared they fight each other now."

"Look," said David. "These crazy wagenis insist on leaving. We've all warned them not to, but they insist on going. So can you take them across and wait. I expect they'll be back."

THE TIN BOAT

"Which way they go?" asked Johnson.
"South, to Nakuru."
"They be back."

Jamie and Matthew paddled easily enough to the mouth of the river, although the heat was severe and their throats were dry. William, Jamie and Nicholas had all brought hats with them. They dipped them in the water and put them on. They all remained fairly cheerful. They had hoped for an adventure and here it was. It never occurred to them that they might not be rescued. Only William was struggling to keep his sense of humour. His new resolve to join in and be one of the gang was being severely tested. Once they emerged into the first stretch of open water there was a bit of a breeze against them which made paddling harder, though it helped to cool them down.

"I'm choka kabisa!" said Matthew about half way across to the beginning of the floating islands. "Somebody else have a go."

"I will," said Nicholas, taking over Matthew's paddle. The change wasn't a great success. Jamie was much stronger than Nicholas so the boat tended to go round in circles. Nicholas became tired very quickly.

"I've got a bit of a headache," he complained. "Can you take over, William?"

"O.K." said William. "Helen can take over from Jamie when he's tired."

"You O.K. Jamie?" Helen asked.

"I'm fine," Jamie assured her. He was determined to keep going, though he did look rather red in the face.

"Right. I'll try and steer us through these wretched reeds," said Helen.

The wind seemed to drop again as they came into the lea of the floating islands, though Helen could feel it strongly on her face as soon as she stood up to try to guide them through. Even in that short time the channel had changed. The islands were on the move all the time.

THE TIN BOAT

Some of the channels through which Helen guided them were very narrow indeed. Sometimes it was impossible for paddles to be used on both sides of the boat at once. On one occasion they even had to pull themselves along on the reeds.

"Ow!" screamed Matthew as the sharp leaves cut his hand.

"It's bloody stuff!" William agreed.

"Can't we punt it?" suggested Nicholas. They tried but the water was too deep for the paddles and they hadn't brought a long pole.

"Can't we go another way?" asked William. The channel had virtually disappeared. Helen agreed. They pulled themselves painfully backwards and tried a different channel. At last they found one which became gradually wider instead of narrower. They could start paddling again. They were nearing the open lake.

The reeds were getting smaller and the wind stronger. Helen took over from Jamie and they paddled with renewed vigour, but their hopes of things becoming easier were quickly dashed. It soon dawned on them that they were making very little headway against the wind. If they paused for even a second to catch their breath they were blown back towards the floating islands

"It's no good," gasped Helen, her throat beginning to dry out in the heat. "We'll never make it far in this wind."

"Better wait till it dies down," said Jamie. "It usually does later in the morning, doesn't it?"

"Yeh, but gees, they'll have rescued us by then!" exclaimed Matthew.

"So we just wait here?" asked William.

"I still think we ought to get right out past all the reeds where we can be seen," piped up Nicholas.

"O.K. You row then!" snapped Jamie.

"All right, I will," said Nicholas, although the glare from the water was making his headache worse.

"I'm sure you're right, Nicholas," said Helen. "We must give them every chance of finding us. But I think the strongest should row." That stirred Jamie into action again. He took the paddle uncremoniously from William.

"Let's go then," he said to Helen.

They put in a determined effort. Not daring to stop, they forced the boat out into the open water again as far as the old dead trees where they had seen the cormorants. From there they were at last in sight of the island, though it was a long way off. Matthew climbed up onto the bow and took hold of the painter.

"Just get to that first tree and I'll tie her up," he said. Jamie and Helen were gasping and pouring with sweat. It was extremely hot, but they kept going until at last Matthew was able to grab the tree.

"Stop!" he yelled as the tree nearly knocked him into the water. The rowers were only too pleased to obey. Groaning they flopped over their paddles. William helped Matthew to tie up.

"You O.K. Jamie?" croaked Helen.

"Yeh, sort of. And you?"

"I'll live. God, I need a drink though."

"Me too!" gasped Jamie.

"That was an amazing effort," said William generously. Helen looked up for a moment and smiled at him.

"Yeh, great stuff," admitted Matthew. A change came over their mood. Their joy ride had turned into an adventure. Now the adventure was becoming a problem. They didn't yet see it as a danger, but they all had the feeling that it mattered what they decided to do next. The sun and the lack of liquid were becoming serious.

"Can we drink the lake water? Is it safe?" asked William.

"The watu drink it all the time," said Matthew.

"They're used to it though," William pointed out.

"Yes," Matthew agreed, "but think how much of the stuff you take in when you're getting out of the water on skis."

"Anyway," said Nicholas, "the camp drinking water all comes from the lake."

"Oh, yeh!" said Jamie. "That's filtered, you idiot."

"Please, Jamie, let's not argue," said Helen. "It won't help any of us." Jamie felt chastened, and Nicholas was able to continue.

THE TIN BOAT

"It's not filtered really," he explained. He had examined the water system with Morris on several occasions. "It's all pumped up into two big tanks. The mud's allowed to settle and then it comes straight out of the tanks into the taps."

"He's right, you know," said Helen. "I think we're quite safe to drink it, especially this far from the shore, if we need to."

"I still don't fancy it," said William. None of them really liked the idea. It was such a muddy colour. They decided to wait a bit longer before trying it in case rescue came, but it was reassuring to know that they needn't die of thirst.

It wasn't long before Jamie became desperate. He scooped up enough water in his hand to rinse his mouth out.

"That's better," he said. The others plucked up courage and copied him.

"We must keep our heads wet too," said Helen, "I'd dip your hats in the water again, those that have them."

"Do you want to borrow mine?" asked William.

"I'm more used to it thanks," she said, smiling at him again, "but I'll tell you if I need it." She scooped up some water with the baler and poured it on her head.

"You O.K.?" Jamie asked Matthew.

"Yeh, man," he said. Taking his handkerchief out of his pocket he dipped it in the water and laid it over the top of his head.

"Oh, good idea," said Helen. She had a green kikoi wrapped around her over her shorts. She took it off, wetted it, and with great skill tied it as a turban round her head.

'God, she looks beautiful,' thought William. They settled down to wait for rescue.

CHAPTER 16

It was ten o'clock in the morning when the Israelis returned.

"There are road blocks everywhere," their leader told Pam. "The army's all over the place. They seem to be taking up positions all along the road between Kampi-ya-Samaki and Marigat. We thought we heard shooting further south. We can't possibly get through. Sorry."

"O.K." said Pam. "We'll try and fit you in. It may not be very comfortable."

The group leader shrugged his shoulders. Pam went up to the bar where she and Sue poured over the tent list trying to find a way of fitting everybody in. The dreary music on the radio had become so repetitive that everybody forgot about it until it suddenly stopped again.

This time there was silence for several minutes. Nobody in the bar dared speak. At last there was music again, but different music. It was the Kenya national anthem.

"Dis is de voice of Kenya," said a confident new voice. "Long live His Excellency the President!"

"Mneno nakwisha," laughed Stephen behind the bar.

"De forces of Kenya have defitted de enemies of de stet. . ." And so it went on. A curfew was in force. The President was on his way home. Pam waited until the announcement had finished, and returned to the BBC World Service.

"Reports are coming in of a coup attempt against the Kenyan President," said the newsreader. "Rebels from the air force and a group of students from Nairobi University succeeded in capturing the Voice of Kenya radio station in the early hours of this morning. In the last few minutes we have heard that the army, which has remained loyal to the President, is back in control. A dusk to dawn curfew is in force."

"It still won't be safe to let people go," said Pam. "With a curfew in force there'll be roadblocks and trigger-happy soldiers all over the place." The news bulletin was coming to an end.

"We've just received a further report from our correspondent in Nairobi," said the newsreader. "There is some fighting and looting in the capital. An unconfirmed report talks of several people being killed, including a foreign tourist. There are also reports of trouble at the air force barracks in Nanyuki, and in the Rift Valley north of Nakuru among soldiers returning from a military exercise on the Sudanese border."

"That's it, then," said Pam. "Definitely nobody moves."

A long time had passed since the children had tied their boat to the tree. They were all feeling the effects of sunburn and dehydration. They had soon overcome their distaste for drinking the lake water, and they kept their heads wet by filling the baler and pouring it over each other. It was a good joke to start with, but after a couple of hours it had become just a boring necessity.

"The wind has dropped," said Jamie without much enthusiasm.

"Why? Do you want to start rowing again?" asked William.

"Count me out, man," said Matthew. They fell silent for a while. They were all growing lethargic in the sun, and Helen was aware of it.

"I think we should keep trying, or we'll all drop off and roast in the sun," she said. "Let's at least do something."

"We could shout for help," joked Matthew.

"Perhaps we ought to think of finding somewhere on the shore where we could land," suggested Jamie. "At least we would have some shade."

"Then they might never find us," said William. "What about flashing mirrors at the island?"

"What mirrors?" asked Helen.

"What about the baler?" said Nicholas rather weakly. It crossed her mind that he wasn't looking all that well. She looked up at the sun. It was in the right position to be deflected towards the island. She doubted it would do any good, but she wanted to keep them interested and occupied.

"Right. Jamie and I will row again, and one of you try flashing. We'll try and get a bit further out into the lake just to see if there might be anywhere to land."

Samson came to find Pam again and asked her if he could take a boat to the south end of the lake to check on the families of the staff.

"Yes, of course," Pam said. "Take Mandeleo. Johnson's just brought it back from the mainland."

"What about your boss. Don't you think we ought to make sure his household is O.K.?" said David. "He may well want to come over here too."

"You're right," said Pam. "Samson, can you ask Singh to take Islander to the mainland? Tell him to check up on the bwana and bring him and any others back who want to come. Islander will fit quite a lot of them."

So the two boat drivers departed, taking their boats in different directions, one to the south and one to the west towards the mainland jetty. This provided a small distraction for the anxious guests in the bar who watched them leave. Singh in Islander was soon out of sight behind the trees, but they could follow the progress of Samson in Mandeleo most of the way across the lake.

"God, what was that?" asked David.

"Look, a cloud of smoke or dust or something. It's just appeared way down there. See? South-west roughly, behind the trees way on past the lake."

David spotted it just before another one appeared. This time they were all watching in silence. A muffled thud was clearly audible.

"Gunfire, or mortars or something," said David. "It's a long way off though. It must be way beyond the road. Let's have a look through the binoculars." He collected them from behind the bar and went back to the vantage point at the far end of the room.

"Yes, certainly explosions of some sort," he confirmed. "Well, I reckon we're all better off over here. How's Samson getting on? I hope this battle, if there is one, won't spread to where he is going." Samson was some way off now, passing the south end of Teddy Bear Island.

"Now what's going on?" said David anxiously.

"What've you seen?" asked Pam who had come to have a look.

"You look," he said, handing her the binoculars. "See where Samson is? Well just beyond him there are two strange looking boats, rubber dinghies or something. I've never seen them before. They seem to be coming this way."

"Yes they are," Pam confirmed. "Big rubber dinghies with outboards. They're moving pretty quickly this way. They seem to be packed with people...soldiers!.... Soldiers armed with rifles." An anxious murmur went round the guests. Pam wished she hadn't said all that out loud.

"There's obviously some sort of military action going on over there," she said. "I expect they're coming to make sure we don't try and leave. They won't want tourists caught up in the middle of it."

"They're about to intercept Samson," said David. Pam looked again through her binoculars.

"Yes, he's slowing down," she said. "One of the dinghies has gone right up to Mandeleo. It looks as if they're turning him round... no... he's going on. Bloody hell!"

A rifle shot rang out across the water.

"Thank God for that," said Pam. "Nobody's been hit. But

THE TIN BOAT

Samson is turning Mandeleo round. They're all coming this way."

Pandemonium broke out in the bar. Pam had to stand up on a table and shout to restore order.

"Quiet PLEASE!" she screamed, clapping her hands. "That's better. Now, I know it all looks very alarming. The army are obviously going to pay us a call. I need your co-operation. Far and away the most important thing is not to panic them. That's when they get trigger happy. So please, no disturbances. My brother-in-law and I will go down to the jetty and talk to them. It is probably best to do what they say without a fuss. So please stay quietly here until we return."

Sue came in from the kitchen, aware that something had happened.

"Oh good," said Pam. "Can you take over here? They're all a bit agitated because a whole lot of soldiers are about to land at the jetty. They turned Samson back by firing a shot over his head. David and I are going to talk to them. Give everybody a free drink if it would help."

"For God's sake be careful," Sue shouted after them as they left the bar. The idea of a free drink calmed the guests down a little, though it gave Sue and Stephen plenty to do. 'I could do with one of the children to help,' Sue thought.

"My God! The children!" she said out loud. "Stephen, I'll have to leave you to it. I'll send Jackson in to help. The children went fishing over at Mukutan. I'd completely forgotten how long they've been gone. They should be back by now." She ran into the kitchen.

"Everything O.K.?" she asked Rotich.

"Ndiyo, Mensahib,"

"Can you find Jackson and send him into the bar to help Stephen? The children haven't come back. I must go and see if they are on their way."

She went into the dining room, which commanded the best view across the eastern side of the lake. She was hoping to see the tin boat, even if it was only a distant little dot, somewhere on the huge expanse of sun-drenched water, but there was nothing. The Mukutan was the nearest point on the eastern shore to where she was standing. Even so it was more than two miles away. She could make out the cliff-like shape of the Mukutan Hill, but the mouth of the river to the left of it was no more than a long green blur in the midday heat haze. 'Pam's got the binoculars,' she thought. 'I must have them.'

She went back into the bar and pushed her way through the guests to where she could see the jetty. Pam and David were talking to a smartly dressed African army officer. The rest of the soldiers were still disembarking from their dinghies. Samson was tying up Mandeleo. He was clearly very frightened.

The soldiers took up positions on either side of the path which led from the jetty up to the bar. All of them were armed with rifles. It was an unnerving sight, which the guests watched in stunned silence.

Sue was becoming more and more desperate about the children. She pushed her way out of the bar and went down the path. Before she reached the bottom Pam and David were on their way up, accompanied by the officer. They were followed by two of the armed soldiers. Pam looked extremely tense. She caught Sue's eye and made a gesture with her hand. Sue took it to mean that she shouldn't interfere, but she had to do something about the children. When they drew level with her she grabbed David's arm. He knew immediately what was wrong.

"The children!" he whiskered to Pam.

"Binoculars, quick!" said Sue. Pam handed them to her, trying not to do anything which would alarm the soldiers, though they were eyeing her suspiciously. Fortunately they were distracted by the sight of the crowd of guests watching them as they reached the bar. Pam led the officer in. The two soldiers halted in the entrance, rifles at the ready.

Sue ran back to the dining room, followed by David.

"You look! Your eyes are better than mine," she said, handing him the binoculars. "What's going on with the soldiers?"

"They're evacuating us," said David, scanning the lake. "I can't see them."

"Evacuating us? Why? When?"

"Right now. They're escorting a convoy through to Nakuru. There's obviously about to be a hell of a battle between this lot who have remained loyal to the President and the ones who mutinied when they thought he'd been ousted. Hang on..... I thought I saw something flashing. No. Perhaps not."

"Keep looking," said Sue.

"They've got these rebels on the run and they're pushing them north towards Kampi-ya-Samaki. Apparently the police in Marigat panicked and released those prisoners from the police cells, you know, the ones they rounded up here. They seem to have run off and joined the rebels. This officer is worried that it will give them the advantage of some valuable local knowledge. I can't see any sign…yes…wait. Yes, there is something flashing in front of that green bit of shoreline. They must be in trouble."

"You'll have to take the speedboat. Take John with you."

"Right," said David, "but we must explain to our military friends exactly what we are doing and why. They're very jumpy. This evacuation thing is a direct order from the President's office. They don't want any more wasungus caught up in the fighting. Apparently one tourist really has been killed in Nairobi. They're getting sensitive about how all this looks to the rest of the world."

"But they must let us rescue the children!" Sue insisted.

"Yes, yes. But we must talk to them in the right way. You saw what they did to Samson."

"Why did they do it?"

"They want every available boat here now for the evacuation. They're very jumpy and they want to be seen to be obeying the President's orders. They reckon he's firmly in control again, and none of them want any suspicion attached to them that their loyalties might have wavered."

"Well, talk to him, for Gods sake!"

The bar was emptying. The officer, obviously satisfied that

everybody was going to do what they were told, was on his way back to the jetty. Pam had gone to summon the rest of the boat drivers. David stopped her outside the kitchen

"The children are obviously in trouble. We've got to go and rescue them," he said. "Can I take John with the speedboat?"

"Yes of course. You must," said Pam, "but for God's sake clear it with this officer. He reckons time is not on our side and he's very impatient. JOHN! KUJA! WATU YA MELI YOTE! KUJA! HARAKA! HARAKA!"

David waited for John to appear and told him the situation.

"The speedboat is at the back jetty," said John. "I fetch it. You talk to the army. I collect you from that jetty. All the boats here, Memsahib. But not Singh. He went in Islander. He is not back."

"Yes, I know," said Pam. "I sent him to collect the bwana, but the army say they've already evacuated all the mainland wazungus to Nakuru."

Singh was surprised to find the mainland jetty deserted when he arrived. The cars and minibuses of the Pelican Camp guests were still there, apparently unharmed, but there was nobody to be seen. He brought Islander alongside the jetty very slowly. It was a difficult manoeuvre in such a heavy boat without help, and he bumped the first post a little harder than he would have liked, but without causing any damage.

Once he had switched off the noisy diesel engine he could hear shooting somewhere just inland from the jetty. He guessed the sound was coming from the main road north of Kampi-ya-Samaki. He had expected the jetty to be crowded with local people wanting to escape to the island, so he couldn't understand why nobody was there.

The shooting couldn't have been more than a mile away, and seemed to be coming closer. He decided to go up to the house as quickly as he could, so that he could get back to the safety of the island as soon as possible. He didn't get very far. As he stepped up off the jetty into the car park, soldiers armed with rifles appeared from behind every car, from the bushes, and from the night watchman's hut. He stopped, his heart thumping. All around him rifles were pointing at him. There was no hope of escape.

Slowly the circle of men closed in on him, making him edge backwards towards the jetty. Their combat uniforms were covered with dust, their eyes wild and frightened. A man whose face Singh thought he had seen before pushed his way through the circle. He was dressed not in military uniform but in the white shorts and T-shirt worn by prisoners. He looked at Singh and turned to the sergeant who seemed to be the leader of the group.

"This one is a Pelican Camp driver," he said in Swahili. To Singh he said with a sneer, "Yes, I know you lot. It was your wazungu bosses who put me and my rafikis in prison. Now you can do us a favour. You take us to Pelican Camp NOW! Or you are dead." Singh heard the click of safety catches. He was in no position to argue.

The drone of engines could be heard across the bay. Two army lorries and a land rover were heading their way along the bumpy track from Kampi-ya-Samaki.

"MOVE!" shouted one of the soldiers on the jetty. Singh was pushed down the steps. He boarded the boat with a rifle in his ribs and started the engine. The soldiers climbed on board in a panic, trying to push ahead of each other.

"Keep us covered!" shouted the sergeant, who was already on board, to some of the men still on the jetty. They opened fire on the approaching army convey, which promptly stopped and disgorged its own troops who returned fire.

Two more men in prison uniforms appeared from the bushes, followed by more fleeing rebel soldiers, who stopped and fired at the advancing army as they fled. Islander was becoming seriously overloaded. One of the prisoners who was sitting up in the bows cast off the bow painter and tried to push the boat away from the jetty while others were still fighting their way on board.

"Don't wait! Go now!" shouted the sergeant. As Singh put Islander into reverse a deafening crack rang out right next to him.

THE TIN BOAT

A man who was trying to climb aboard fell forward into his colleagues in the boat. As Islander left the jetty they heaved him overboard and left him floating face downwards in the water.

The occupants of the boat kept their rifles trained on those who were left standing on dry land, staring at the departing Islander in disbelief. After a moment the shooting started again behind them. They turned and fled northwards along the shore.

Many of the guests were already down at the jetty when David arrived. They were mainly members of the Israeli party whose bags had already been packed for their previous departure. The officer was busy lining them up in an orderly queue so that there would be no undisciplined rush for the boats when Samson returned. The officer indicated to him to take up his position in Mandeleo. This done, he started boarding the first of the guests.

John arrived, driving the speedboat flat out from the back jetty. David approached the officer to explain what he wanted to do as John slowed down to bring the speedboat alongside one of the rubber dinghies tied to the jetty. The officer thought David was queue-barging and pushed him away. He tried again.

"I must talk to you!" he insisted. This time the officer looked up at his sergeant and nodded. The huge Luo sergeant grabbed David by the arm and marched him off the jetty to the end of the growing queue of guests with their luggage. Nothing David could say was going to make the sergeant listen.

He looked at John hopelessly, but didn't struggle. John still had the speedboat engine running. He had one hand on the steering wheel while he clung to the dinghy with the other. He was all ready to make a dash for it. The sergeant, obviously satisfied that he had brought David into line, released his arm. David waited until he had backed off a little, and made a desperate break for the jetty before anyone could stop him. He had one foot in the dinghy by the time they set on him. This time they weren't going to let him go.

"I get them!" shouted John, revving up the engine and

THE TIN BOAT

slamming it into gear.

"Stop him!" ordered the officer.

"No!" screamed David. "No! You can't!"

Fortunately for John the only soldiers on the jetty who were not occupied holding David had to push through the queue of guests before they could get a clear shot at the speedboat. By that time it was about to round the point of the island. Two shots were fired. The first threw up a spout of water just behind the speedboat. The second produced a metallic thud. David saw John look round anxiously, but he didn't stop. The boat had clearly been hit, though it seemed that John was unharmed. He disappeared from view round the end of the island.

"NOW! No more trouble!" barked the officer. "Let him go." he ordered David's captors.

"Listen. I'm sorry but. . ." David started again.

"David!" Pam was calling him from up in the bar. Sue was standing with her. They beckoned him to join them.

The evacuation started. Half the soldiers departed with the sergeant in one of the dinghies to accompany the first boat. The other boats quickly took their places at the jetty. They too were filled with tourists, as many as could be crammed into each boat.

"What can we do?" sobbed Sue, who had been watching with her sister from the bar. "Even John's not going to make it over there now."

"Memsahib!" a voice whispered behind them. Sion was trying to attract their attention.

"What is it, Sion?" asked Pam. He wouldn't come into the bar, so Pam went to talk to him.

"Memsahib. I seen John. He take the speedboat to Fig Tree Island, round the other side. I think it not go any further. I have ngadich. You want go see John?"

"Yes. Take Bwana David. Thank you, Sion." David went with Sion.

"We've still got a bit of time." Pam said to Sue. "One of the boats will have to come back to take us all off. I've insisted they

THE TIN BOAT

take the up-country staff too. The Njemps have all gone north."

David followed Sion out past the swimming pool and through the fence into the African village. It was deserted.

"Where they all gone?" he asked Sion.

"They all scared. All these soldiers and shooting. They go up north end of the island. Maybe they cross to Longicharo. Safer there." There were two ambach boats pulled up on the shore, opposite Fig Tree Island. Sion and David launched them and paddled across the hundred yards or so of water. John must have been watching for them, because he came down to the shore to meet them.

"You O.K., John?" asked David.

"Niyo. Nzuri sana. The speedboat has big hole on the water line. Is no good. But you not worry. Go now, or there be more shooting. I find the children, I promise. I take care of them. There is a village over there."

"But how will you get there?"

"I have ngadich. The wind blow that way soon. Make it easy. But it is too far for you."

"Well you're right there. I'll try and persuade this idiot to take a boat over. If not, I trust you."

"They be O.K. All friends of mine over there. They have African life for a few days. That not kill them." He smiled reassuringly. "Go quick. I think there be more trouble."

Sue was on the opposite shore waving frantically for David to come back.

"Thank you John. Tell them we're all safe," he said, and paddled back as hard as he could.

"Look, John's going across by ambach. He swears he'll look after the children."

"We've got no choice," said Sue gloomily. "Some of the rebels have landed just a bit further up the island. They're coming this way. Mandeleo is back. All the staff are on board. This is our last chance to escape."

Samson had returned with reports of fighting at the mainland jetty. Islander had been seized and he had seen it full of rebel soldiers heading for the island. The troops escorting the tourists were still holding the track into Kampi-ya-Samaki. He thought that the tourists would all escape, but he had been told to take the last boatload to a point further south on the shore. From there they would have to walk inland to the road, where Chogi's bus had been commandeered to take them into Nakuru.

Sion accompanied them down to the jetty.

"Not cry, Memsahib," he said to Sue. She couldn't help being touched by his concern. "I stay here with John. We look after the children. They be safe." As Mandeleo set off the rebel soldiers could be heard entering the north end of the camp.

"Go quickly," said Sion.

"Don't let them find you, Sion," said David,

"I be O.K. I hide. Kwaheri."

"Kwaheri, Sion."

Sion crossed the camp close to the southern point where he was hidden by the trees. He tried to clamber northwards along the eastern shore, but it was too steep and rocky. He decided he would be quicker and almost as well hidden swimming as close to the shore as possible. He could hear the rebels talking loudly, obviously relieved to have found the camp deserted. They sounded as if they were in the bar or the dining room. He knew he couldn't be seen from there unless he swam quite a long way out.

He reached his ngadich safely, but he thought that he was likely to be spotted if he set off openly towards Fig Tree Island. So he decided to paddle it through the reeds all the way round the bay and cross to the eastern side of the little island which was invisible from the camp.

He found John struggling to sink the speedboat when he finally arrived.

"Why are you doing that?" he asked.

"I don't want them to know anybody's been here," explained John. "We can hide easily enough on this island, but if they come looking round here by boat they will see the speedboat and suspect

THE TIN BOAT

someone is here. There is a lot of water in it. It is too heavy to pull up into the bush. Come, help me sink it."

"The engine's gone. Have you lost it?" asked Sion.

"I've hidden it," said John. They both leaned on the stern with all their weight until at last the water started to flow over the transom. Soon the little boat slid to the bottom. It was invisible in the muddy water.

"Now, we hide," said John. "In an hour or two the wind will blow from the west. Then I set off. What did you see at the camp?"

"All the wasungu and the up-country staff have gone. The Njemps have all gone to the north of the island."

"What about Singh?"

"I don't know. These rebels came ashore at Samson's village outside the camp in Islander. I don't know what happened to Singh after that."

"I must go and look for the wazungu children. I promised. But Singh might need help too."

"I'll stay. I can hide. I can spy. I'll find Singh."

"O.K." said John, "but be careful."

CHAPTER 17

"The sun must be getting to me," said William. "I keep imagining things."

"What things?" asked Matthew.

"I keep thinking I hear explosions, or shots or something, as if they were a long way away so you're not sure whether you've heard them or dreamed them."

"Yeh, well I don't think you're imagining them, 'cause I've been hearing the same thing," said Matthew.

"Me too," said Jamie. "It seems to be coming from way over the other side of the lake. I've been seeing clouds of dust, like dust-devils, only they're not the same shape."

"There must be an army exercise over there," said Helen, "although a couple of shots sounded closer, almost as if they came from the island."

"So you've been hearing it too," said William. "Did you hear anything, Nicholas?"

"What? Hear what?" Nicholas groaned sleepily.

"He doesn't look well," said Helen. "You all right, Nicholas?"

"I've got this headache and I feel sick'" said Nicholas.

THE TIN BOAT

"Come on, we've got to get him into the shade," said Helen. It was now five hours since they had broken down. They were half a mile out from the mouth of the river. From there all they could see was an unbroken line of reeds for miles in each direction along the shore. There was no obvious beach on which to land.

"I suggest we head towards the nearest point of the Mukutan Hill," said Helen. "There must be somewhere at the foot of that cliff where we can get the boat ashore, and there are a few trees there."

The sun had sapped their energy, so that they were able to row only in short shifts. William and Matthew alternated with Jamie and Helen. The breeze had just begun to stir again, and this time it was helping them. Matthew in particular was finding it difficult to keep going in the heat, so on one occasion Nicholas volunteered to take his turn. After a few strokes this proved to be a mistake. Nicholas suddenly swayed and slumped into the bottom of the boat. Helen reacted quickly, taking off the kikoi which was wrapped around her head and dampening his forehead with it until he came round. He raised his head feebly, only to start groaning and vomiting.

"My God!" cried Matthew.

"C'mon," said Helen. "He must have shade. Jamie, you try and keep him cool. William and I will row. You can keep going, can't you, William?" She gave him such a warm and encouraging smile that he would have rowed for her until he dropped. He was also encouraged by the fact that they had drifted in the wind more or less the way they wanted to go.

Jamie continued to dip Helen's kikoi in the water and soak Nicholas's head. He grew quieter and quieter. His eyes closed and he lost consciousness again. He lay absolutely still in the bottom of the boat.

"No! He's not dead, is he?" Jamie screamed. He placed the dripping kikoi over Nicholas's brow and covered the top of his head and the back of his neck with it. He bent down and put his ear to Nicholas's mouth.

THE TIN BOAT

"Ssh!" he whispered. The rowers stopped. Everything was still except the gentle breeze and the call of a fish eagle far away to the north. "I can just hear him breathing," he said. He sat in the bottom of the boat and put Nicholas's head on his lap, and he cried.

"Let's keep going," Helen said quietly to William. They both put all their remaining strength into paddling. By the time they reached the reeds they were both worn out. William's hands were very sore and in danger of becoming blistered, so Matthew had to take over for the last little stretch. Jamie offered to relieve Helen, but she didn't want him to have to move Nicholas. He was breathing a little more easily now, though he was still unconscious.

There was an easy channel through the reeds which led them to a rocky little beach. It smelt of frequent visits by goats and cattle. However it did offer them what they most needed. On the steep bank which rose from the beach to the base of the cliff were acacia trees whose thin foliage gave a surprising amount of shade.

It was difficult to pull the boat up on to the beach. There were too many large rocks to lift it over and the children hadn't the energy left. They pulled it into a lump of reeds where it couldn't bang against anything hard, and wedged the knotted end of the painter under a heavy rock.

"We can make a better job of it later," said Helen. They were all happy to leave it there and forget about it for the time being. "Bring some life jackets to make him comfortable," she suggested to Matthew and Jamie as she and William carried Nicholas with difficulty over the rocks and into the shade.

With four life jackets they improvised a bed for Nicholas and laid him down on it. Then they made themselves as comfortable as they could. The shade was a relief. They felt as if they never wanted to see the sun again.

Nobody spoke for a long while. Each of them looked at Nicholas anxiously for signs of him regaining consciousness, but he was sleeping peacefully. As they were all perfectly well aware they were in a mess. Coming ashore had solved the immediate problem of finding shade, but they were no longer in the place where anybody might come looking for them. The long hours in the sun had left them all too dazed to be able to think what to do next. The old tin boat was out of sight, but they could hear it rhythmically brushing against the reeds with the movement of the water. They struggled to stay awake, but one by one they were overcome by drowsiness.

Helen awoke with a start. Nicholas was stirring and groaning beside her. The other three boys were asleep in the most uncomfortable positions. At first she couldn't bear to look beyond the shade. The glare of the sun was too dazzling.

She felt Nicholas's head and thought that he felt a little feverish. He opened his eyes but quickly covered them with his hand.

"How do you feel?" she asked.

"I've got a headache, a really bad one, and a tummy ache," he said. "My eyes hurt."

"Can you see though?" she asked anxiously.

He uncovered his eyes but only for a moment.

"Yes. I can see, but I can't bear the sun. I hate it. I want it to be dark. Is it nearly night?" She looked at her watch. It was almost midday. To her relief she realized that she hadn't nodded off for more than about ten minutes.

"It's only noon," she said. Nicholas groaned.

"Where are we though?" he asked. "Is this the island or where?"

"We're back at the Mukutan, I'm afraid," Helen explained. "We're just under the hill. You must have got a bit of sunstroke, that's all. We thought we'd better get you into the shade."

"So nobody's rescued us," said Nicholas, obviously alarmed.

'He looks dreadful,' Helen thought. 'We must do something.'

"Jamie! William! Matthew!"

"Hey, Helen, cut it out!" squeaked Matthew, startled out of his sleep. Jamie sat up abruptly.

"How's Nicholas?" he asked immediately.

"Not good. Can you wake William," said Helen.

THE TIN BOAT

Jamie shook William by the shoulders. He woke up groaning.

"What now?" he said without enthusiasm.

"Where's the rescue team?" squeaked Matthew.

"Look, they won't find us here," Helen said firmly. "We don't even know if they are looking for us. Can somebody take the boat out beyond the reeds again and see if anyone's coming?" They all protested vigorously. They'd had enough of the boat, and their hands were sore from rowing. Jamie had another idea.

"There should be a good view from this hill behind us," he said. "One of us could climb up there and have a look."

"Great idea man," said Matthew. "You do that."

Jamie looked pleadingly at Helen.

"You don't want to leave Nicholas, do you?" she asked.

"I'll go," volunteered William.

"Thanks, William," said Helen. "You go with him, please, Matthew. I don't think anyone should go off by themselves."

"What? Because of snakes and things?" asked William.

"Yes. Well, anything really. You know this is Africa," said Helen. "Anyway, you ought to have Matthew with you because he speaks Swahili."

"Why? Are there people living here?"

"Not exactly here, but it's all Njemps country. There'll be a village around here somewhere. You might easily come across somebody grazing cattle or goats."

"What if we do?" asked William.

"Well, ask for help. They're bound to know somebody from Pelican Camp staff. They'll probably be friendly O.K."

"C'mon then Matthew," said William. Matthew reluctantly got to his feet.

It was a hot and exhausting climb, and it was a relief to be able to stop and sit on a rock at the top. Even Matthew had never climbed the Mukutan Hill before, so the view took both of them by surprise. Looking east, away from the lake, they could see the skyline of distant hills which was familiar enough to them. What they never expected to see was the vast plain which stretched from the hill where they were standing to where the first distant slopes began. It was quite invisible from the level of the lake, and even Matthew was totally unaware that it existed.

Through the parched landscape the course of the Mukutan River could be traced by the line of greener vegetation snaking away from them. Another area of relatively lush green was visible way to the north towards Rukus. The rest of the land was the usual dry earth and bleached grass broken up by low bush and acacia trees, and criss-crossed with cattle paths.

There were several herds of white boran cattle stretched out in long unhurried columns each tended by one or two Njemps tribesmen in pink shukas carrying sticks and spears. A few clouds cast their shadows on the otherwise sun drenched land.

It was a glimpse of the Africa which never changed, the Africa which was untouched by power struggles or political upheavals, the Africa which lived through dry cycles and rainy cycles, and didn't thirst for progress. At least from that distance it was a peaceful, friendly sight.

The view across the lake was much more alarming. Smoke was rising from the island at a point quite close to the camp.

"Something bloody odd is going on," said William. "It scares me stiff."

"It's almost as if the village just outside the camp is on fire," Matthew commented.

"Yes," William agreed. "Hang on. Look over there. Is that a boat coming this way? D'you see? Just a dot, between here and Pelican Camp, about level with Gibraltar."

"Yes. Yes, got it," said Matthew "Must be an ambach. It's too small for any other boat. Even so, it means if we hang around we might find out what the hell's going on."

"But I'm worried about Nicholas," said William. "It'll take ages for that guy to reach us, won't it? We can't just hang around here for hours watching him get iller and iller."

"Surprising how quickly those ambaches can go," said Matthew. "He's got the wind behind him. Still, perhaps you're right. Maybe we should ask one of those guys down there for help."

The hill fell away very sharply towards the plain. Immediately below them one of the long strings of cattle was being herded south by a man with two totos helping him. They spotted the boys on the hill and stared up at them with passive curiosity. William and Matthew shouted and waved at them.

"Ngoja! Wait!" The herdsman stopped. William and Matthew clambered down the rocky side of the hill, carefully avoiding the treacherous falls of loose shale. As they descended they lost the breeze which had made the heat tolerable on the top of the hill. Their unprotected legs were scratched by thorns. In spite of everything they hurried on in the hope that at last somebody would be able to help then.

The cattle slowed and came to a halt. The herdsman stuck his spear firmly in the ground and waited for the boys to approach him.

"You ask him," William said to Matthew, aware that the very few words of Swahili he'd picked up wouldn't be of much use. He lost the thread of the conversation after the initial greetings.

"Jambo."

"Jambo sana. Habari yaku?"

"Nzuri."

Matthew addressed him quietly and respectfully, not in the boisterous way he would talk to the Pelican Camp staff. It was one of those meandering, long-winded, conversations which seemed to be usual in that country between strangers or people who hadn't seen each other for a long time. William noticed how they gradually stopped looking at each other and talked as if half their attention was on the cattle or the far horizon. On the other hand, the two totos who were not involved in the conversation stared at Matthew and William remorselessly. At last some agreement seemed to have been reached.

"Mimi na kuja," said the tribesman, looking Matthew in the eyes once more.

"Asante sana," said Matthew, returning his gaze. "C'mon William. He's coming with us. He says he'll take us to his village. His name is Lemeriai."

"Asante, Lemeriai," said William.

"Ndiyo," said Lemeriai, plucking his spear out of the ground and following them round the north end of the hill, which seemed an easier route. The two totos were left to guard the cattle.

Nicholas was awake when they returned, feeling a little stronger although he still complained that the sun hurt his eyes and that he had a stomach ache.

"Lemeriai, this guy here, says we can come with him to his village," Matthew explained to Helen and Jamie. "We can't see any sign of a Pelican Camp boat, but there is an ambach way out by Gibraltar which seems to be coming this way. There's a lot of smoke from the village just outside the camp. Something odd's going on."

"I wish we knew what was happening," said Jamie. "We must get moving with Nicholas, though. Do you think one of us should stay here and say where we've gone if it is somebody coming from Pelican Camp?" Helen discussed the problem with Lemeriai.

"One of those totos will stay," she said. "Apparently the cattle more or less find their own way back, so the other toto can manage by himself." Neither of them had looked more than eight years old. William was struck by how young they were given responsibility.

William and Jamie offered to carry Nicholas, but he said he could walk. They all soaked their headgear in the water once more to keep themselves cool. They knew it would be a long hot walk.

Lemeriai led the way, his spear across his shoulders. They headed south, between the cliff face and the lake, which was hidden by the thick growth of ambach plants. The path turned away from the lake once they passed the southern end of the hill. The land was flat and must have been part of the lake bed in years gone by when the water level was much higher. It was dominated by a series of huge termite chimneys, at least three metres high.

THE TIN BOAT

The further they went from the lake the more oppressive the heat became. Nicholas began to fall behind the others, so Helen waited for him.

"You O.K.?" she asked.

"Yes," said Nicholas, although in fact his head was starting to swim, and he longed to reach the shade of the thorn trees which he could see in the distance ahead of them. Shortly afterwards, with a faint cry of "Help!" he fell to the ground.

"Ngoja!" shouted Helen. The others looked round, and hurried back to where she was tending Nicholas. She looked up at Lemeriai and asked him how much further they had to go.

"What does he say?" asked Jamie.

"Another mile," Helen told him. "Let's try and carry him to the trees and go and get help."

Lemeriai came to the rescue. He gave Jamie his spear to carry and hoisted Nicholas onto his shoulders.

CHAPTER 18

Nicholas came round to find himself in almost total darkness. His head hurt badly and he was very thirsty. He didn't feel like moving, so he lay still and tried to work out where he was. A myriad of tiny cracks of light filtered through a wicker screen next to the bed on which he was lying. He felt the bed with his fingers. It was no more than a web of ropes strung on a wooden frame. Although there was no mattress it wasn't uncomfortable. He reached down and touched the floor. It was just dry earth. He was in an African hut.

The events of the day came tack to him, and he remembered what difficulties they were in. This made his head worse. He put his hand to his forehead and groaned.

"Neecola! Neecala! Nzuri sana. Nzuri. Nzuri." A wrinkled old Nemps woman was bending over him, stroking his hair with her rough lingers and almost tickling his nose with her long dangling earrings.

"Where's Helen... I mcan... wapi Helen?" Nicholas groaned.

"Wapi Helen? Ndiyo, Helen iku hapa. Watoto wote wapo hapa. Nzuri sana. Neecola." She gabbled on in her awful

THE TIN BOAT

screeching voice, though she didn't worry Nicholas. She reminded him of Eleru's mother, and he remembered how kind she had been to them at John's wedding. However he was longing to see the others, and he tried to get up. She pressed his shoulders lightly back down onto the bed.

"Ngoja," she said reassuringly, and hobbled out. Soon he heard the familiar voices of his friends thanking the old lady.

"Don't lets all rush in and bother him," suggested Helen. "Jamie, why don't you and I go in and see how he is?" The hut darkened as they came through the doorway, which was the only source of light. Soon the faces of Helen and Jamie appeared round the screen.

"How're you feeling, you poor chap?" asked Helen.

"You any better?" said Jamie.

"I'm so thirsty," complained Nicholas in a parched voice. "Is there anything to drink?"

"Well only the lake water which they carry up here in drums on their donkeys. We've boiled some up so it won't do you any harm. It's still a bit warm, though," said Helen. Nicholas knew he had to drink something, but how he longed for a lovely cold glass of fresh orange.

"That'll do O.K." he said.

"I'll get it," said Jamie, and slipped out. Helen felt Nicholas's head.

"You don't feel too bad," she reassured him, "but I'd lie still till your head feels better."

"What's happening, though? Where are we?"

"We've been taken in by these kind Njemps people. This village is somewhere between Mukutan and Fort Baringo. You fainted, and Lemeriai carried you here. They've been so kind. Lemeriai has moved all his family into two other huts so that we can use this one. They've even killed a goat for us. We've all agreed to try and be as little nuisance to them as we can. They don't have much, and yet they seem to be prepared to share everything with us, so we mustn't take advantage of them."

THE TIN BOAT

Nicholas appreciated how kind the Njemps people were being, but he still wished he was back in his bed in Pam's house.

"What about Mum and Dad and Pam?" he asked. "Why haven't they come to rescue us?"

"We don't know exactly what's happened," said Helen. "I'm sure you needn't worry. One or two people have come into the village with stories about a coup attempt in Nairobi."

"What's that? I don't know what you mean."

"It means that some people have tried to get rid of the President, you know, the ruler of Kenya, and put somebody else in his place. They say there is even some fighting on the other side of the lake. They think that everybody from Pelican Camp might have been taken to Nakuru where they will be safe from the fighting, so I expect they're all O.K."

"They won't come and fight here, will they?" Nicholas asked. Helen wished she knew exactly what was going on. It was difficult to answer Nicholas's questions without making him even more worried.

"No, I'm sure they won't. There are no towns or roads, or anything to fight over here," she said. "Look. Don't worry. I expect we'll get more news very soon." Jamie reappeared, breathless and excited, clutching an open bottle of sprite.

"Heavens!" said Helen. "Where did you get that from?"

"One of Lemeriai's friends gave it to me. I couldn't get his name."

"But I thought we'd agreed...."

"I know," said Jamie, "but they're all so friendly, and they just made me take it. It will do Nicholas good."

"You bet," said Nicholas, suddenly feeling well enough to sit up. The sprite was warm but wonderfully refreshing all the same.

"Do you want some?" he said to Jamie,

"No, I brought it for you, to make you better," Jamie insisted.

"It's all right. Let's share it. I do feel better now," said Nicholas generously. Jamie took a quick swig and passed the bottle on to Helen. It was pleasant to get rid of the muddy taste of the lake water.

"Matthew says someone's seen John Boat coming this way," said Jamie, wiping his mouth with the back of his hand.

"Oh, great!" said Helen.

Nicholas was so heartened by the news that he sat on the edge of the bed and prepared himself to find out what standing up would feel like.

"Is it still hot outside?" he asked. He still felt nervous of the sun.

"Not bad," said Jamie. "It's about half past four so it's much cooler than it was." Nicholas stood up and walked cautiously towards the door. His legs felt weak, but the drink had done wonders for his headache.

The sun was far less dazzling than he had feared, and a pleasant breeze from the lake helped to make the heat tolerable. He looked around at the village. It was much the same as all the others he had seen, except that there were more trees breaking up the open ground between the bomas, and therefore more shade. Their own boma enclosed three huts, widely spaced so that there was some degree of privacy. As usual there were goats, dogs and chickens wandering around apparently unattended. Cattle were being herded here and there around the village by tribesmen.

William and Matthew were standing under a big fever tree surrounded by a crowd of noisy children. When they saw Nicholas they rusted over to greet him shouting "Jambo! Jambo!"

"They say John Boat's on his way," said Matthew. "We're watching out for him."

"Yes, I heard that," said Helen, who had followed Nicholas out of the hut. "Is it really true?"

"Let's hope so," said William. "We might find out at last what's going on." They didn't have to wait long. The little boy who had been left at Mukutan came running down the path out of the trees pointing behind him shouting,

"Ye nakuja! John nakuja!" The children were already running up the path when John emerged from the trees. He looked hot and

THE TIN BOAT

tired and a little anxious, but still managed his old warm smile when he held out his arms to greet them.

"We are pleased to see you," said Helen.

"We got stuck here, 'cause the sheer pin got jammed," Jamie explained.

"What's going on over there?" asked Matthew. Nicholas said nothing, but flopped into John's arms and burst into tears. John picked him up and carried him back to the boma, while the other children continued to fire questions at him.

"O.K. O.K. I tell you everything soon," he assured them. He wanted a little time to catch his breath before he told them the whole story. "Iku mneno mgubwa sana. Big trouble. But all O.K. Pam, Sue, David, yote nzuri ."

"And my Dad? Have you heard anything about my Dad?" asked Helen.

"Ndiyo, and the Bwana. He O.K. too. I heard this."

"Oh, thanks, John," said Matthew. "I sure feel better for hearing that."

Once inside the boma John left them and went with Lemeriai into one of the other huts. After a few minutes he returned looking refreshed, carrying a mug of strong tea. He sat down with the children under the tree, and in the clear, friendly evening light they listened to him tell his story. He told them of the coup attempt and the battle between the loyal troops and the rebels. He described how Pelican Camp had been evacuated just in time before it was taken over by the rebel forces, and how he made his own escape.

"So you see everybody escape," he concluded. "There is only Singh who is in trouble. I very worried about Singh. I hope Sion find where he is."

"Yes, but I hope Sion is careful," said Jamie. "I'm frightened he might be caught."

"Sion very clever boy. Akili mingi. He not stupid. I think he be O.K.," said John.

"Can't we go and rescue Singh?" asked Nicholas.

THE TIN BOAT

"These are bad people," said John. "Rebel soldiers and criminals. They all have guns. We have no guns. But you not worry too much. I think they not harm Singh. They stuck on that island. They need boat driver."

"Well yes, unless one of them knows how to drive a boat," said Helen.

"They have Islander. Not easy boat," said John.

"What do we do, though?" asked Matthew. "Can we escape round the lake and through Marigat?"

"I think it is not safe," said John. "There has been shooting down there all day. I think the army stop everybody. We must try to hear more news."

"News from where?" asked Matthew.

"The chief in the next village. He has a radio. They go to ask him for news. They come back soon."

"So all we can do is wait here?" said William.

"Yes," said John with a heartening smile. "You be O.K. here. All friends here. You hungry? Nataka chukula?"

"Yes, please!" they all said in unison. They had been too tired and anxious to think about food, although they hadn't eaten all day. Now that they knew roughly what was going on, and in particular that their families were safe, they suddenly felt ravenously hungry. Only Nicholas was a little unsure about the idea of eating. He was still feeling rather dizzy.

"I am very hungry too," said John. "They kill a goat. They say you very special guests. Perhaps tomorrow we catch some fish. Is not Pelican Camp food, but not bad?"

Helen took him aside and explained their anxiety to him.

"Everybody's been so kind, especially Lemeriai and his family," she said. "We must be an awful nuisance to them. We really don't want them to do special food. We can share whatever there is, and of course we'll pay for and replace what we eat."

John shook his head.

"You are wageni here. They are very happy that you are their guests. Please, don't try to pay. Maybe one day you offer a gift, something to make them remember you." The children understood because they had all experienced the hospitality of the Njemps people before, and they had no wish to risk offending those who were helping them so generously.

The goat was eaten in their hut, just before dusk. John was there with Lemeriai and a couple of his male relatives, but not the women or children who seemed to eat separately. Nicholas sat next to John. In fact he had hardly left John's side since his arrival. He ate a little of the meat, but he was finding it hard to keep his eyes open. William noticed this and whispered to Helen.

"I think we ought to put Nicholas to bed." Helen looked at him and agreed. She explained to Lemeriai, and the Africans all bid Nicholas goodnight.

"Kwaheri, Neecolas. Lala salama."

"I'll cope with him," William said to Helen. "You look worn out."

"O.K., thanks," said Helen, relieved to be able to share the responsibility for Nicholas. "Shout if you need help." William took Nicholas out briefly before putting him to bed behind the screen. He returned to the table.

"Everything all right?" asked Helen.

"Yeh, fine," said William. "He'd like Jamie to say goodnight to him." While Jamie was gone Helen said,

"Shall we go out and leave him to be quiet?"

"No," said William. "I think he'll go to sleep anyway, and he'll feel safer if he knows we are all here." Matthew translated and everybody agreed.

Lemeriai continued to offer them more and more meat, slicing it off the bone for them to eat with their fingers. Though it wasn't their favorite taste, the children were hungry enough to enjoy it, and they found the strong, sweetened African tea refreshing. They were already beginning to feel at ease sitting on the little wooden benches in the dark crowded African hut.

Some of the totos peered through the door to stare at the strange sight of wazungu children eating in one of their huts. Lemeriai firmly shooed them away, and was rather more instantly obeyed than a European father might have been.

Presently an older boy peered in. He seemed more purposeful, and spoke urgently in Maasai to Lemeriai, who followed him out, returning alone a few minutes later. When the boy's story had been retold in Swahili Helen translated for Jamie and William.

"That boy has just come back from the village behind Fort Baringo," she explained. "The chief there has a radio. According to the news the generals have stayed loyal to the President, and so has most of the army. They are back in control and the President is on his way home. There has been some fighting in Nairobi but they say it is more or less over. The two trouble spots are here and at the air force base at Nanyuki. The problem here is that some of the soldiers coming back from the exercise up north joined the rebel side thinking they were going to win. Now they are on the run with some criminals who were released by mistake this morning."

"But do we know what's happened to everybody from Pelican Camp?" asked William.

"Yes, it just said the area had been evacuated of foreign tourists without casualties. The trouble was that a tourist was shot in Nairobi. That's why they wanted everybody out of the way of the fighting."

"Good Lord!" said William.

"Gosh, I'm glad they're all safe," said Jamie. "Can't we get out to the road at Marigat and go to Nakuru?"

"Marigat? Its miles!" said Helen. "I don't think Nicholas would make it. Anyway, there's a curfew and roadblocks everywhere, so there won't be any transport to take us. Besides, we don't know quite where the fighting is going on."

"So we're stuck here," said Matthew. He was very tired and his sense of humour had finally deserted him,

"We're safe and among friends," said his sister. They all fell silent until she added "C'm on. We've all had it. Let's get some sleep. It's almost dark now, and there isn't much to do in an African village after dark except sleep."

The first stars had appeared, and the evening wind was beginning to blow quite strongly. The goats, together with the cows and calves, had been driven inside the boma, and Lemeriai's young wife was closing up the entrance with thorn branches to keep out the baboons.

Outside the hut the children thanked their African hosts. John went off with Lemeriai to the hut where he was to sleep. For a long time they could be heard talking and laughing. Lemeriai was obviously enjoying the visit from another young mzee of his own age-group.

Dust was being blown around by the wind, so the children were glad to be back inside the hut. The smell of goat lingered on, though even inside the wind seemed to have driven away the flies.

Jamie and Matthew chose the crude wooden bunk beds where Lemeriai's younger children normally slept. On the raised area which was Lemeriai's own sleeping place there was an old mattress.

"You have that," William said to Helen.

"Where will you sleep, then?" asked Helen.

"I'll make myself comfortable with the life jackets somewhere," he assured her.

"You're a very kind fellow," said Helen. "If you're very uncomfortable we'll swap over, so that at least we'll all get some sleep. Take the blanket off the mattress. It looks a bit old and dirty but it might help."

CHAPTER 19

William was so tired that he dropped off to sleep in spite of being acutely uncomfortable. It wasn't a very restful sleep, and he awoke in the middle of the night aching all over from lying on the hard ground. There was silence in the hut, only broken by the familiar sound of Jamie snoring. He decided to check that Nicholas was sleeping peacefully. He put his head round the screen and listened. He could hear Nicholas breathing steadily, if perhaps a little faster than usual. He was certainly asleep, which was the best thing for him.

So William returned to his uncomfortable bed and tried to go back to sleep, but he knew it wasn't going to work. As he lay there wondering whether there was any way of rearranging his bed to make it tolerable, he became aware of other discomforts. He felt dirty and he smelt, and this became increasingly annoying as the night wore on. They had all been too tired to work out a way of washing themselves, and now he regretted their laziness.

He started worrying about how long they might have to survive in the clothes they had on. He tried to work out how far they were from the nearest point on the lake. It would be quite a walk, but he thought it would be a good idea for them to go there early when it was cool and wash themselves and their clothes, which would dry quickly in the sun.

He wasn't particularly worried about the troubles on the island or way over on the far shore of the lake. It all seemed a long way off, and he couldn't imagine the circumstances which would bring the fighting in their direction. He never doubted that in time they would all be happily reunited with their families. What he couldn't foresee was how much time they would have to spend living the life of Njemps tribesmen.

He would have been much less worried if Nicholas hadn't become ill. He wondered how much Helen knew about those things. Perhaps she had looked after Matthew when he was ill at some time. He assumed that the Africans had their own ways of dealing with illnesses, but that idea didn't encourage him much.

The night was very still now. Through the open doorway he could see that the village was bathed in moonlight. It looked inviting, and as sleep seemed impossible he decided that he might be more comfortable sitting outside in the fresh air. He took his blanket and a couple of the life jackets to sit on, and went out into the moonlight.

The cattle and goats stood or lay on the bare earth absolutely motionless, as if frozen in a black and white photograph. The full moon was almost directly overhead, casting the same sort of shadows as the equatorial sun, but picking out trees, animals, the huts and the boma fence of thorn branches more clearly because there was no glare. The loudness of the night noises from the crickets was as astonishing as the brightness of the moonlight.

"Hi!" whispered a soft, friendly voice behind him. He turned and saw Helen sitting on the ground with her back to the outside wall of the hut. "Can't you sleep either?" William shook his head. She looked different somehow, perhaps because of the strange shadows cast on her face by the colourless light of the moon. She seemed almost to have become an adult, with the look in her eyes of carrying adult cares and responsibilities. "Come'n talk," she whispered, patting the ground beside her.

"D'you want something to sit on?" asked William. "I've brought these things out."

"Yeh, great. I'm beginning to get a sore bottom," Helen joked. She stood up and they folded the blanket a couple of times and laid it down where she had been sitting so that there was room for both of them. They each took a life jacket to lean against.

"Wasn't your mattress comfortable, then?" asked William.

"Bit lumpy, but I can't complain," she said. "It must be ten times better than what you had to put up with. D'you want to try it? See if you can get some sleep?"

"Thanks, but I don't feel as if I'm going to get to sleep anyway at the moment," said William.

"I agree," said Helen. "Anyway, it's rather pleasant sitting out here. Probably better to sleep through the middle of the day and enjoy the cool of the night in a place like this."

"That's true," said William. "I've seen quite enough of the midday sun for a long while."

"I think it was feeling so dirty and smelly that really kept me awake. We must get organized about washing. I wonder what they all do about it."

"Yeh, it's bothering me too," said William. "I thought we ought to go down to the lake early in the morning when it's cool and wash ourselves and our clothes. How far d'you reckon it is to the lake?"

"It seemed miles when we walked here, didn't it? But I suppose, what, a mile and a half or so by the shortest route. I thought boys didn't mind about things like that, being dirty and so on."

"Perhaps the younger ones don't, but it drives me mad. How worried are you about Nicholas?" he said, changing the subject. Helen looked at him anxiously.

"I hoped you might know something about these things," she said. "I mean I could cope with a little bit of sunstroke or a mild tummy bug or something like that, but if he gets really bad I'm not sure I'd know what to do. You seemed so good with him this evening."

"I don't think I'd do any better than you," said William. "I thought you might have had to look after Matthew sometimes, you know, because your mother isn't here and.... sorry, I'm prying into things that are none of my business." She turned towards him and rested her hand lightly on his arm.

"Hey, I don't mind you talking about that," she reassured him with a smile. "We're both rather in the same boat anyway in that way, aren't we?"

"Sort of," said William with a touch of sadness.

"Well, then. Yes, my parents are divorced, and I have had to look after Matthew to a certain extent when we're with my Dad, but he hasn't been ill much. Actually one thing does come back to me, but more from seeing the African children who are brought to the house when they are ill. I know that the thing everybody worries about if they get a tummy bug is dehydration. It can happen so quickly in this climate if they don't have enough liquid. It's something we must watch if that is what he's getting."

"Well that's a useful thing to know," said William. He was silent for a while, troubled suddenly by the thoughts of all the things which might be wrong with Nicholas. He tried to shake it off, telling himself that all they could do was face the problems as they came along, and not dream up new ones.

"Look," he said at last, "there are obviously things which might happen which we would find hard to cope with, in which case we would have to try and get through for help, and risk getting caught up in the fighting. We're not in that situation yet though, and with any luck it's just a bit of sunstroke and he'll be fine in a day or two. Perhaps the fighting will be over soon anyway. All we can do is keep an eye on him and take things as they come."

"What a sensible guy you are," said Helen. "Isn't it odd though. Here we are talking about the younger ones almost as if we were their parents. I suppose for the moment we are, in a way. It all seems terribly grown up. I mean we're only fourteen."

"Do you find it scary?" asked William.

"Oddly enough I don't really, but I'm sure I would if I didn't have you to share it with. You've been great. You keep taking me by surprise."

"I know. I know. You must have thought I was a complete dead weight! I'm sorry. I'm just not much good at letting my hair down and enjoying myself, am I? I suppose it's because I had to spend too much time fending for myself when I was younger and never got into playing and having fun."

"Why?" said Helen. "Sounds awful!"

"You wouldn't want to hear about all that," said William. "It's all rather boring."

"Of course I would, if you want to tell me," Helen said to him with an encouraging smile.

"Well the truth is my Mum has always been a bit of a problem. She only married my Dad because I was on the way, and he disappeared when I was a baby. I've never even met him, not since I can remember."

"That's bad," said Helen.

"Yes, but it gets worse," said William. "My mother re-married and had two more children. My stepfather and I just don't get on. He drinks a lot, I think I told you that, and he's pretty foul to me - makes me feel that he really doesn't want me around."

"But doesn't your Mum stand up for you," asked Helen sounding genuinely concerned.

"Not really," said William. "She sort of makes out that it's all my fault. And anyway, she only really cares about the other two children who are much younger than me. Anyway, from very early on I've been left to get my own food and so on most of the time, and I even have to do a lot of the cleaning in the house because my Mum's hopeless about it and I hate the mess. The truth is that she's thoroughly lazy, and my stepfather's even worse. He does nothing. Hasn't even got a job."

"So you mean you go around doing the…..?"

"Please don't laugh at me! I know it sounds a bit pathetic for a boy to be doing all that sort of thing." 'God! I wish I hadn't started this conversation,' he thought. He glanced nervously at Helen and found her looking almost angrily at him. She took his hand in hers and said earnestly,

"I'm not laughing at you, I promise. Please don't think that. Actually it explains a lot about why you seemed to be so good at looking after Nicholas and all that this evening. Anyway, go on."

"If you really want me to," said William.

"Yes I really do," Helen insisted. "I'm interested. It sounds dreadful."

"I'm not used to talking about it, that's all. I just never do. Anyway, I'll tell you if you really want to know. Things got really bad this summer and in the end the Social Services decided that I wasn't being looked after properly, and I should be taken into care."

"What? You don't mean put into a home or something?"

"Well, no. I was lucky I suppose. My grandmother came to the rescue and I've gone to live with her."

"And you're happy there? You don't sound too sure about."

"Well yeh, I mean she's being very kind," said William. "But you'll understand. When she brought up her family out here in Kenya she would have had endless help, ayahs and so on. She doesn't find it easy taking on a moody teenager by herself at her age. I'm afraid I had an awful row with her. My fault, I know. It was about something quite silly. I feel really guilty about it. I suppose I'd just got in a state after all that had happened. My kind aunt Sue and uncle David stepped in and suggested I got away from it all and came out here with them. They got me a ticket at the last moment. I may not always show it but I know I'm very lucky to be here. I like being with Jamie and Nicholas. They are much more like brothers to me than my mother's other children. But I still feel sort of different from them because they've had the normal family life which I haven't. Do you see that? I think that's also why I'm not good at making friends with other children of my age."

"You mustn't blame yourself," said Helen sweetly. "You've had a lousy deal. I've had a much more normal family life than you, but still I remember what it felt like when my parents split up. It was pretty tough. You feel as if you're the only one going through all this but of course you're not. You talk to other people and you find that lots of children are in the same boat."

"Yes, I know. I've never been good at talking about these things. This is the first time I've ever really done it," said William.

"Perhaps girls are better at yakking away to each other at school," Helen suggested. "There's a lot of it about in Kenya, divorce I mean, so I've got friends in the same boat. Anyway, you can't spend your life mulling over what can't be changed. Somehow we all have to get on with life. Hey, we are getting serious, aren't we? I want to see you laugh."

"Were you hoping for a laugh when you threw that snake on my bed this morning?" said William, his face even then brightening into a smile.

"Sorry, that was a bit over the top," she admitted. "Am I forgiven? In fact, am I forgiven for dragging you out on this fateful expedition? You could be tucked up in a comfortable bed in Nakuru or somewhere if I hadn't made you come."

"No, I really did want to come, I promise," said William. "I'm just hopeless at waking up in the morning. Everyone in the family dreads being the one to have to wake me up. I don't really understand why you bothered with me, though. I'd have thought you would have just said 'Oh, to hell with him,' and gone off without me." He looked at her. She was smiling at him as if to say 'Come on now, I thought we'd got over all that,' so he smiled back and said, "You've been really nice to me. I've been moody and dreary and yet you've always been friendly."

"I can't bear to see anybody come here and not enjoy themselves," she said. "I'm sure there are lots of other places just as good as Lake Baringo, but to me it's the best place in the world and I want everybody else to think so too. Anyway, I like you being here. You're different from all the other boys I meet over

THE TIN BOAT

here."

"How d'you mean?"

"Oh, I don't know. You don't seem to have to put on this tough guy act all the time. You know this Kenya cowboy thing where they all talk with this clipped yarpy accent so you don't have to show your real feelings, man." She said all this in a wonderful imitation of the very accent she was describing, and that did make William laugh. "Don't laugh too loud. You'll wake up the boys," she whispered, though she was laughing too. "So you don't hate me for dragging you out here?"

"It may sound odd, but apart from worrying about Nicholas I've never felt happier," he admitted.

"Do you know, I'm not so surprised?" Helen reassured him. "You look happier. And you look so much fitter. Gosh, am I being rude?"

"No, you're right," said William. "I feel like a different person, as if suddenly I could do anything."

"You know, just a few days ago when we delivered John's calf you wouldn't even break into a run. But today, even after all that rowing you volunteered to climb that hill in the heat of the day. You did wonderfully. It was a great effort. And now look at you. You look as if you've spent your whole childhood leading an outdoor active life. You may be tired and bruised and sun burnt but you look fantastic!" William blushed and looked away from her. He didn't know how to answer that, so after a long pause he changed the subject.

"I just hope it's not all going to come to a sudden end. You must be worried, aren't you, about what's going on over there?" he said.

"I'm trying not to think about it, but yes, of course I am. You know, it's not just the camp but our house as well, our whole lives really, abandoned to the mercy of these people who aren't likely to be great respecters of other people's property. It doesn't bear thinking about."

Thinking once more about the horror of what might be going

just across the lake reduced them both to silence for a while. It was hard to imagine any strife or destruction when the night was so perfectly peaceful and still. Occasionally there was a call or a screech or even a laugh from some wild bird or creature which William couldn't identify, or a bored moan from a cow somewhere in the village, but otherwise there was only the high-pitched pulse of the crickets.

The shadows from the moon were lengthening as it moved west, but the stars seemed more and brighter than ever. Looking up at them William felt that he should be more worried or even frightened by the predicament they were in, but he couldn't make himself wish for things to be any different than they were at that very moment. He had never felt more at peace with the world or with himself. However briefly, he had found a friend and had unloaded his troubles in a way he had never been able to do before.

He looked at her, but for a while she continued star-gazing as he had done. He wondered if he was really seeing tears in her eyes, or whether it was just a trick of the moonlight. He wanted to tell her how beautiful she looked, but he knew he wouldn't dare to in a million years. At last she broke the silence, still looking up at the sky and murmuring softly.

"You'd think this one peaceful place could have been left alone by power struggles and strife, wouldn't you? And yet I suppose I've often thought that our life here was too good to be true, and would just turn out to be a dream and vanish." William was silent, wishing he knew how to comfort her. "Oh, let's face it," she continued with a sigh. "It's not really our world. We've just been lucky enough to be allowed to enjoy it. The Njemps people's lives probably won't be disrupted in any serious way, just as they weren't by colonialism or the Mau Mau, or independence, or any of the upheavals in the past. People with such simple needs are probably much better able to survive these things. I sometimes think it's these sort of people who would be left to carry on if the developed world blew itself up nuclear war or something."

"Isn't there something in the bible about the meek inheriting the earth?" said William, almost as if out of a dream.

"What was that?" asked Helen.

"My Gran drags me off to church sometimes," admitted William.

"I think I prefer the idea of the earth inheriting the meek," suggested Helen.

"Wow! That's getting a bit deep!" said William laughing.

Suddenly an owl flew silently into the tree opposite them. It sat there looking at them with great curiosity.

"Isn't that a lovely sight," said Helen. "There are so many different sorts of birds here, but I still think the owls are my favourites."

"It doesn't seem too bothered by us, does it?" said William. In fact it was so untroubled by the sight of them that eventually it flew down and started circling around the roof of their hut as if it was going to land there. Helen leaped to her feet, apparently terrified.

"Quick, William, make it go away!" she gasped. "Throw something at it! Don't let it land, please!" William couldn't understand what had suddenly troubled her so, but he picked up a stone and aimed it at the owl, not very accurately but enough to divert it. It dipped behind the hut and they saw it fly off away from the village.

Helen clung to William. He could feel her shaking.

"What on earth was that about?" he asked. "Are you afraid of them? Surely it won't harm you, and you were brave enough with that snake this morning. Anyway, you just said you liked owls."

"I know, you can laugh at me now," she said, pulling herself together. "You must think I'm quite mad. Normally I wouldn't think twice about it. We often have owls on our roof at home and I love them. It's just me being silly because we're in an Njemps village and sleeping in an Njemps hut. You know they regard an owl settling on their roof as a very bad omen. Well, actually, it's a symbol of death to them. Sorry, I don't really know why it got to me like that. It must be because I'm tired. Come on, we'd better try and get some sleep."

"Sure you're all right though?" said William gently. "You won't have nightmares or anything?"

"No, really, I'm fine, thanks," she assured him. "Anyway, thanks for reacting to my silly little whim. Oh, William. I'm really glad you're here. I'd hate to be coping with all this without you."

"You'd manage," said William. "You've been fantastic today. Still, I'm glad I'm here too. I'll just go and check on Nicholas. Sleep well."

"You too," said Helen. "No snakes with your early morning tea tomorrow, I promise."

CHAPTER 20

For Sion too the night had brought little sleep. He had been afraid to venture back into the camp in daylight. Once the evacuation had been completed and the camp had been overrun by the rebels he had taken refuge in the cave which he had used to hide John's calf. He had witnessed to his horror the burning of many of the huts in the village by the rebels, and hoped that they would suppose the place to be deserted now. But even if they came searching that way again he was reasonably sure that they would never find the mouth of the cave amongst the tangle of thorn bushes which hid it from view.

The bushes grew almost to the top of the rocky outcrop, and gave him enough cover to climb to a point from which he could see the area around the swimming pool. From there he had caught a brief glimpse of Singh, alive and apparently unharmed. In the middle of the afternoon he had seen two rebel soldiers hustle poor Singh past the swimming pool at gunpoint and lock him into the

THE TIN BOAT

little storeroom where the sunbathing mattresses were kept. They had remained outside the store all afternoon, keeping guard.

'I have found out where Singh is, as John told me to do, but John is not here.' thought Sion. 'Nobody is here to help. What can I do, just myself alone? I cannot fight two men with guns and rescue Singh. I must fetch help.'

At first he thought of finding an ambach and paddling across to the Mukutan as John had done, but he knew it would be a tremendously long way for a boy of his age, not yet fully grown and not particularly strong.

'I will do it if I must,' he told himself, 'but it would take me many hours and many hours more for anybody to return this way, for how often does the wind blow from the east?' He thought of the villagers who had fled north over the central hill of the island, and wondered whether they had all crossed over to the mainland. The north coast of the island was two miles from the camp, so he supposed that many of them would still be there. 'That is what I must do,' he decided. 'When it is night and the moon is up I must go to the other end of the island. There I will find help. If nobody is there, I will try and cross the lake to Longicharo.'

So until nightfall he remained hidden. When darkness came he thought, 'I will not find my way over the hill until the moon shines, but maybe in the darkness I can go into Pelican Camp and see what these bad people are doing.'

He left his cave and crossed to the western shore, keeping close under the boundary fence. Undressing and leaving his clothes by the fence where he could find them again, he slipped into the water and swam silently as far as the back jetty. There he found not only Islander but Blue Banana too, tied up at the end of the jetty. 'So they have stolen that boat too,' he thought. 'More soldiers must have come here.' He wondered if another of the camp drivers had been captured, but he had seen no sign of any of the others. Perhaps one of the soldiers had been able to operate a simple outboard motor by himself.

He crawled out of the water onto the rock below the back jetty.

THE TIN BOAT

He could hear voices from the manager's house above him, but there was no sign of anybody near the jetty, so he climbed up onto it and started up the path. In the darkness, for they had not managed to start up the generator, he thought he could creep close enough to the house to hear what they were saying.

When he was half way up the steep path the voices grew suddenly louder. People were coming towards him. He scampered back noiselessly in his bare feet, ran across the jetty and hid behind the shelter which housed the generator. He couldn't see what was happening, but he could hear that the footsteps and the voices were coming straight towards him.

Suddenly a torch was flashed on.

"Iku generator hapa," said a familiar voice. It was Singh. 'They must have brought him down here to show them how to start the generator,' thought Sion. That meant that they were heading for the very building behind which he was hiding, and besides that, if Singh did get the generator started, the whole place would be flooded with light any minute now. Quickly he looked for a better hiding place.

A few yards behind him he could just make out in the darkness the upturned hull of an old wooden coffee-smuggling boat. It had been holed in an accident some two years back, and had been lifted up onto the rocks to be repaired, but the repairs had never been carried out. It lay upside down straddling two large rocks, in between which there was enough room for him to crawl underneath and hide inside the hull.

Once in there, not only was he totally hidden, but the unrepaired hole enabled him to see what was happening on the jetty. All he could make out in the darkness was the light of the torch waving around but coming ever closer to him. Whoever was holding it was crossing the concrete yard towards the generator. Sure enough the torch disappeared into the generator shed, and in the light it gave out from the building Sion briefly caught sight of Singh and at least four other men, two of whom waited outside, guns at the ready. They were so close to Sion that he hardly dared breathe. He was naked and still wet from his swim, and he began to feel cold. He was satisfied that he would still be well hidden even if the lights did come on, and he longed for the noise of the generator to drown any sound he might make. He was terrified of sneezing.

At last he heard the familiar sound of the handle being turned, followed by the deafening banging of the engine and the smell of exhaust smoke being blown in his direction. Then the light on the corner of Morris's workshop came on dimly and quickly brightened. Immediately Singh was led back up the path towards the house. This time Sion could see him clearly. Though he looked anxious and frightened, there was no sign that he had been hurt.

Sion longed to know what they would do with him. It seemed unlikely that they would kill him while he was still useful to them. But how long would they stay on the island, and what would Singh's fate be if they left? 'I must find out what they mean to do,' Sion told himself.

There was an unlit path running between the back of the manager's house and the kitchen. Sion knew that if he went round by the staff quarters he could make his way along this path and hide behind the house. The kitchen staff had often told him that they could hear everything that was being said in there as they walked down that path going to and from work. If, as seemed likely, the leaders of these rebels had taken over the house, he might learn something about their plans. He still had an hour or so before the moon would rise to light his way to the north end of the island, and this seemed to be the best way of using this time.

There were voices coming from the little green huts of the staff quarters as he passed them, so he kept himself in the shadows. Once on the path he ran silently as far as the house, and slipped down the bank to where he could crouch against the back wall under the eaves of the thatched roof.

At the end of the path was the bar, from where he could hear a tremendous amount of shouting and argument. The voices from the house were sober, though there too an argument was in progress.

"What use is he as a hostage? You're mad! An Njemps tribesman! That won't stop them for a minute."

"So what do we do? They could cross the lake at any time. What chance have we against them?"

"Half our lot are drunk!"

"Yes! For God's sake! Go and put a stop to that!" Sion heard the tread of heavy boots leaving the house. "The army know they've got us cornered here. They'll come in their own good time, when they've finished with the fighting over there. We must get off this island."

"But which way? North?"

"No good. They'll be more troops still coming back from the exercise that way."

"Got to be east then. What is there east of here?"

"You! You say you know this place. What if we go east? That way?"

"It is a wild place. A few Njemps villages near the lake. After that wild. I never been there. No roads. Nothing."

"We must go that way. We must take food with us, and maybe some tents from this camp. We must go across that wild place until we reach the forest of the Aberdares. There we can hide like the freedom fighters did, until the time comes for us to win our freedom."

"The Aberdares! It is a long way. They will find us before we reach there."

"Yes, it will take us many days, but it is our only way out. We must take it. We start by making ourselves a camp that side of the lake. Tomorrow, early, I take some men in the blue boat. We must find a place for a camp, far from a village, where we can bring food from here and make ourselves ready for this long journey. We will be safer there than waiting here."

"It would be safer if we had taken a more important hostage, a mzungu cven. Then we could have made them leave us alone until we reached the forest."

"It is, true, but we have no hostage, only this man who is of no value, so we must take this chance. Take some men who are sober. Look round this camp and see if there are tents which we could take with us. If there are, pack one up and put it in the blue boat. Find food in their kitchen which can be stored. Put that that in the boat too. We will find a place over there where we can make a camp without being seen, and we will build up a store of food. If that works ….."

Suddenly a shot rang out from the bar, making Sion almost jump out of his skin. It was followed by the sound of a terrifying amount of breaking glass. People started staggering out of the bar, some of them heading down the path in his direction. He flattened himself in the little ditch between the house and the steep bank.

The men who tottered down the path were far too drunk to notice him, and he thought he was safe until one of them fell and rolled half way down the bank, where he lay groaning. His companions laughed and went on their way, leaving him lying there.

Sion felt ants crawling all over him and was desperate to move. The drunken man appeared to be conscious still, although he was making no effort to get up. He had past Sion when he fell, so Sion decided it was safer to move up towards the bar rather than try and go past him. There was no longer any sound from the bar. He crawled to the end of the house and looked around. Everybody seemed to have gone, so he climbed up the bank and slipped into the bar through the service entrance

One man was slumped over a table at the far end, snoring loudly. He wasn't about to wake up. Otherwise it was deserted. The floor was a horrendous sight, covered in broken glass and awash with drink. There was an overwhelming stench of alcohol. Sion had seen all he wanted to see. He was about to leave when he noticed a pad of bar chits and a pencil lying beside an upturned table near where he was standing. He grabbed them and ran.

Keeping to the shadows he made his way up towards the swimming pool. He crouched down below the wall which enclosed the swimming pool area, breathing hard but trying not to make a sound. After about five minutes he was convinced that nobody was after him. Very carefully he stood up so that he could see across the swimming pool to the little store where he knew Singh was being held. The two guards were sitting outside, but they were watching the store with their backs to him.

There was a light on a post attached to the swimming pool side of the wall which shone on the steps just beside him. Looking around to make sure nobody was watching, he rested the pad of bar chits on the bottom step, so that he could write without raising his head high enough for the guards to see him. On the top bar chit he wrote in Swahili,

"Hello Singh. I am Sion. What is the news of you? I have seen you, but I have not been seen. I go now for help." He tore the chit off the pad and crumpled it into a ball.

Now he had to find a way of reaching the little storeroom without the guards seeing him. While they weren't looking he dashed across the steps and crawled as quietly as he could behind the wall and then behind the back of the swimming pool bar. Now he no longer had the guards between him and the storeroom, but he still had to cross the brightly lit lawn where the barbecue stood. The guards were still watching the store and would certainly see him if he came out of the shadows. Unless they moved or looked the other way he could go no further. He waited for a long time, growing more and more fearful and not knowing what to do. He might have stayed that way well into the night if the problem hadn't suddenly been solved for him.

Another soldier appeared up the steps at the far end of the swimming pool, and shouted to the guards to bring Singh back to the house.

"The sergeant wants to find out what he knows about the land on that side of the lake," he said pointing towards the east. One of the guards unlocked the door, and they both escorted Singh past the swimming pool, down the steps, and out of sight. They had left the door wide open and the storeroom was unguarded. Sion dashed across the little lawn and went it.

THE TIN BOAT

Singh had made a bed for himself out of the sunbathing mattresses, and Sion put his crumpled message on top of the bed at the far end, where he hoped that Singh, and only Singh, would find it. He doubted the guards ever went inside the store. They probably just pushed Singh inside and shut the door behind him. Then Sion checked the gap between the top of the wall and the thatched roof, and made a mental note of where he should put his hand through from outside to drop in any notes in the future so that they landed on the bed. Satisfied that he had achieved all he could, he slipped out and, keeping to the shadows, went round the back of the store and down to the gate in the bamboo fence which in normal times it was his job to guard.

He was dry by now, but he was still pleased to find his clothes again. The wind was blowing from the west, and he felt quite cold. He dressed himself and went back to his cave, where he left his precious bar chits and pencil. There he rested for an hour until the first light of the moon showed on the eastern horizon.

Setting off on his journey north, he had to pass the hut in the village where his uncle Samson lived. He was pleased to discover that it was not one of the ones which the rebels had burned down. He went inside and helped himself to a blanket which he draped over his shoulders in the Maasai way like a long shuka. He wasn't sure where he might finally lay his head down that night, but a blanket might well add to his comfort.

Once past the village at the north end of the peninsular he felt able to relax and forget about the possibility of anybody seeing him. The moon was vast and orange, its base still flattened against the skyline. It lit his way as he climbed the winding path which would take him over the central hills. He climbed to the top and looked back at the camp, the lights still twinkling at the end of the black finger of the peninsular in the silver lake.

There were fewer lights over on the western mainland. Kampi-ya-Samaki must have been more or less deserted because of the fighting. There was some activity further north. He could see the headlights of vehicles on the road and the occasional flash of an explosion. Here and there fires seemed to be burning. He was glad for his own people that any fighting still going on was up in the country of the Pokot tribe.

The valleys beyond the central peak of the island were all uninhabited. He wasn't expecting to meet anybody until he reached the northern shore. He began looking forward to telling the wazee what he had done. He felt proud of his foray into the occupied camp, and longed to show that though he was only a boy and still uncircumcised, he had faced danger as well at any moran.

Most of the northern shore was very steep, and the only village was built on the one small stretch of flat land on the edge of a bay. Sion was relieved when he came over the shoulder of the last hill and saw the round thatched roofs in the moonlight. As he drew closer, he became aware of the persistent bleating of a large number of goats. Soon he caught sight of them, herded together in a huge boma just beyond the village. They must have driven all the goats on the island north to this one village. This cheered him because it meant that some people at least would have stayed there with the goats. He would have been happier still if he could have seen some sign of human life, but at first glance there seemed to be nobody. He was anxious about taking whoever was still there by surprise. Knowing that the south end of the island was occupied by unfriendly soldiers, they would be on the alert, or so he assumed, against anybody wandering into their village. He would have liked to have been seen and recognized from a distance. He even supposed that somebody would have been on guard throughout the night.

He approached the nearest hut, wondering whether he should enter and wake the occupants. He was just deciding that it would be wiser to go on to the house where he knew the head man of the village lived, when a tall figure leaped up out of the shadow and barred his way with a spear. Sion jumped back in alarm.

"Mimi Sion!" he gasped. "I have found Singh."

CHAPTER 21

William was awakened soon after first light by the sounds of the village coming to life. Dogs barked and cocks crowed, and from all around came the shouts of men moving their cattle out of the bomas for the day. Women too were screeching, either at their children or at their goats, or maybe even their husbands. Though he had slept soundly for a short time, William ached all over from the hardness of his improvised bed.

He looked at Helen's bed but she wasn't there. He remembered that they had agreed to walk down to the lake while the day was still cool to wash themselves and their clothes, and hoped she hadn't left without him. Matthew and Jamie had also gone, but he found Nicholas in his bed behind the screen.

"Oh, hello. How are you?" William asked. "Feeling any better?"

"Yes, a bit," said Nicholas. "Just a bit wobbly and very hungry."

"You must be recovering then," said William with relief. "Where did the others go?"

"Just outside, I think. They were waiting for you to wake up, but they thought you'd like to be left to sleep for little while."

"Right. I'll just go and find them and I'll be back in a minute," said William.

"Ah! Here he is!" said Jamie as William emerged into the clear morning sunlight. There was a smell of wood smoke in the air which he hoped meant that somebody was cooking something for breakfast.

"Morning," he said. "Is everybody O.K.?"

"Yeh, fine," said Matthew. "Not a great night's sleep but we've all survived." William went over to Helen.

"Did you sleep O.K. in the end?" he asked.

"Eventually," she said. "That bed wasn't too bad. We'll swap over tonight if we're still here."

"Oh, no, I was fine," William insisted. "Nicholas seems better."

"Yes, thank God. I think he'll be perfectly all right if we manage to keep him out of the sun today. Are you as hungry as the rest of us?"

"Yes, why? Any chance of breakfast?"

"John's having some posho cooked up for us, and some tea," said Jamie.

"Tea sounds great," said William, whose mouth was parched. "What's posho like?"

"Porridge," said Matthew. "Just pretend it's porridge. That's all it is really, made out of maize meal,"

"Doesn't sound too bad," said William.

"They only eat once a day normally, in the late afternoon," Helen explained. "They're doing this specially for us because they know we're used to eating more often. Really kind of them, but I reckon this'll have to do until evening."

"Any news from across the lake?" William asked. "No chance of returning to the island, I suppose?"

"Nobody's heard anything yet this morning," said Matthew.

"I'm still keen to get down to the lake to wash, aren't you?" Helen asked William.

THE TIN BOAT

"Yes, lets, as soon as we've had breakfast," he replied. Just then they heard John's voice calling them from the next hut.

"Chukula tayari! Kuja hapa yote!"

"He wants us to go and eat over there," said Helen.

"Yes, even I understood that," said William. "What about Nicholas?"

"Oh, he can come," said Helen. "It'll be good for him to get out of that stuffy hut before the sun gets too hot. It won't do him any harm now."

"I'll get him," said Jamie.

Soon they were sitting on the ground outside Lemeriai's mother's hut drinking tea and helping themselves to handfuls of posho out of a communal wooden bowl. They all agreed that it would be better if it wasn't quite so solid, but they ate it gratefully. John came to talk to them, though he didn't share the meal.

"You like this posho?" he asked.

"Yes, thank you very much," said Helen. John smiled. He knew it was an unusual diet for them.

"You like catch some fish?" he asked. "I think you like fish better."

"Yes, please," said William, "and we'd like to wash in the lake and get our clothes clean."

"Nzuri. I take you. We take donkey too, and drums to fetch water for you. These people carry water for themselves a long way. It is better for you to have your own."

"That would be good," said Helen, "but Nicholas shouldn't be out in the sun all morning. One of us had better stay here with him."

"I want to come," Nicholas insisted. "I'm better now."

"You'd be mad to come," William told him. "The sun will be really hot again by the time we get back. Give yourself a chance to get better. It would make things really difficult if any of us became properly ill out here."

"Matthew, would you like to stay with him?" Helen asked her brother. "Better to have a Swahili speaker in case he needs

THE TIN BOAT

anything."

"Sure thing," said Matthew. The walk down to the lake didn't appeal to him at all, and washing wasn't one of his top priorities.

A boy came into the boma leading a donkey with two tin drums strapped to its back.

"Look! This must be our donkey. Isn't it lovely," said Jamie, and immediately went over to stroke its head and make friends with it.

"How do we get it to go where we want?" asked William. John laughed and said something to Helen in Swahili.

"He says the donkey knows much better than we do where to go," Helen explained. "He reckons we should just follow it. He's going to catch us up." William and Jamie found hats to protect them from the sun, and the three of them set off towards the lake at the donkey's comfortable walking pace.

"What shall we do?" Matthew asked Nicholas.

"You know how to play Bau?" asked John.

"Not properly," said Nicholas.

"I do. I'll teach you," said Matthew

"Kuja," said John, and led them out of the boma to the shade of a large acacia tree in the middle of the clearing. There in the hardened mud were the four rows of little holes containing pebbles which form what has been the most popular game over a large area of Africa for more than a thousand years. The boys squatted like Africans on either side of the game, and Nicholas's lesson began.

The donkey led the children out of the village along a different path from the one along which they had come the day before. For about a quarter of a mile they followed it in single file through the trees, When they came out into the open, they could see that they were making for the wide bay about half way between the Mukutan Hill and Fort Baringo.

"Oh, great," said Jamie. "It's much closer than I thought."

"Yes. Not much more than a mile altogether," said Helen.

"It seemed much further when we walked it yesterday," said William.

"We've come out a little further south," said Helen. "This bay is much closer to the village than where we came from. It really isn't going to be such a long walk as we thought." Encouraged by this discovery they tried to make the donkey go a little faster, but it had a mind of its own and nothing was going to persuade it to speed up, so they had to settle for continuing at the same plodding pace.

Nicholas had found the game of Bau fairly complicated, so Matthew had decided to teach him the simplified version which he had first been taught, using only one row of holes on each side. This idea proved very successful and Nicholas was really enjoying the game. They were distracted by the sudden appearance of half a dozen fully armed morans led by a man of the young mzee age-group who came running across the clearing from the north looking as if they were on some urgent business.

"I wonder what they're up to," said Matthew.

"Do you know them?" asked Nicholas.

"I think the older one is one of Rapili's sons from Longicharo," said Matthew. "Let's go and see what they want. No. On second thoughts, perhaps you'd better stay here in the shade. I'll come back and tell you what they say." Nicholas watched him saunter over to the group of young Africans, taking on an African way of walking, and using an African posture and African gestures as he talked to them. 'It would be nice to be able to become one of them just like that,' Nicholas thought, knowing that he hadn't even tried very hard to speak Swahili himself.

The Africans appeared to be looking for somebody, and they soon hurried off after Matthew towards the boma. Nicholas watched them disappear behind the thorn barrier, but the air was growing warm, and he must have dozed off, because the next thing he knew was that Matthew was standing over him saying,

"Wake up, Nicholas, man! Listen, to this!"

"What?" asked Nicholas, forcing himself awake. "What's happened?" He was anxious suddenly that there might be bad news.

"Hey! They're off to rescue Singh, or so they reckon."

"Why? What's happened to Singh?" Nicholas was now fully awake and anxious for the safety of one of his friends.

"He got captured with Islander by those rebels on the island," Matthew explained excitedly. "They say that it was Sion who found him. He hung around the camp and saw that they were holding Singh and using him to drive the boats and work the generator. Apparently Sion turned up on the north end of the island late last night with the news that they were going to make Singh drive a few of them over to the Mukutan to set up a camp from which they can make their escape to the east."

"When are they meant to be going to do that?" asked Nicholas.

"Any minute, I think. This morning, some time. Anyway, Rapili sent his son over here to get some morans and young wazee together to try and surprise these guys and snatch Singh.

"Wow!" said Nicholas. At first it seemed an exciting prospect - a battle in which his friends would triumph and rescue Singh - but more frightening possibilities soon came to mind as he thought it all through. "Is John going with them?" he asked nervously.

"Of course!" said Matthew enthusiastically. "I wish I could go too, but they won't let me." This didn't surprise Nicholas at all.

"But they haven't got any guns, have they?" Nicholas went on. "Those rebels are bound to have guns. The Njemps will only have spears and things. They won't be much good against people with guns, will they?"

"Well, no, not sort of face to face, they wouldn't," Matthew admitted. "I think they reckon on taking these guys by surprise." Nicholas was silent for a long while. Matthew could see that he was worried. "They're brave and clever, these people," he reassured him. "They may lead rather peaceful lives here, but deep down they are Maasai warriors." Not much use against guns though. Nicholas was right there, he had to admit.

"S'posing John gets killed," said Nicholas gloomily, and a new worry clouded his thoughts. "The others won't get caught up in it will they? Jamie and William and Helen? There won't be a battle where they've gone?"

"Oh, God! I hope not," said Matthew. "No, surely not. They'll be way south of Mukutan." He smiled and tried to appear relaxed about it all. "No, don't you worry. They'll be O.K. I tell you."

CHAPTER 22

"Getting a bit warm," William said to Jamie.

"Yeh, I'm beginning to feel it too," Jamie agreed.

"You both look rather red in the face," laughed Helen.

"All right for you. You're used to it," replied William good-humouredly.

"So's the donkey," Jamie quipped. "I bet neither of you would be so happy in the winter in the north of England."

"I'd hate to try," Helen agreed. "In fact I think we're going to be lucky. It's going to cloud up a bit. I don't think we're going to get that burning sun like we had yesterday. Not till later in the day, anyway."

"Still, it'll be nice to jump in the lake," said William. "I suppose this donkey knows where he's taking us." They were crossing the huge flat area of dried up lake bed which William recognised from the previous day. The donkey plodded on at his unhurried, unvarying pace. He obviously had an African attitude about not rushing things unduly. He never looked round to see if they were following.

"I s'pose it's a daily routine to him," William speculated. "He just seems to assume we're following."

THE TIN BOAT

"I wonder. Let's try," said Helen. They came to a halt and stood quite still. The donkey still didn't look round, but after two more paces he stopped and hung his head in an attitude of patient endurance, as if to say 'I'm doing this for you. If you don't want to go on that's fine. Suits me.'

Helen beckoned the boys to move forward very quietly, but the donkey wasn't fooled. Once they had made up the extra two paces he had taken he was on his way again. They walked on in silence, watching the wall of ambach plants growing taller as they reached the edge of the lake.

"I see the boat. It is coming here." A young moran who had been posted in the low bush on top of the Mukutan Hill as look-out had come back to report to John.

"I come to see," said John. The rest of the tribal band, all armed with spears or bows and arrows, rose to follow him, but John signalled for them to stay out of sight. They were hidden below the crest of the hill on the east side, away from the lake.

As John reached the point from which the lake became visible, Blue Banana was entering the bay below them through the reeds.

"Good," he said.

"Stop the boat here!" the rebel sergeant in charge of the boat ordered Singh. They were still out in the middle of the bay. Singh cut out the engine and took up the paddle to bring the boat under control.

"What's the matter, Sergeant?" asked one of the others. "You do not want to land here? This is a good place. From that hill we will see a long way. If we make our camp below the hill we can keep a watch over it from above. Is that not true?"

"Yes, you can see very far from that hill," replied Singh.

"That may be so," said the sergeant, "but we must be careful. From that hill we can also be seen. We cannot tell if anybody is up there watching us. Maybe units of the army have been moved round here. They will have seen us, but we cannot see them. No.

Let us proceed south. Switch off the engine and use the paddle," he ordered Singh. "Keep close behind these bushes where we cannot be seen. We will find a landing place further on and some of us will approach the hill from behind. When we are sure it is clear the rest of you can take the boat back to the place below the hill and unload."

"Yuk! It stinks!" cried Jamie. "I'm not swimming here!" The donkey had led them to the edge of a very shallow bay, and there he had stopped. It wasn't the colour of the water which put the children off. The whole lake was pink with mud. They were used to that. It was obvious, though, that this was the main watering place for all the goats and cattle around the south east corner of the lake.

"Do you think they really fill up with drinking water here?" William asked Helen.

"I s'pose they've built up a few immunities that we haven't got, but it seems unlikely," she admitted.

They all stared enquiringly at the donkey. It had been his idea after all. But it seemed that he wasn't about to change his mind. As if to rub it in he took a drink of the stinking lake water which dribbled from his mouth as he stood there, with his head hanging, and refused to come up with any better suggestions.

"Oh, let's leave him here for the moment and look for somewhere cleaner," William said. "South, d'you reckon?"

"Who knows?" said Helen. "Either direction must be better than here. I'll tell you what. I wouldn't mind a little privacy, so why don't you two guys head south and have a good swim and a wash, and I'll head north. Meet you back here, and we'll see who's found the best place to fill up with drinking water."

"Fair enough," said William. "I wonder why John hasn't caught us up yet. There's no sign of him. He was going to help us catch some fish, and we'll need his help to load up the donkey."

"Well, no hurry," said Helen. "I expect he'll show up soon. See you later. Watch out for crocks and hippos!"

"You too!" called out Jamie as they parted.

William took the occasional backward glance at Helen as she strode off in the other direction. For the moment he was in no hurry for this little adventure to come to an end. He had meant it when he had told her last night that he had never been happier. He loved the fact that she needed him here. Nobody had ever made him feel so important. But it was more than that. He had reached the age where he and the other boys at school talked about girls, discussed their looks and scored them out of ten and all that. But what he had discovered in Helen was something completely different. There was something so warm and direct and uncomplicated about the friendship she showed him. He had no illusions that Helen would every think about him again once all this was over and they had gone their separate ways. Her friendliness towards him was just part of her nature, he knew that. It wasn't special treatment. Still he wondered whether he'd spend the rest of his life searching for somebody else with the same qualities he'd found in her.

"She's great, Helen, isn't she?" said Jamie seriously, catching William out with one of his backward glances. At first William blushed, but seeing that Jamie was not trying to tease him he wasn't so worried about showing his feelings.

"Yeh, I think she's terrific," he confessed.

At the next little bay Jamie went and inspected the water.

"It's a bit cleaner here, isn't it? Not so smelly," said Jamie.

"Yeh, it is," William agreed. "It might be nicer still if we slipped through that gap in the ambach to where the water's deeper. I'm going to take my clothes off here and give them a good wash while I'm swimming."

"Good idea. Me too," said Jamie. Washing clothes wasn't usually one of his top priorities, but right now he wanted to appear grown up. They waded out naked, carrying their clothes, beyond the ambach. There they stopped and looked around.

"No hippos?" said Jamie.

"No crocks?" said William.

"All clear, I think," Jamie declared and they plunged into the water.

Singh paddled Blue Banana quietly southwards, keeping as close as he could to the ambach plants which hid the boat and its rebel crew from the shore. The water there was just deep enough with the engine tipped up. It would have been easier to abandon the paddle and use the pole, but that would have meant standing up, which his captors forbade for fear of him being seen.

He was used to doing exactly what he was told by now, used to having a gun pointed at him all the time except when he was locked up. For the present he was not afraid of being shot so long as he did what the rebels asked. He was useful to them for the moment, but he was terrified of what they might do to him if he no longer served a purpose for them.

In the short term he was more nervous about what his own fellow tribesmen might be up to. He couldn't believe that they would have remained indifferent towards the invasion of their land, or to his own plight. But if they were planning some action he would have liked to have known where they were. He didn't want to be the one to help their enemies, nor did he wish to be the victim of an attack by his own friends.

Wondering how he could best hinder the cause of the rebels, he decided to try and take them as far south as he could to a point where the land was much more open and bare, and they would have very little cover.. He pushed on as quickly as he could without arousing suspicion, but the order soon came to stop.

"We land here. Take the boat in."

"Ndiyo," he said, pretending to agree. He deliberately steered towards what looked like a shallow spot, and sure enough the boat ran aground long before they reached the shore. "Not enough water here," he explained. "We have to get out and pull the boat in."

As the man in the bows prepared to jump overboard Singh called out,

THE TIN BOAT

"Chunga sana. Many crocodiles here." The man lay frozen along the gunwale with one foot in the boat and one dangling just above the surface of the water.

"Crocodiles?" exclaimed the sergeant. "Here?"

"Yes," said Singh. "Bad place for crocodiles. Safer further on." The rebels took little persuading to let Singh push off and paddle a few hundred yards further south.

'Time I went back and found the others,' thought Helen without much sense of urgency. Lying back in the soft, warm water of the lake she was luxuriating in the feeling of being clean again. She had washed her clothes and spread them out to dry. She'd had a quick look round to make sure nobody was in sight before jumping into the water with nothing on. The place was totally deserted, so it had seemed sensible to wash and dry her only set of clothes while she had a chance. Once in the water she had allowed herself to relax from the fears and tensions of the last two days. Her head was light with lack of sleep. It took an effort if will to drag herself to her feet and wade back to the shore.

The sun had almost dried her clothes already. She turned them over, and found a reasonably smooth rock on which to lie down and allow herself to dry before getting dressed again. 'This is stupid,' she thought. 'I must get back to the boys. God, I'm so tired though. I'll just give myself five minutes.'

She never knew whether she had actually dozed off before the sound of voices made her leap to her feet and grab her clothes. She hid as best she could amongst the ambaches and dressed herself. Then she stood still and listened. There was nothing but the sound of the birds. 'Stupid,' she thought. 'I must have dreamt it, or perhaps it was the boys coming to find me. I'll go and see.'

Singh had brought the boat in towards the shore once more. The rebels had disembarked and pushed their way through a gap in the ambach barrier before they realised what a hopelessly unsuitable landing place he had chosen for them. He had brought them far too far south. To get round to the east side of the hill they would have to cross a huge expanse of flat, parched, open ground, broken only by a few termite chimneys. If anybody was watching them from the hill they would be all too easily visible.

The sergeant was about to round on Singh when one of the other men tapped him on the shoulder and pointed in a southerly direction.

"Hey, sergeant. What's that now?" With a sharp intake of breath the sergeant stood and stared in disbelief. A mzungu girl, dressed in shorts and a striped shirt, and carrying a little bundle of other clothes, had emerged from the line of ambaches not thirty metres from them. She seemed to be alone, and was looking away from them, as if in search of something or somebody further south.

"Well now, I'll tell you what that is," said the sergeant. "That is a mzungu woman. What she is doing here I do not know, but she could buy us our freedom."

"Looks like just a child to me'" said the other man.

"Even better," said the sergeant. "She will be all the more valuable." At that moment she turned and saw them. With a scream she ran off.

"Get her!" ordered the sergeant. "Stop her! Shoot, but don't hit her. We need her alive." The other man put his rifle to his shoulder and fired one round into the ground a couple of yards to the left of the girl's feet. She swerved to the right and disappeared into the ambaches.

"After her!" shouted the sergeant, setting off at the double towards where she had vanished, followed by his five companions. In the excitement they had forgotten about Singh. He had only caught a glimpse of the girl, but he knew it was Helen.

He hurried back to Blue Banana and pushed the boat into the water. He punted for all he was worth until the water was deep enough to lower the engine. For a moment he hesitated about making a noise by starting it up, but speed was his only hope of rescuing Helen. It was a chance he had to take. Only later did he realise that he had been free to make his own escape. At the time it never crossed his mind.

Helen was paralysed with fear. She had crashed into an impenetrable growth of dead ambach. She knew there was no escape behind her, and very little chance of losing her pursuers even if she managed to push her way through to the water. Her situation seemed utterly hopeless. All she could think of was to try and hide, although she knew that it would only delay her fate for a minute or two. She tore frantically at the ambach with her hands. Because it was dry it broke up easily, so that she managed to make the beginnings of a tunnel towards the lake. She had time to crawl far enough into it to be completely hidden before she heard the voices of the men who were chasing her.

She kept as quiet and still as she could, hoping against hope that they would misjudge the distance and look in the wrong place, but there were enough of them to make a fairly wide search in a short time. In the dusty half-darkness, scratched by broken branches and covered with insects, it seemed as futile to stay where she was as to try and go forward. It almost seemed preferable at that moment to break the unbearable tension and give herself up.

Suddenly, from the direction of the lake, she heard the sound of a boat engine. She had no way of seeing who was there, but the noise gave her a glimmer of hope. Painfully she fought and pulled her way through the dead ambach. Changing course slightly to her right where there seemed to be more light, she burst unexpectedly into a gap in the plants. Already her pursuers could be heard hacking away at the bushes behind her.

She was right at the water's edge. Beyond that point the ambaches were alive, green and flowering and tangled with reeds at the waterline. The branches were less easy to break, but were more flexible and easier to push aside. As the water became deeper and the reeds thicker it was her legs, not her arms, that were having to struggle. By the time she reached a point where she could see the open lake, she knew that further progress was almost impossible.

To her overwhelming relief she saw Blue Banana gliding slowly towards her with Singh on board.

"Singh!" she cried out. "Saidia mimi! Help me!"

"Mimi nakuja!" he replied. "Ngoja!"

"Well I can't move!" she said.

The bows of the boat came to a halt in the reeds only three feet or so beyond her reach. Without switching off the engine Singh went forward and lay along the bow, stretching out to take her own outstretched hand. She managed to touch his finger tips before she saw the look of wide-eyed horror come over is face. The next moment an irresistibly strong arm grabbed her round the waist and pulled her back. Singh stood up in the boat with his hand in the air. Out of the corner of her eye she glimpsed the muzzle of a gun.

CHAPTER 23

William and Jamie had spent less time in the water than Helen. They were busy trying to persuade the donkey to move to where the water was cleaner when they heard the shot. There could be no doubt that it had come from the direction where Helen had headed.

"My God! Helen!" cried Jamie.

"C'mon!" said William. "Leave the donkey. She must be in trouble." They ran northwards as far as they could, keeping close to the ambach barrier because instinct told them to stay out of sight as far as possible. Their flip-flops were hopeless running shoes, so they took them off and carried them, moving more comfortably in bare feet on the dried mud.

"How far d'you reckon?" gasped Jamie.

"Can't believe she would have gone that much further," said William breathlessly. Suddenly he signalled to Jamie to stop. They both crouched in the shadow of the ambaches. He had heard the sound of a boat engine only a little way beyond them. Almost immediately the engine stopped.

THE TIN BOAT

"Let's see if we can get closer," whispered William. "We've got to see what's going on."

"Careful we're not seen," said Jamie. They had to go very carefully because the sun was still the wrong side to give them much shadow. Soon they froze rigid again when a tall African in combat dress crashed out of the ambach carrying a rifle. Two others followed, dragging Helen between them.

"What the hell are they doing to her?" exclaimed William. "I'm going after her."

"NO! You're mad!" said Jamie. "What can you do? They've got guns."

"But we can't just….."

"It's much better if we see where they go and stay out of sight. Then we can get help," Jamie suggested. He couldn't think what help they could find against this lot, but he knew they would be no help at all if they showed themselves and were captured as well, or even shot. Helen and her captors only stayed in view for a minute or two, but even that was more than William could bear to watch. There was no sign that Helen had been hurt, but she looked so helpless and scared. Once she managed to glance behind her but the boys couldn't tell whether she had seen them or not. Soon she disappeared behind the ambach bushes again. The soldier who was not manhandling her remained in view, obviously making sure that they weren't surprised, until the boat engine started again. Then he too disappeared.

The boys ran forward, and were in time to see, through a gap in the bushes, Blue Banana heading north, driven by Singh. In the centre of the boat they could just see Helen sprawled on the canvas in the middle of the boat surrounded by African soldiers.

"Why on earth should they want to take her?" asked William desperately. "What good can she be to them?"

"Perhaps they've kidnapped her so they can ask for money," suggested Jamie.

"Yeh, I suppose that must be it," William agreed gloomily. "Either that or she's some sort of hostage, so that if they're not allowed to escape they might threaten to… Oh, come on! We've got to try and help her."

"But how? If they're taking her over to the island we've no way of getting there."

"Yes, but I'm not sure they are. Look! They seem to be going further up the shore. They won't see us now. Let's follow!"

"The boat is coming back," the moran who had been on watch whispered to John. "Singh is still there. He is still driving. I think they are going to land here."

"Good. At last," said John. It had been a long, frustrating wait for the Njemps war party hiding below the crest of the Mukutan Hill. They had no interest in attacking the rebels unless it would result in Singh's rescue. They had seen him bring the boat in just below them once, but then they had watched helplessly as he had been forced to push off again and head south. Now that he was on his way back, their chance might finally have come.

"This is what we do," John told his companions. "I will take one man with me and we will go round this way." He indicated with a broad sweep of his long arm a route round the back of the hill towards the lake. "All you others, keep out of sight and watch from the top of the hill. When you see us in position, make a big mneno, much noise so they think you attack them, but do not let them see you. While they look for you we will take Singh. Remember they have guns, and we have not. I know you are all brave. Let us be clever too. If we can rescue our friend without fighting, then we have done well."

As he led the young moran round the side of the hill, he had grave misgivings about the whole idea. They had all agreed that they couldn't just leave Singh to his fate, but he knew that if things went wrong their attempt to rescue one man could end in the loss of many.

They descended to the flat ground south of the hill and made for a break in the ambach through which they would be able to see the boat come in, but by the time they had edged close enough Blue

THE TIN BOAT

Banana had already been pulled up onto the shore. Everybody had disembarked except Singh and one of the rebel soldiers who had been left with the boat. Only these two were visible from where John was hiding. 'Good,' he thought. 'As soon as the others start their diversion, a single arrow from my bow should deal with the guard, and Singh will be free.' He fitted a monkey arrow with a barbed point to his bow, took aim, and waited.

There was a rustle behind him followed by urgent whispers. Irritated that his companion should not have seen the need for quiet, but at the same time not wanting to take his eyes off his target, he signalled with one hand behind his back for him to be still. 'Come on,' he thought, 'start making a noise up there on the hill before we are seen.' Fortunately the lapping of the water against the stones had been enough to drown the noise behind him.

"John! No! Don't shoot!" a voice whispered in English almost in his ear.

"What?" he exclaimed, and swinging round he saw Jamie and William crouching behind him, sweating and panting for breath. "Nataka nini, Jamie? What you doing here?"

"John. They've got Helen," Jamie whispered. "Taken hostage or something. They might kill her if you shoot. Please! Please don't!"

"O.K. Wapi Helen?"

"She must be just the other side of the ambaches with those men. They're pointing a gun at her." John signalled to them all to retreat out of sight, and the boys heaved a sigh of relief that they had stopped him causing a disaster. They followed the path between the ambaches and the cliff face of the hill, keeping out of sight, until they saw the group of men with their captive in their midst. At that moment there was a tremendous noise of shouting and whooping from the warriors on top of the hill.

The sergeant looked up, and then turned and barked an order to the man holding Singh in the boat. Singh was forced at gun point to disembark and join the other rebels on the shore. The sergeant looked up at the crest of the hill once more and started shouting at the top of his voice, trying to make himself heard over the war cries of the warriors.

"What's he saying?" whispered William.

"Dunno," Jamie admitted. "Telling them to come out, or something."

"He say they must go away or Singh will be shot," said John. "Boys, wait here. Stay out of sight. Keep very low and be very quiet. They must not see you. I leave you with this young moran. He is son of Chief Rapili. He speak English. He clever boy. He will look after you. Do what he says." The boys nodded to show that they had understood. John left them and moved silently through the bush in the direction the rebels, still being careful to remain out of their sight.

Then started a strange shouting match between John and the rebel sergeant. Each time John shouted something he swiftly moved positions, so that the sergeant never knew where his voice was coming from next. Each time he answered angrily and threateningly, frustrated that he couldn't see where John was, while John's voice remained calm.

Jamie and William looked anxiously at their moran companion, desperate to understand what was going on. The moran translated for them in a low whisper.

"John, he says to this bad man, release your prisoners, the boat driver and the girl, and we will not stand in your way."

"And will this rebel guy agree?" asked Jamie.

"No. He says he will not. He say show yourselves and leave this place or we will shoot your friend. Then he say, he has also mzungu girl. If they still not go, he kill her too."

"No! No! They can't!" whispered William, almost loud enough to be heard by the rebels. The others signalled to him to be quiet, but he wouldn't keep still. "I've got to see what they're doing," he whispered frantically. The moran put a hand on his shoulder to calm him down, and then beckoned the two boys to inch forward very slowly to a point where they could see the rebels through a gap in the bush.

They could only just see Helen, completely surrounded by rebel soldiers near where Blue Banana had been pulled ashore. Singh was much more clearly visible, and as they watched they saw two of the rebels push him forward into the open space in front of the sergeant, who took up his rifle and pointed it at him. He drew back the bolt.

"NO!" said Jamie. "Come on, John! You can't let him do that!" At last John spoke again. The moran translated once more for William and Jamie.

"He say again, let go of your prisoners and we will not harm you. He say, leave our land in peace and go away." There was a good deal of murmuring, even arguing, among the rebels before the sergeant addressed John once more.

"He say O.K. He say, if you want your tribesman back, let your men on the hill show themselves. Let me see them leave this place." Before John could answer the sergeant emphasised his point by firing a shot into the ground which just missed Singh's feet. This was enough to persuade John to come out into the open and show himself. He called to the warriors and they stood up and appeared in a line along the ridge of the hill. He waved to them to move off, and they set off following the ridge south away from the rebels. The sergeant spoke to John once more, and again the young moran translated for the boys.

"We give you back your tribesman, he say. We send him with a message. Once all your warriors have gone you may take him." They watched Singh being spoken to before being pushed roughly away towards John. But Helen was held fast. It was obvious they were not going to release her. John shouted a protest but received a mocking reply.

"He say, you have your tribesman back," the moran explained to the boys. "He say, we keep the mzungu girl. He say, what she matter to you? She a mzungu. Stay away from us! Any more trouble from you and your tribesmen and she dies!"

"I'm going after her!" said William desperately, but Jamie and the the moran grabbed him and held him back before he could show himself. Several of the rebels now had guns pointed in the direction of the retreating Njemps war party. They waited until the warriors had descended the southern end of the hill. Two of the armed rebels followed the Njemps until they were satisfied that they were all heading away to the south east. Then they climbed the hill to make sure that nobody was left up there. Meanwhile the others returned to the boat and helped unload the tent and the supplies, which they hid in the thick bush between the hill and the lake. Once this was done Helen was bundled back into the boat, and most of the rebels clambered aboard after her.

All this time John and Singh hadn't been allowed to move. The sergeant had kept his rifle trained on them until at last a shout from the top of the hill told him that the area was clear. He was the last to climb on board. With a shout of "Kwenda! Sasa!" he stood up in the boat and fired a shot over John's head

Throughout these exchanges the boys and their new moran friend had managed to stay hidden and observe what the rebels were up to. They saw them push the boat out and, after some argument about how it should be done, succeed in starting the engine. But it soon became clear that, as well as the two who were now making their way back down the hill, a third rebel had stayed behind with the supplies. He stood pointing a rifle at John and signalling for him to hurry up and take Singh and leave. Another shot was fired, and at last John led Singh away. By this time the boat had been turned and was carrying Helen across the lake towards the island.

"Come on, before we are seen. Nothing else we can do here," Jamie said to William, but his cousin was reluctant to move. "We'll think of something," he said rather hopelessly, "but it doesn't help poor Helen if we're caught. We must hurry back to the village to tell Matthew what's happened to his sister. It will be dreadful for him, but he's got to know," said Jamie.

"Kuja!" said the moran who had been translating. "Come. I will take you."

THE TIN BOAT

"But somebody's got to think out a way of rescuing her," said William desperately. "You go on. I'll catch up John and Singh and go back with them. I want to talk to John and see what he thinks we can do. See you later."

"You'll have to hurry," said Jamie, and then hesitated. "But for goodness sake don't let yourself be seen and don't do anything stupid, will you?"

"Of course not," said William. "On you go."

Things began to go wrong for William almost as soon as the others had left him. He quickly discovered that trying to follow the route John and Singh had taken without being seen meant pushing his way through some very thick bush. It was slow going and after a few minutes he realised that John and Singh would already be way ahead of him. It took him fully half an hour to reach a point far enough round to the east of the hill to dare break cover. Cautiously he emerged onto the cattle path and looked towards the east, but there was no sign of them.

He started to climb the hill, looking back over his shoulder as he went, until at last he was high enough to catch sight of the two men maybe half a mile away, running across an open stretch of ground. There was no way he could catch up with them now. Soon the path took them back into the thick bush and he lost sight of them again. He didn't even know now where they were heading, so following them seemed futile. He looked to see if he could spot Jamie and Rapili's son, but the path they had taken was also hidden by bush. He knew now that to get back to the village he faced a long walk on his own, with very little sense of the direction he should follow. He suddenly felt very tired. He decided to sit for a while and try and think what to do next.

He climbed up the hill to where he could see the lake and sat in the shadow of a tree where he could not be seen from the beach below. From there he stared at the island until the sun was well passed its zenith. Later in the afternoon he was surprised to see Blue Banana return. Suddenly he decided that the most valuable

THE TIN BOAT

thing he could do was stay here and keep an eye on what these rebels were up to.

There was only one man on board the boat this time, and it looked as if he had come with more supplies and another tent. He was obviously not an expert boat driver, and had some difficulty controlling the boat in the strengthening wind and mounting waves before he made the shelter of the reeds.

The other three men who had stayed behind went to help carry the new load ashore. Once on dry land they were hidden from William's sight under the hill but he could hear their voices below him. After a while a serious argument seemed to break out, and all four men reappeared racing and pushing each other through the shallow water towards Blue Banana. Eventually they all managed to clamber on board and they set off towards the open lake once more. He guessed that none of them had been willing to stay behind and guard the supplies overnight and were all determined to get back to the island before dark.

'So they're all going,' he thought. 'I'll be on my own.' A plan formed in his mind. As soon as they were well out in the middle of the lake he would go and look for the tin boat. Hopefully it would be easier to remove the bent sheer pin when he could work with his feet dry land. If he could get that done in daylight he could wait until darkness fell and take the boat over to the island in the hope of finding Helen.

By this time the wind was blowing so strongly in his eyes that he had to shield them from the dust as he watched. Once out beyond the reeds the boat pitched violently in the waves. The driver, obviously alarmed, did what even William knew was the wrong thing and turned the boat across the wind. It seemed that it must surely roll over. The passengers made things worse by panicking and moving around. When all seemed lost one of them grabbed the tiller and brought them safely back into the shelter of the bay. They beached the boat and disembarked, wet and angry. William guessed that they wouldn't be going out into the lake again that day. 'Damn!' he thought.

THE TIN BOAT

For the time being that seemed to be his chances gone. He knew anyway that his plan was a foolhardy one which was not properly thought out and had little chance of success, but somehow he didn't care. It seemed to him that nothing could possibly matter as much as reaching Helen right now. He wasn't even sure that he really hoped to rescue her. All he could think about was how lonely and frightened she must be. He wanted to be with her. He wanted that so desperately that he minded little about his own safety.

However he was worried that nobody, not even Jamie, knew where he was. He knew he had created another major worry for his friends by disappearing. For a while he thought about trying to find his way back to the village while it was still light. From the top of the hill he thought he could make out where it was. There was quite a high hill on the horizon behind it, and he reckoned that as long as he could see this hill above the bush it would show him the right direction. But the thought of what Helen was suffering held him back. 'No. I must try and get to her,' he told himself.

Moving very cautiously he left the shadow of the tree and sought out a new hiding place in what little cover there was right on the edge of the hill. He found a spot almost immediately above the place where the four rebels had returned to guard their stores. He wanted to be able to keep an eye on the whereabouts of all four of them without them being able to see him. He had the advantage of being downwind from them, so that they were unlikely to hear any sound he made.

As he looked down on them from the top of the hill he saw three of the men begin to struggle with erecting one of the tents. It obviously wasn't an easy task. The tent was designed for a fixed camp where it would be partly suspended from a permanent thatched roof. It was heavy and cumbersome, and the ground was hard and uneven. The thick thorny bush gave them very little space to work in. The wind too was hampering their efforts. It was certainly going to take them a while to get the job done.

THE TIN BOAT

He wished he knew where the fourth man had gone. He was pretty sure he would have been able to see anybody who tried to climb the hill, so he assumed that the man must be somewhere down at the level of the lake, but he didn't dare make a move until he was sure.

By the time the sun was beginning to turn a golden colour in the sky beyond the island he had become frustrated with inactivity and was becoming desperately thirsty. 'I can't bear much more of this,' he thought. 'At least if I was in the reeds with the tin boat I would have something to do, and there would be water to drink. I'll go to pieces if I hang around here any longer.'

At last he caught sight of the fourth man running back towards the others from the south, looking over his shoulder as if alarmed by something. But his companions quickly put him to work helping them to put up the second tent. Satisfied that all four men were now busy down there, William crawled back away from the edge of the hill until he was in the shadow of the tree again. He stood up and looked around. There was no sign of anybody, nothing to tell him that he wasn't totally alone on the hill. He looked carefully in every direction, and stood still and listened for a long time.

'Right then. I'm off to find the tin boat,' he thought, but no sooner had he emerged from the shadow of the tree than he heard something move in the bush beside him.

"Eh! Mzungu! Ngoja!" The voice stopped him in his tracks.

CHAPTER 24

"Hello, donkey, where are your friends?" said Nicholas, stroking the patient animal's nose. "Did you go too fast for them?" The donkey had just wandered into the boma alone. Nicholas was cheered by the fact that Helen, William and Jamie must be on their way back. He was feeling very much better, his headache gone, and if he was still a little weak he was determined that he was now well enough to join whatever adventures the others were involved in. He was longing to tell them how well he felt now. He also hoped that they might know what had happened to John and his Njemps war party.

Matthew had been playing around with some of the older totos, but Nicholas could see him hurrying across the open space of the boma. He too must have noticed the donkey's arrival.

"Where are the others, man?" he asked as he inspected the donkey.

"Perhaps they couldn't keep up. I expect they're tired," said Nicholas.

"Seems unlikely," said Matthew. "This guy doesn't walk very fast, I shouldn't reckon." He patted the donkey on the rump and then banged one of the water drums on its back with the palm of his hand just for good measure. It gave out a dull but unmistakeably hollow ring. "Hey! This thing's empty!" he exclaimed. Nicholas banged on the other one.

"So's this one," he said.

"They've been gone long enough," Matthew complained, "and yet they don't even seem to have filled up the water drums which is one of the things they went specially to do. I hope they're O.K. I'm worried." By this time several of the totos had gathered round them, asking,

"Wapi rafiki yaku?"

"C'mon, let's go and look for them," said Matthew.

Out on the open ground beyond the trees they encountered a dispirited looking line of warriors approaching the village from the north, their heads bowed and their weapons carried limply at their sides. Nicholas knew immediately something was wrong. Matthew ran forward a little to question the leading moran, but the man turned his head away and wouldn't speak. Likewise did the second and the third.

"Ambia mimi!" he cried out, but they would not speak to him.

"There's Jamie!" said Nicholas behind him. Back towards the end of the line of warriors Nicholas had spotted his brother looking even more crest-fallen than the Njemps people. Nicholas thought he might have been crying, though it was hard to tell at that distance. Lemeriai was with him, an arm round his shoulders, obviously trying to comfort him. There was no sign of William or Helen.

Both boys ran to meet him, though Matthew outran Nicholas, whose legs were still a bit weak. By the time he caught up with them Matthew had already spoken to Jamie, and he too was in tears.

"What on earth…?" asked Nicholas, very anxious indeed. "Where's Helen and William?"

"Helen's been kidnapped by those horrible rebels," Jamie sobbed. "They've taken her to the island."

THE TIN BOAT

"Not really?" said Nicholas.

"Yes, I promise," said Jamie desperately.

"What about William? Have they got him too?"

"Yeh, where is William?" asked Matthew.

"He's O.K." Jamie reassured them. "He's gone to join up with John. I think he was hoping to work out some plan for rescuing Helen. He wanted to talk to John. I'm sure John won't let him do anything silly. They'll be back soon."

"But William's right!" Matthew insisted. "We've got to rescue her."

"Why would they want to take her, anyway?" Nicholas asked.

"Let's go back to the village. I'm dying of thirst," Jamie said. "I'll tell you exactly what happened."

After drinking two mugfulls of muddy water Jamie sat with Matthew and Nicholas under the tree outside the boma and told them all he and William had done and seen.

"So Singh's O.K.?" Nicholas asked, relieved at least to have good news of one of his Pelican Camp friends.

"Yeh, Singh's fine," said Jamie. "He's been used as a boat driver and generator starter, and kept locked up the rest of the time, but they didn't hurt him."

"I hope that means they won't hurt Helen," said Matthew without much confidence.

"I'm sure it does," said Jamie, trying to sound encouraging.

"How come they let Singh go, though?" asked Matthew.

"They said they'd release him if the Njemps promised not to stop them all escaping to the east," explained Jamie.

"They've got Helen as hostage, haven't they?" Jamie wished that he had not put it so abruptly. He could see that he had made Matthew miserable again. Still, he decided, Matthew had to know the truth. "In fact, it turns out that they let Singh go to act as a messenger."

"What sort of messenger?" Matthew asked.

"He was told by the rebels that somehow he has got to get a message to the army commander to say that the rebels will kill

Helen if they are not promised a safe conduct to escape to the east in the next two days."

"Will they let her go then?" asked Matthew, his head buried in hid hands as he heard more and more of the awful situation his sister was in.

"That's what they say," said Jamie.

"Which way's east?" Nicholas asked.

"That way," said Jamie rather impatiently, pointing inland. "I don't know what good it will do them. It's all wilderness for miles that way."

"Yeh, well I know what they're up to," said Matthew, sitting up and pulling himself together. "If they keep going that way they'll eventually get to the Aberdare forest. That's where the Mau Mau freedom fighters hid and fought from for ages before independence. It'd be difficult for the army to control them once they were in there. It's the last thing the President would want them to do. Dad knows the President, but God, I'm not sure he'd let this lot run a terrorist campaign from the Aberdares just to save Helen. Oh, hell! What can we do?"

"You know a lot about it," said Jamie, duly impressed.

"Why not? We learn our country's history just like you learn yours. But listen, we've got to do something."

"I'm sure John and William will be here in a minute," said Jamie. "Surely they won't want to harm Helen before there's even been time to get a message to the army."

"P'raps you're right," admitted Matthew. "O.K., we'll wait till they come. But I'm not going to sit here for ever doing nothing."

Later in the afternoon Lemeriai brought them a meal of goat and posho. They made themselves eat because they knew they would need all their strength, though the day's events had taken away their appetites, and they didn't find the African food very tempting anyway. Only Nicholas ate hungrily. It was good at least for Jamie and Matthew to see that he had recovered.

THE TIN BOAT

They enquired of Lemeriai where John might be. Gone with Singh to the chief in the next village, they were told, to ask for a runner to be sent to Marigat with the rebels' message.

It was after sunset and the first stars were appearing in the evening sky when John came to find them. He tried to sound reassuring.

"The chief has sent a man to Marigat, to tell the army what these rebels have done and what they are asking for," he said. "Now another man has come back from there. The army have the message, we are sure of this. Also this man has news. The army has stayed loyal to the President, and he is still in control. The trouble is over, except here and in Nanyuki, where some of the rebels will not give themselves up to the army."

"But will they do what the rebels ask?" said Matthew. John was clearly trying to find a way of breaking the bad news gently. "They won't, will they? I knew they wouldn't," Matthew went on hopelessly.

"They do not want these bad men to escape. Other people could be killed. But they say they will not attack the island yet. They try to find a way to rescue Helen first."

"Have they got any ideas?" asked Nicholas. John shook his head.

"Not yet. I don't think so," he said.

"Have you got any ideas?" Matthew asked him.

"Be patient," said John. "I talk to Lemeriai. We not leave her. We think of something."

"Where's William?" Jamie interjected almost casually. John looked around.

"William not here?" he said, surprised.

"No!" Jamie insisted. "I last saw him back at the Mukutan Hill. He was looking for you." John became very agitated.

"I not seen him," he said. He turned to the group of morans and totos who had gathered around them. "Wapi William?" he asked, hoping that one of those present would have the answer. "Wapi kijana mzungu William?"

THE TIN BOAT

They all looked at each other but nobody seemed able to help. All of a sudden a little boy of about Nicholas's age was pushed forward towards John by his friends, with a good deal of prompting. The child was clearly reluctant. He hesitated for a moment and ran back into the crowd.

Encouraged by John he was pushed forward once again. This time John crouched in front of him so that their eyes were at the same level, and put his hands on the frightened boy's shoulders, talking to him in a kindly voice. At last the child began to speak, first hesitatingly and then more confidently with much pointing and gesticulation. When the story was finished John patted him on the back and sent him away with a smile on his face, obviously having told him that he had done well. John relayed the boy's story.

It seemed that the child had been reluctant to speak because he knew he had done wrong and had broken one of the tribal laws.

"This mtoto, he has a brother who has just been circumcised two weeks ago. You know these boys must go to live in the bush for one month. They must shoot birds and find their own food."

"Yeh, we met one of them at your wedding," said Jamie.

"That is right," said John. "Well, this mtoto, he has been taking food to his brother in the bush. Now that is not allowed, but they all do it, everybody knows that. Still they must not be caught. The mtoto was not happy to say this, but he has just seen his brother, and his brother say he has seen William."

"Where?" said all the boys together.

"He is still on the Mukutan Hill. He is hiding. He speaks no Swahili, you know that, and this boy speaks no English, so they not able to talk to each other."

"Stupid idiot!" said Jamie. "Why on earth couldn't he have said what he was doing? He's mad!"

"What's he doing, man? Have you got any idea?" asked Matthew.

"He talked about trying to rescue Helen. I didn't think he'd actually try anything alone. I can only guess that he thinks he can

THE TIN BOAT

get the tin boat working and go after her. We'd better go and find him before he gets into trouble too," said Jamie.

"No, it is very dangerous," said John earnestly. "It is nearly dark. You will not find him now before the moon is up."

"Oh, surely we can find our way well enough," Jamie insisted. "When we get near the hill we can start shouting for him. Surely he'll show himself if he hears us, if he knows we've gone all that way looking for him. He can't be that stubborn."

"You cannot shout," said John. "The rebels will hear you."

"Rebels? Are they still there?" asked Jamie.

"This boy, he say the boat come back but now the water is too rough. They are not good boat drivers, these people. Now they wait, four of them, on the shore by the Mukutan Hill till morning. They have guns. They dangerous."

"He saw them, this guy, did he?" asked Matthew. John nodded. "And did they see him?"

"Yes, one of them see him" said John. "He say he scared of him." John almost broke into a smile.

"Scared of him?" asked Matthew with considerable interest.

"Ndiyo. He has this costume, you know, all these birds and feathers on his head, and his long black ngombe skin. They never seen anything like that. Maybe they only scared for a moment. He escape quickly. Then he find William hiding."

"I see," said Matthew.

Lemeriai came to tell John that there was food for him, so John left the boys, telling them that he would return and they would talk together about what could be done. He promised that once the moon was up he would at least go and find William, and persuade him to come back to the village.

Gradually the little crowd dispersed. Jamie and Nicholas remained sitting under the tree in the gathering darkness. Murmuring something to himself to the effect that at least William was trying to help Helen, Matthew followed the little boy whose brother had found William, and started an earnest conversation with him.

CHAPTER 25

Matthew returned to the other boys, followed by the little toto.
"What on earth are you up to, Matthew?" Jamie asked.
"You won't say a word to John or anyone?" he insisted.
"O.K. then, no."
"Right. We've got to move fast, man. I'm going to find William. I'm going with him."
"You're mad! You heard what John said."
"Yeh, but listen. She's my sister. I can't sit here doing nothing."
"But they'll see you, those men with the guns," said Nicholas, really frightened for him.
"I'm going in disguise," said Matthew confidently, as if it was bound to work.
"Disguise!" said Jamie, deciding that Matthew really had gone mad. "What sort of disguise?"

THE TIN BOAT

"C'mon. We're going to find this guy's brother. You know he said those men didn't harm him. In fact they seemed rather scared of him. Some of these towny guys are a bit superstitious. They get windy of tribal customs they don't understand. Quick, now, while we've still got a little daylight."

Suddenly the idea seemed exciting. Just the feeling that they were doing something was a boost to their moral. Following the toto through the village Matthew expanded his thought.

"William's a brave guy but I'm worried about him going off on his own. At least I speak Swahili and I know a bit about Africa. He knows nothing. I've got to reach him before he does anything stupid."

They headed west out of the village along a cattle path, but they had not gone far into the bush when the toto told them to stop and be quiet. They could hear the wind blowing through the tops of the trees, but they were sheltered by the bush where they were standing. The little boy waited for everybody to be still before he began to imitate the call of an owl.

At first nothing happened. They all looked round, expecting to see the little boy's brother appear from the bush, but there was no sign of him. He repeated the owl call. This time it had the amazing result of summoning a real owl, a very small one, into the branch of a tree above their heads. The owl and the boy carried on an owly conversation, much to the delight of Jamie and Nicholas, but Matthew was growing impatient.

Another owl seemed to be joining in the conversation from somewhere beyond them in the bush. This alerted the toto, who varied his own call, and a boy clad in a dark skin, with a black ostrich feather and the bodies of several little birds tied to a band round his head, emerged from the bush opposite them.

"How did you know he was there?" asked Matthew, but the toto put his finger to his lips. "Oh, of course, nobody is supposed to know where the initiates are when they are out in the bush, but they obviously keep in touch with their friends in case they need help. This little chap's still worried about getting into trouble. We met him by accident, didn't we?" He said in Swahili to the boy, "We won't get you into trouble."

The toto smiled and said something to Matthew.

"Now we are to wait here a minute," Matthew explained to Jamie and Nicholas. The toto went over to his brother, and engaged him in a long conversation which the boys were unable to hear. The initiate, who must have been about sixteen, stood very still, nodding occasionally while his little brother pointed and gesticulated. It seemed at length that agreement had been reached. The toto beckoned to the three boys to follow him and his brother.

They were led still further away from the village. Nicholas was worried because there was very little light left in the sky. He knew it would be dark before they returned.

"How will we find our way back?" he whispered to Jamie.

"Oh. I expect this little boy can find his way, and we can easily follow him," Jamie said. Nicholas hoped he was right.

They must have walked for another quarter of a mile before the older boy led them off into a thick part of the bush. There, well camouflaged, was a disused African hut which he had obviously made into his home while he was supposed to be living rough in the bush. They were amazed to find that he even had a fire going in the hut, on which some meat was cooking, which gave him a bit of light.

"Naughty, naughty," laughed Matthew. "Still, it's our good luck." The initiate took off his elaborate headdress and tried it on Matthew's head.

"Great!" said Jamie. "But we'll have to make you black." The two African boys seemed to have thought of that already. They took the headdress off him again, and told him to remove his T-shirt. Then they took some black ash from the fire and mixed it with some of the fat which dripped from the meat as it was re-heated over the flames. Once it was made into a thin paste they smeared it onto Matthew's face.

"Wow, it'll stink after a bit, but never mind," said Matthew.

THE TIN BOAT

"You look great," laughed Jamie, and indeed his face was the right shape to look convincing as an African, particularly his nose, which was very straight like many of the Maasai related people. "You'll need to do your arms too," Jamie went on, but the two Njemps boys were having difficulty in obtaining enough fat to make a new batch of paste.

They took the long black skin from the initiate's shoulders, and put it on Matthew. He was smaller, of course, but tall enough that with an adjustment to the knot at the shoulder the cloak didn't touch the ground. Now they could see how much more of him needed to be blackened.

They covered what could be seen of his shoulders, but the business of trying to gather enough fat was taking too long, and Matthew grew impatient. He was obviously in a highly nervous state.

"Can't they use water?" suggested Jamie.

"Yeh, good idea," said Matthew edgily, "As long as it doesn't rain."

"Oh, surely it won't rain," said Nicholas.

"Yeh, well, nataka maji, chaps," said Matthew. Even this suggestion was improved on by the ingenious young Africans. They mixed the water with some soil to make a clay base, into which they mixed the ash, and with this new material the job was quickly finished, even to the blackening of Matthew's blonde hair. By the time they had replaced the headdress he looked most convincing, at least in that dim light.

Finally, and with some ceremony, the initiate handed Matthew the bow and gummed arrows which were the other essential part of the disguise. Matthew shook his hand and bade him an elaborate and grateful farewell in Swahili, saying that one day his act of friendship would be returned. Matthew knew how to behave like an African. Even his walk assumed the loose-limbed gate of the Njemps.

"Perhaps he really can fool them," Jamie said to Nicholas as the toto led them back to the village. Just as they reached the first huts Matthew said,

"I won't go any further. I'll wait here till the moon rises. I don't want to be seen." Now that the moment for parting had come Jamie and Nicholas were afraid for him once more. It was hard to say to him what they felt, except to say "Goodbye," and "good luck."

"Yeh, sure. Go on now, or we'll be missed. Pretend to John that I'm asleep or something," he replied. And so they parted.

Since his encounter with the young Njemps initiate William hadn't dared move from under the tree. He was terrified of the dark, of every noise which filled the African night, and of the men camped below the hill who had guns. He had been scared out of his wits by the appearance of the Njemps boy, and realised that he had been taken by surprise all too easily. Now the whole idea of crossing the lake by himself and rescuing Helen seemed like madness. How he had fooled himself into believing that he could play the hero he had no idea.

The boy had tried to help him. He had given him a drink of water from the gourd he carried, and indicated with gestures that William should follow him. He should have gone with him. Even if they had not been able to understand each other, at least he would not now be alone in the darkness, terrified by every sound, until he clapped his hands over his ears and wept.

While William was paralysed with fear, Matthew had become restless and impatient. He was in no mood to hang around waiting for the moon to rise. The night was clear and starry, and he hoped this would give him just about enough light to find his way. His plan was to find the cattle path which he had seen from the top of the Mukutan Hill. This would bring him round the east side of the hill, and he would be able to reach the tin boat without going past the place where the Njemps boy had seen the soldiers.

It wasn't easy going. The bush was thick, and though his cowskin cloak gave him good protection against the thorns, it was bulky and cumbersome, and was forever being snagged on branches which he hadn't seen. His ostrich feathers too kept becoming tangled in the thorns, and were difficult to extricate in the dark.

The grease used for his black make-up was beginning to smell, and his hair was itchy. His arms, unprotected by the cloak, were constantly being scratched. The further he went the more irritated he became, longing to be on an open path where he could move freely. When at last he did break out into the open, it was not onto the cattle path he had been seeking, but onto the wide expanse of dried-up lake bed which lay between the village and the lake. His sense of direction had failed him badly.

Utterly exasperated, he threw down his bow and arrows and swore at the top of his voice. He knew that if he was going to pass to the east of the hill he would have to fight his way back through that dense bush, and he couldn't face it.

'Oh, to hell,' he said to himself, picking up his weapons again. 'I'll go round the lake side, and if I bump into these guys my disguise had bloody well better work.'

It was his experience that Africans could go to sleep more or less anywhere, so he hoped that by now they would all be sound asleep, even the sentries if they had thought of posting any. There was no reason why he shouldn't creep silently by without waking them. Comforting himself with this thought, he set off toward the hill which even in that light he could just make out as a dark shadow against the starry sky.

As he made his way across the open landscape, the sky lightened from the east. The moon rose, vast and orange, and flattened almost into an oval until it was well clear of the horizon. At last it took on its normal size and shape, and lost its colour until it was cold and white. He had seen it happen many times before, though never in a place so far removed from human life. He felt as if he had been caught out in a place where he had no business to be. He shivered and moved on.

Gradually though, he found himself more at home in the coldly lit nocturnal world. His shadow was not his own, but that of the boy whose disguise he wore, and this helped him to think himself into his African role. There was something of the actor in him. He checked his shadow to see how convincing he could make his African loose-limbed gate, and he began to think only in Swahili, with the few Maa phrases he know thrown in. By the time he reached the shadow of the hill, and had started to pick his way along the path between the cliff and the lake, he had fully immersed himself in the part he was playing. This probably saved his life, for when the huge figure of an armed man rose up and blocked his path, asking him who he was and where he was going, he answered automatically in the way an Njemps boy would have spoken to a stranger. His head was bowed, for the initiate has to be humble in the face of anybody he meets on his wanderings.

"I am an initiate of the Il Chamus," he said, using the proper Maasai name for the Njemps. "I must wander alone and speak to no man. Let me pass." But the armed man would not move.

"Throw down your weapons and turn back, or I will shoot you," he commanded. Matthew, as if inspired, stood his ground, and with his head still bowed invented some unlikely folklore of his own, calculated to scare a superstitious African city dweller.

"All initiates are protected by snakes who are the souls of our ancestors. If you try to harm me, then for evermore you must watch the ground beneath your feet, for my ancestors will surely take their revenge." Having said this, he raised his head for the first time, and though his heart was pounding with fear he looked his challenger hard in the eye.

It was a long time before the big man moved. Matthew felt his nerve about to break. Gradually, though, the man's eyes opened wide and wider with apprehension. He looked anxiously at his feet, then at the ground each side of him, and finally with a scream he took off.

When it was over Matthew's legs went weak from under him and he looked for a rock to sit on. Only then, in the very spot where the man had stood, did he notice a great fat puff-adder. He knew how dangerous these snakes could be, particularly at night when they were at their most active. When the snake turn its head towards him and let out a low hiss he knew he had no time to waste. Quick as a flash he brought his bow down on its head and beat it to death. After that he really did need to sit down.

'My God,' he thought, 'I'm glad that guy didn't hang around to see how I treat my ancestors.'

CHAPTER 26

Helen was wakened from a nightmarish sleep by two shots, merciless cracks from immediately outside her little prison. She sat up with alarm, still feeling sick and shaking, instantly recalling her desperate situation, which was worse than her nightmares.

They hadn't hurt her, though nobody could claim that they had been gentle. Their behaviour towards her seemed to be designed to intimidate her, so that she would be too scared to try to escape or play any tricks. They had locked her in the little storeroom by the swimming pool which had also been Singh's prison. This meant that at least she had a soft bed of sunbathing mattresses to lie on, though there was very little space. The only light filtered through the gap between the top of the wall and the thatched roof where the sisal poles rested. She had a great fear of the long hours of darkness ahead.

Her captors had at least given her some food, a tin of grapefruit clumsily opened with a knife, and a lump of cheese. Obviously they had found their way into the food store. She had made herself eat, because she knew she must, though she was too sick with fear to have any appetite. After that she had lain down and cried from exhaustion and helplessness. She must have cried herself to sleep until she was wakened by those shots.

All was quite again now, except for the sound of the wind, which was blowing strongly. She didn't know how many men were guarding her, but there must have been at least two because they started talking excitedly to each other. She moved as quietly as she could towards the door and pressed her ear to it to try and hear what was being said. It wasn't difficult. Other men seemed to have been attracted to the swimming pool area by the shots, and something of a shouting match had developed. She learnt that somebody had thought he had seen a mtoto prowling around in the shadows. Two shots had been fired in the general direction of the intruder, but they had lost him. This information brought accusations of negligence against the guards, but one of them defended himself by saying it was probably just a baboon he had seen.

'I wonder,' thought Helen with a flicker of hope.

Soon all was quiet again outside, and Helen lay back on her mattress. She found herself lying on a little crumpled piece of paper which she was sure had not been there before. It seemed to be one of the little yellow Pelican Camp bar chits. She spread it out. There was something written on it, but it was too dark to read. She stood up on her bed and held the paper up to the fading light which still came through the gap above the wall. She had to hold it still in the wind which howled through the gap.

There was a message written in uneven block capitals, mostly in Swahili, but with a few English words thrown in here and there. As with most African letters it was largely preoccupied with greetings.

"Hello Helen. How is it with you? I am Sion, nephew of Samson. I am well. How is Matthew? What is the news of Jamie and Nicholas and William?" and so on until it came to the point. "These bad people, they think maybe we don't know where you are. But I am here. I know where you are. I have seen you. I will find help. Kwaheri."

She hid the message quickly under her mattress. The darkness she dreaded was almost complete, but Sion's message had kindled a small flame of hope, though what he could do for her she had no idea. He had at least taken away the feeling of being totally abandoned. That gave her renewed courage. She began to think positively again.

All that was visible now as she lay back on her mattress was the single unshaded light bulb dangling from the roof at just the right level to catch the very last crack of light, and swaying slightly in the wind. 'Perhaps it will come on,' she thought. 'Perhaps they know how to work the generator. Singh might have shown them. Maybe the generator is already working, and all I have to do is find the switch.' She thought it unlikely that she wouldn't hear the generator from there, particularly with the wind coming from the west, but it was worth a try. She groped around by the door frame and found the switch. It was already on. She flicked it up and down just in case it had been fitted upside down, but to no avail. She wondered if they had broken the generator or run out of fuel. It was far more likely, she decided, that none of them knew how to work it. They probably hadn't even tried. She called to the guards.

"Nataka nini? What do you want?" asked a voice, not friendly, but not threatening either.

"Do you want the lights on?"

"Nini?"

"Lights. Electricity. I know how."

"Hakuna electric," said the guard.

"Yes I know," Helen persisted. "But I can work the machine. The light engine. I know how."

"Eh? You can make electric?" said the guard, more interested now.

"Ndiyo," said Helen.

"Hey! Kuja!" the guard said to his companion. "Yeye na wesa wakisha taa." They seemed to have taken the bait. She sat back and waited for events to take their course. When after a few minutes the door of her prison was unlocked, she was dazzled by the light of a torch shining in her eyes. She sensed that there was now a large group of people outside. She shielded her eyes from the light. The rebels' leader, the sergeant, who held the torch, took the hint and dipped it towards the ground.

"Light engine. How this thing work?" he demanded.

"I'll show you where it is," said Helen hopefully.

"No!" he shouted. "I know where it is. That Njemps boy, he worked it for us. Now you tell me how. We work it." It shocked her to hear him, an African, refer to another fully grown African as 'boy', though, like most Europeans, she did it all the time.

"If I come with you I could…" she tried once more.

"You not come. You tell!" he insisted angrily.

"O.K. There's a starting handle. But you must make sure the power is off first. That's the red button. Turn the handle to start the engine. Then press the green button." There was also a fuel switch to be turned on, but she wasn't going to tell them that. Let them try, she thought, and come back to her for help.

Locked in her darkness she tried to listen for the sound of the generator being started, but the wind was making too much noise by now for any other sound to be clearly distinguishable. Suddenly the light flickered on. 'Damn,' she thought, but it went out almost immediately. 'That's better. Starved of fuel.'

Sure enough they returned, their manner more aggressive still because they had to concede that she now had some hold over them.

"O.K. You come!" said one of the heavies guarding the sergeant. "Now you show how this thing work."

"O.K Ndiyo. I…"

"SIYO MNENO! You understand?"

"No trouble," she agreed. She hadn't planned on causing any trouble or playing any tricks this time round. All she wanted was to establish a job for herself which would hopefully mean her being unlocked four times a day if she could persuade them to save fuel by switching it off in the mornings.

They only seemed to have one torch working between them, which must have been why they were so keen to get the generator going. This was to her advantage, because she had to take the torch to inspect the generator. Bending over the oily old diesel engine, she was able to make it impossible for any of them to see what she was doing when she pressed the little fuel valve. Then she pretended to fiddle around with every part of the machine which might conceivably be adjustable, without actually altering anything.

When she came to use the cranking handle she found that she just wasn't strong enough. The compression kicked it back at her. She was going to have to ask one of her captors for help. The large body-guard was already standing over her waiting to grab the handle. She didn't want them to think that she was not needed any more, so she deftly flicked the fuel switch off again.

The big man turned the handle several times. Each time the machine spluttered and died. He straightened up and looked round despairingly at the sergeant.

"Bure kabisa!" he said.

"No," said Helen. "Let me look again." She pretended to fiddle once more, switching the fuel back on when she hoped they couldn't see.

"Now try," she said. This time the engine thudded loudly into action, belching out smoke from the exhaust. Helen pressed the green button on the little control panel and the lights in the generator house came on. Everybody, including Helen, smiled and cheered, and for a moment they shared their mutual triumph, but not for long. Helen was marched swiftly back up the now well lit path to her prison. The big man who had turned the handle did thank her as her locked her in, but this drew a rebuke from the sergeant.

So she was locked up and alone once more, but the little expedition had brought several benefits. For a start, she was now useful to them as more than just a hostage, which made her feel safer. Secondly, she had probably established a routine which meant that they would have to unlock her at regular intervals. How that could be developed into some plan of escape she couldn't work out, but it gave her hope. Thirdly, and of most immediate benefit, she had light, and her little prison seemed less fearful for that.

To her amazement there was another little yellow ball of paper on her bed. She smoothed it out and read it.

"Jambo Helen. Mimi Sion. I have seen you at the generator."

Exhaustion must have overtaken William and he must have fallen asleep, because the next thing he knew was that the moon was rising over the distant hills to the east. The wind had dropped. Everything was quiet. He listened for sounds from the rebel camp below but could hear nothing. Acutely aware that any sound he made would be audible, he crawled slowly and carefully back to the place from where he could look down on the rebels.

Because the moon was behind him and still low in the sky their camp was in shadow. It was very difficult to see anything down there. Out at the edge of the lake he could still see Blue Banana tied up in the reeds, so he presumed the four men were still there. He waited a long time but nothing moved. He edged his way back towards the tree, still crouching low until he was sure he couldn't be seen from below.

It was only when he finally dared to stand up that he saw to his horror that he was not alone. Over the top of the low scrub to the south of him he could see the head and shoulders of an African in a military berry. The man appeared to be sitting at the edge of the ridge looking down at the camp below him. He showed no sign of having seen William. He sat very still. Perhaps he was asleep. What was clearly visible was the end of a rifle barrel resting against his shoulder.

William crouched down again and crawled back into the shade of the tree. 'It's now or never,' he thought. He positioned himself so that the trunk of the tree hid him as far as possible from the sentry and moved as quietly as possible towards the northern end of the hill. From there he could begin his descent down to the level of the lake. He knew this route would keep him out of sight from the camp, and prayed that the sentry would not hear him until he was safely in the cover of the bush below.

The descent was steep and rocky but to start with the ground was firm and the bright moonlight enabled him to pick out his footholds without too much difficulty. But he was aware that this same moonlight made him very conspicuous, particularly because of the bright white T-shirt he was wearing. He decided he would be better camouflaged by his skin which was now quite brown, so without slowing down he started to pull it off over his head. It was a bit of a struggle because he was sweating, and for a moment he was blinded and didn't see the firm rock beneath his feet give way to a loose bank of shale.

Suddenly he began to slip and slide. It was all he could do to stay upright and he was unable to control the speed of his descent. The stones he dislodged went clattering down the hill ahead of him. Disturbed by the noise, a hornbill flew screeching out of the bush below. He felt sure the sentry would have heard the commotion, but didn't dare look back for fear of loosing his footing completely until he reached the firmer ground at the bottom. When he did turn to look up the hill behind him he saw the sentry standing on top of the ridge, bringing his rifle up to his shoulder. He flung his T-shirt to one side and ran for the cover of the bushes. Almost at the same time he heard the shot from the top of the hill and the crack of the bullet hitting the rock near where his T-shirt had landed. The sentry had picked it out as his target. It had saved William's life.

Matthew's encounter with the rebel soldier had convinced him that it wasn't safe to continue his journey along the narrow strip of land between the Mukutan Hill and the lake. If he came up against any more rebels he would be trapped there with very little chance of escape and he couldn't count on them all being scared of him. He'd been lucky once, but he had reluctantly decided to retrace his steps and make his way round the eastern side of the hill.

It was a long way round, but he reached the tin boat without seeing anybody else. He looked around hoping to see William there, and was surprised when there was no sign of him. He dithered about going off to search for his friend, but he had no idea

THE TIN BOAT

where to start looking. The tin boat was the one point where William was likely to be heading, and to have two of them wandering around alone was only going to make the situation more dangerous. He decided to stay where he was and hope that William was unharmed and would find him there. If he was going to help his sister he needed this brightly moonlit part of the night to repair the engine.

The boat had not been disturbed. He pushed it back into the water and towed it to an open part of the rocky beach where he could see what he was doing. He had imagined that returning fresh to the task of removing the sheer pin would make things seem easier, particularly since he could work on it out of the water. But the problem remained the same. The sheer pin was bent in such a way that without the necessary tools it could not be removed, nor could it drive the propeller in that position.

'The arrows! What about the arrows?' he though. 'I wonder if they have proper points underneath the gum.' He took one of his arrows and rubbed the gum off against a rough stone. It did indeed have a good sharp metal point. He snapped the shaft about an inch from the base of the point to make it into a less cumbersome tool. The point was much harder than the soft metal of the sheer pin, so that it bit nicely into the end of the pin. Using a stone as a hammer he knocked against the broken end of the shaft. Gradually the sheer pin edged its way through the hole, the force of the blows partly straightening it and partly sheering off the soft metal at the edges.

The task became more difficult once the end of the pin disappeared into the hole. The point of the arrow was too wide to push it any further. He banged at it impatiently, but he could make no more progress. He thought he heard something moving in the reeds. He listened for a while, but could hear nothing. Returning to his task, he tried to grip the other end of the sheer pin with his fingers and pull it through, but it was still stuck fast.

He was sweating, more with frustration than exertion, and he discarded his heavy skin cloak and his headdress, which were beginning to annoy him. Without them he felt less encumbered and he could think out the problem more clearly. He needed something of smaller diameter than the sheer pin and the hole in which it was stuck. In the end the split pin which held the propeller onto the shaft provided the solution. With this he was able to tap the sheer pin a little further through, and at last it came free.

He found the new sheer pin in the little rusty box with his fishing hooks. He took it out, but he was so nervous that he dropped it into the bottom of the boat. He had to swivel the whole boat round and tip it up so that the moon shone into it before he found it again. He was panicking partly because he knew this job was nearly finished, and he was totally undecided about what to do next. He fitted the sheer pin and fixed the propeller and the washers back onto the shaft with the split pin. The tin boat was ready to go.

By now the moon was over the lake, making it the colour of ice. He could see the island where Helen was being held. He wanted to go straight there, but equally he didn't want to abandon William without knowing what had happened to him. If William was all right he would come looking for the tin boat. He would be desperate because he couldn't find it. 'Stupid idiot!' he thought. 'Why couldn't he have agreed a plan with all of us?' It made things impossible not knowing where he was.

At that moment he heard the shot from the top of the hill. Was someone shooting at him? He had no idea. Terrified he climbed into the boat and curled up in the bottom between the thwarts. It seemed the safest thing to do. He lay there very still for while, listening. He began to hope that he hadn't been seen. Then the awful thought came to him that it may have been William who was the target. He had to try and find out what was going on. Cautiously he climbed out of the boat again, but as he did so there was a shout from behind the ambach bushes.

"Matthew! Get down! Quick! He's got a gun!" William burst onto the beach gasping for breath. He seemed to have lost his shirt and was pouring with sweat.

The tin boat was their only possible cover. As William ran towards it Matthew tried to duck behind it, but caught his forehead on the sharp corner and opened up a deep cut. The pain made him cry out and fall back.

"Behind the boat! Move!" he screamed to William, grabbing his arm, but it was too late. The rebel appeared in the gap between the ambaches, his rifle trained on them.

"No hope now," whispered William.

"Nope," said Matthew, grabbing William's wrist for comfort in what must be his last moment. Blood was pouring down his face but that no longer seemed to matter. As the shot rang out and they realised that neither of them had been hit, they saw the rebel keel over and fall face down on the beach. He had a long Njemps spear in his back.

"John!" they both cried out together, recognising the slim, unmistakeable silhouette of their friend standing over his victim. He removed the spear contemptuously from the man's back, and brought it down swiftly on his neck to make sure he would never bother them again.

William and Matthew were standing facing him now, Matthew still clutching at William's wrist and both of them shaking from their close brush with death, and from having seen a man killed in front of them. John read their feelings and led them away. Matthew looked up at him.

"You weren't meant to know we were here," he said. "But man, what if you hadn't come? Asante, John. How did you know where we were?"

"You must say thank you to your friends Jamie and Nicholas. They worried for you. They tell me where you go, but I nearly too late."

"Traitors!" said Matthew, partly in jest. "They showed more sense than either of us though."

"You my rafikis, and you both brave boys, brave like morans. But we work together now."

"Sure thing," said Matthew. "Sorry sana."

"Thanks, John," said William. "It was my fault. I tried to follow you and Singh but I couldn't catch up with you. Then I thought I could mend the tin boat and go off in search of Helen." He bent down and scooped some muddy lake water into is mouth.

"You want to go to the island to find Helen?" asked John. "Still want to go?" William nodded. "O.K. This is what you do. Go now, while the moon can show you the way. Take Rapili's son with you. He needs to return to Longicharo, so take him there keeping close to this side of the lake. Then cross to the island by the hot springs and come south close to the shore. Do not go take the boat to the camp. Leave it on Fig Tree Island, on the side away from the camp where they will not see you. Do not try to go into the camp until you have found Sion."

"Sion? He there?" asked Matthew.

"Sion has been hiding there all this time. He find Singh. He hide in his cave. You know the place?"

"Yes. He hid your calf there," said William. John smiled at the memory of happier times.

"O.K. Find him there. He will be impatient now for somebody to come. It is good for him you go now."

"I'm coming too," Matthew insisted.

"We all go," said John. "But let William go now. It will be quicker. Time is short. By morning these men will be missed, then what they do to Helen I don't know. Somebody must warn Sion now, and you cannot go till we mend your head."

"My head? Oh, yes." He had forgotten about it, but now he put his finger to the cut and felt how much blood was there. Now that he was reminded of it he felt the pain again.

"Come!" said John. "I have first aid box in Blue Banana."

"Blue Banana? Have you found Blue Banana?" asked Matthew excitedly.

"Ndiyo. Jamie and Nicholas and me. We find Blue. The boys, they wait there now. Is not far. Help William out, then we go. William, do not be foolish. Learn where Helen is, then wait for us

THE TIN BOAT

on Fig Tree. We come soon. We bring food too."

"Hey, what about that guy's rifle? Why don't we take it?" suggested Matthew. John went back to where the dead man lay and prized the rifle out of his hand. He pulled back the bolt, and then remover the magazine and examined it.

"Hakuna bullets," he said. "No use to us." He threw it down into the mud as if it was a piece of rubbish.

"Pity," said Matthew. "Anyway, good luck, William. Don't know why you're risking quite so much for my sister. Still, as John says, don't be stupid, man."

"I'll be O.K," said William. John called for Rapili's son who appeared on the beach and helped push the tin boat before climbing aboard with William.

"Don't let those other guys catch you," said William, casting a last horrified glance at the body on the shore. "There's three more of them out there somewhere."

"They not harm us now," John assured him. "My morans surprise them. They chase them off. They run away. They gone now."

William started the engine. It worked like a dream, and they were off through the reeds towards the open lake.

CHAPTER 27

'What are they doing, those wazungu?' Sion thought. 'Why are they not coming now? If they not come soon it will be too late for Helen.' He was worried for his own safety too. They knew he was around, those bad men, he was sure of that. Consequently he didn't dare go spying into the middle of the camp as he had done before. He still felt reasonably confident about going unseen to the back jetty and watching the comings and goings there from his hiding place under the upturned boat. He had caught a glimpse of Helen when she had turned on the generator for them, and decided to return at dawn when, like Singh, she would probably be taken to switch it off. This enabled him to keep some sort of watch over her, to make sure she was not being treated badly, although he had no idea what he could do about it if they did harm her.

He also hoped to be able to continue delivering his messages to her over the wall of her prison, though this was a much more risky business for which he had to pick his moment with extreme care. Still, he hoped she had taken heart from knowing that he had seen her. When the others came to find her, if they ever came, at least he could tell them where she was.

He had returned from the village at the north end of the island with some food and two blankets, which made his life in the cave more tolerable. He supposed there would be nobody left up that end of the island now. They had decided to take everybody off to Longicharo, in case there was a revenge raid as a result of their planned attack at Mukutan to rescue Singh. He wrapped himself in his blankets and tried to sleep. He had slept for perhaps an hour earlier in the night, but the bright moon had shone directly into the cave and awakened him. Now the moon had passed overhead, leaving the cave in darkness again.

He thought he heard a rippling of waves in the reeds way below him. He sat up smartly and listened. There was definitely something moving in the water. He went out of the cave and climbed up the rocks a little way to where he could see the whole of the channel between Fig Tree Island and the camp.

Somebody was swimming towards the shore below him from Fig Tree Island. The moon was bright enough for him to see even at that distance the white arms and straight hair which told him it was one of the wazungu boys. Sion calculated that he would be out of sight of the camp, but only just. He decided to slip down to the shore to greet him.

By the time he reached the shore the boy had disappeared into the reeds. Though he could have stood there, he must have decided to keep his head down for as long as possible. A movement in the reeds gave away his position. Sion stayed in the shadow of the cliff until the boy's head and shoulders emerged.

"William! Kuja hapa!" he called as loudly as he dared, stepping into the moonlight for just long enough for William to see him. William looked up and down the beach, and seeing nobody made a dash for Sion and the shadow.

"You are cold," said Sion when they reached the cave. William, dressed only in his wet shorts and his flip-flops was

THE TIN BOAT

shivering with cold and exhaustion. Sion draped one of the blankets over William's shoulders, and William pulled it gratefully round him.

"Thank you, Sion," he said, feeling his tense body relax a little in the new warmth. "Have you seen Helen then? You said you knew where she was."

"Yes, I see her," Sion reassured him.

"Is she O.K.? Have they hurt her?"

"She O.K. Ndiyo. Nzuri. She scared, but she not hurt. I don't think so."

"Oh, thank God!" sighed William. He sat with his arms folded across his knees. He was utterly worn out. His head drooped lower and lower until it rested on his arms. He felt like crying from exhaustion, but would not let himself do so in front of Sion.

"Can you take me to her?" he asked in a voice drained of energy. "I want to see her."

"Not now," said Sion soothingly. "Sleep now. At dawn I take you."

"You mean we'll see her? But where can we....?" His question trailed off into silence. He was asleep.

With the very first light of dawn, when the stars were still bright in the west, Sion had brought William to the old upturned boat by the back jetty. They had come from the cave by a circuitous route round the back of the village and along the western shore. They had crawled inside the hull, and Sion has shown William how it was possible to see the jetty and the generator house through the hole in the side. He let William sit in front of him to get the best view.

"How do you know they won't leave it on?" William asked. "I can't see why they'd bother to turn it off." He had to shout to make himself heard over the machine's deafening noise.

"I think they turn it off," said Sion confidently. "Yesterday Singh turn it off for them. He tell them the light engine use minge fuel. Maybe they finish all the fuel, then no light."

THE TIN BOAT

"I see," said William. "Well, let's hope you're right." He had been longing for a sight of Helen, to see for himself that she was still alive, and that there was still hope. The longer he waited though, the more frightened he was of seeing her suffering. What if they had harmed her? Anything might have happened in the long night since Sion had watched her last from that very spot. The sky lightened, but still nobody came. He knew he should be back on Fig Tree Island where he had agreed to meet John and the other boys. He hoped that they would see the tin boat and know he had arrived. His plan had been to be with them by now, with news that he had seen Helen, but it was not working out that way. He waited and waited, imagining them cursing him for having gone off on his own again.

"One of us should go to Fig Tree Island to meet John," he said to Sion.

"John? Wapi John?" asked Sion. "Is John here?"

"Yes, he should be. He's got Blue Banana. His plan was to meet us round the back of Fig Tree. The other boys are with him."

"Wait!" said Sion. William was still. People were approaching from the direction of the manager's house, down the steep rocky path. From there they would have to cross the landward end of the jetty to reach the generator. William steeled himself for what he knew was going to be a distressing sight. He had imagined that he would see her tired, frightened, with sunken staring eyes, hair dishevelled and clothes filthy. He had even thought what it would be like to watch her being roughly handled by desperate, unsympathetic captors. What he was totally unprepared for was that when the time came he could hardly see her at all. There were so many men round her, pushing her forward, that he glimpsed only her feet and the top of her head before she had crossed the jetty and disappeared into the generator house.

"For God's sake! She's only a little girl! They don't need to bully her like that!" William shouted in a fury. Sion signalled desperately for him to be quiet only just in time, because at that moment the generator suddenly slowed down and was silent.

"What can we do, though?" William whispered. "We'll never snatch her from all that lot."

Sion was looking over William's shoulder, and drew his attention to two men who were hurrying down the path towards the jetty.

"See this first man? He is the leader of these people," he whispered. William recognised the sergeant who had led their little expedition to the Mukutan.

"Yeh, he was one of the bastards who captured her," said William. "I seem to have seen the other one before as well, but I can't think where." The second man had his hair cut very short. He was wearing dirty white shorts and T-shirt.

Suddenly William realised who it was, though he looked very different from the last time he had seen him. "That's the man the police took away, the one who stole the money from tent fifteen, isn't it?"

"That is right," confirmed Sion. "That man, he bring these rebels here. They let him out of prison."

The two men went to the end of the jetty, where they seemed to be examining the water below them on all sides. To judge from the shaking of heads they couldn't find what they were looking for. The sergeant turned and shouted in English to the men gathered around the generator house.

"Bring her here!"

The men dragged Helen back onto the jetty, and pushed her towards the sergeant and his convict henchman. She stumbled forward a couple of paces and stood facing them. The other men stayed back. Now at last William could see her.

The sun rose behind the water tanks, picking out blond streaks in her tangled hair. She still wore her green striped rugby shirt and her kikoi over her shorts. William could see no obvious marks of injury on her, though she was rubbing her wrist as if she had been tied up or roughly pulled around by her captors. Her face was in the shadow, but this didn't prevent William from seeing here eyes which seemed to stare ahead of her without focusing.

THE TIN BOAT

William had always thought of her as being strong and athletic, but alongside the huge Luo soldiers she looked so small and vulnerable, utterly defenceless against powers which could overwhelm her at any moment. She reminded him suddenly of John's little bride.

The agony of having to sit there and watch her and do nothing was almost more than he could bear. It was as if his mind and soul were straining to tear away from his body and be with her. Sion must have seen the danger of his reaction, because he took him by the shoulders and pulled him back a little deeper into the shadows for fear that he would be seen.

The sergeant took three paces towards Helen. As he did so she stiffened and raised her head to look him unflinchingly in the eye.

'Wow! She's got some guts,' thought William. 'I couldn't have done that in her situation. However harshly they've treated her they haven't broken her.'

"What happened over there?" the sergeant demanded. "Why have my men not returned in the blue boat?" Helen replied in a thin, croaking voice, but without hesitation.

"I expect they stayed over there last night because the lake was so rough. It was very windy."

"You EXPECT!" roared the sergeant. "I expect your friends, those savages who live there, have tricked us. The lake is calm now, but the boat is not coming."

"Perhaps they've escaped by themselves. That's what I would have done," said Helen. The words came out smoothly, but William could see that the muscles in her face were tense with fear. The sergeant took another pace towards her, his face sweating with rage. It seemed certain that he would hit her, and she shouted "NO!" and shrank back from him.

Sion had to restrain William with all his strength. At the same time the sergeant too was being held back by the convict.

"Ngoja! Nataka meli ngini," he said. The sergeant refrained from hitting her, but took her by the arms and shook her.

"A BOAT!" he roared. "Is there another boat?"

231

"But you've still got Islander. OW! Let go!" squealed Helen.

"Islander?"

"Yes, the big diesel boat."

"We cannot all fit in this one boat. We need another. We leave this place tonight. All of us."

"You could make two journeys," Helen suggested vainly.

"NO!" he roared again. "Your savage friends, I do not trust them. How I know they not attack us, maybe damage the boat so it cannot come back? No. We all go together. Then we are a strong army. Your friends not stop us. Now, where is another boat?"

"There's only one, but it's got a hole in it," said Helen. "I think you could mend it in a day though, good enough to get you across."

"Where?"

"Here. Right here." She turned and pointed to the old wooden hull where Sion and William were hiding.

"Stay back," whispered Sion, crawling back deep into the shadow. But William wouldn't move.

"Show me!" ordered the sergeant. Helen led him off the jetty, past the generator hut, and down the bank towards the upturned boat.

"Hide! Quick!" whispered Sion. Still William could not force himself to move. He heard her voice so close now, heard the weariness in it and the determination not to seem afraid.

"There's wood and tools in the store," she gabbled on nervously, obviously humouring the sergeant and playing for time, for anybody could see that this old thing couldn't be made to float in a day. "There's some pitch here too. It would take time to dry, but I reckon you could get away easily before dawn tomorrow." They were almost on top of them now. William jumped as a hand slapped the wood of the boat above his head.

"This is the hole. This is all you'd need to mend." William could hardly hear what she was saying because of the pounding of his heart. Suddenly her face was there, looking straight into his. It only lasted for a moment - the look of horror, the blood draining

THE TIN BOAT

from her face, then the merest shadow of a smile returning his smile - before she plunged them into darkness by leaning over the hole, pretending to look for damage on the other side.

It was quick thinking on her part. She prattled on about how the rest of the boat looked fine and there were engines in the repair shop and one of them was bound to work. By the time she stood up again for the sergeant to inspect the damage William was safely back in the shadows.

"See," said Helen with a noticeable new brightness in her voice. "If you screw some planks across inside and outside and cover them with pitch it will do fine for this one journey. To make it last of course you'd have to repaint it, but you needn't worry about that. I'll show you where the tools are, and the wood."

'She's brilliant,' thought William, listening to her with unbounded admiration. 'She's drawing them away so that we can escape.' But the sergeant wouldn't take the bait. Infinitely slowly he walked round and round the boat, prodding it and feeling it and at one moment even trying to look underneath it, while William and Sion held their breath, expecting to be discovered at any moment.

"I want to see inside," he said, and their hearts sank. There was no way out now.

"It's very heavy," said Helen. "It will take all of you to move it and you'll have to do it very slowly and carefully or you might make another hole in it." She seemed to be equal to every situation, he mind working like lightening to protect William and Sion despite the danger she was in. "I'd repair the outside first, then you won't have to risk turning it over and back again."

"O.K.," said the sergeant at last. "Show us this store," and she led them away. William and Sion prepared to make their escape, but before they could do so, they heard the voice of the sergeant once more from beyond the jetty.

"I hope this boat work. This is our last chance. If this not work, if we not escape tomorrow, you die."

William and Sion didn't pause for breath until they were back in the cave. The sun was high in the sky by then.

"I must get back to Fig Tree before the others come looking for me," said William. "How the hell are we going to get her out? There's no chance down by the generator. She's too heavily guarded."

"It is a very difficult thing," Sion agreed.

"Yeh," said William. "Is she ever allowed out except to work the generator?"

"No," said Sion. "Never. Maybe they ask her to help with this boat. I don't think so. You see how scared they are she escape."

"Seems to me we will have to spring her from that prison. If only we could even get a message to her."

"I can give her message," said Sion confidently. "I already give her message last night."

"Great, Sion. Great," said William. "That's a start. Now, how can we cross to Fig Tree without being seen?"

"Kuja. Come. I show you," said Sion.

CHAPTER 28

"Yes, sah, I understand your concern for your daughter. I myself am concerned for her too. It is not good for our country to have these troubles. It does not look good with our friends abroad."

"Oh, to hell with your friends abroad!" snapped Helen's father, and immediately wished he hadn't. However the general behind the desk in the fly-blown tin hut of a police station did not show any anger. He held up his hand.

"As I was saying, it is not good for us that a mzungu girl and other wazungu children are caught up in our troubles. But what would you have me do? Let these men go free to make more trouble?"

"If you go in now, either they'll kill her or you'll kill her. And we've lost track of what's happened to the other four. We may be putting them all in danger."

"You see, sah, what may happen if we let these men go. Their only escape would be to the east. It would be a difficult journey, but these men are trained soldiers, most of them. They could make it all the way to the Aberdare forest. You know how long the freedom fighters operated from this place in the struggle for Uhuru. That is the situation which would face us again. We have them trapped on the island. This is our chance to end this rebellion for good.

"Can't you let them off the island, and take them as they cross to the Aberdares?" Helen's father could see that his pleading was making no dent in the general's resolve. No doubt he had his orders direct from the President, and was not likely to disobey them at a time when the army's loyalty was under scrutiny.

"What would they do then?" the general continued, still with studied reasonableness. "They would take your daughter with them until they were safely away. Then what?" He shrugged his shoulders. "These are not honourable men. They are not playing your cricket." He smiled at his own joke. "Once they have no use for her, you know what would happen." There was silence for a moment. It was hard for Helen's father to disagree with the general's assessment. Seeing that he had made his point, the general continued. "Besides this, the stability of our country is at stake. I am sure you understand."

"My country too. I am a Kenya citizen," Helen's father admitted. "But I am also a father."

"I too have children," said the general sympathetically, "but I have decided. We go in tonight. I assure you, the safe release of your daughter will be one of our objectives. I hope we succeed. I promise you this is her best chance as well as ours.

William wasn't surprised to be greeted with anger when he and Sion finally met up with John and the three boys round the east side of Fig Tree Island.

"Why the hell can't you stick to anything we agree, man?" Matthew challenged him.

"Yes, William. We were meant to meet up here, remember, before trying any other escapades," snapped Jamie. But John intervened.

"You must speak quietly. We are very close to the camp. There is no wind. If you talk loud we will be heard." They all fell silent for a moment before the bickering started again in loud whispers.

"If we hadn't found the tin boat we'd have thought you'd drowned." Jamie went on. William held up his hand for silence. They were angry with him because they were tired and tense, but they did want to hear if he had any news.

"I'm sorry," he said. "I know what we agreed, but remember John did say I was to meet up with Sion, and you see I have done that. And with Sion's help I have seen Helen."

"Seen her? Is she O.K.?" asked Matthew, forgetting his anger. He had washed off most of his African make-up, though there were still greasy black streaks on his face and arms. There was a large plaster across his forehead, through which some blood had seeped.

"Yeh, she's O.K. She's not hurt or anything, although I wouldn't say they were treating her gently. She's bloody brave, your sister. But we've got to get her out quick. We haven't got much time." The boys listened with growing admiration and alarm as William related the whole story of how he had watched Helen, and how she had played for time and outwitted her captors. "She's got them all fooled over this generator business, and about the boat."

"Brilliant!" said Jamie admiringly.

"That old Freji will never float," said Nicholas, practical as always.

"I know," said William. "That's why we we've got to move quickly. I don't give much for Helen's chances when it sinks."

Silence again. They all understood what he was saying.

"O.K.," said Matthew at last. "How're we going to do it? Any ideas? John, what d'you reckon?" They had learned to rely so heavily on John that they almost took it for granted that he would think of something. For once, though, their friend did not have the answer at his fingertips.

"Come. I have brought food," he said. "Let us sit together and eat. While we eat, we talk. Each one think of an idea. We talk about it. Like that, if it can be done, we will find a way." They were all tired and hungry, so they needed no persuading to do what he suggested.

The days when they found goat distasteful seemed a long time ago as they sat in a circle in the shade, chewing at a piece of cold meat which John carved for them. John acted as chairman and invited William to speak first.

"I've no idea," he admitted, "but if it helps us think it out, I'd say we've got two main choices. Either we try to rescue her from the store where Sion says she's locked up, or we make use of the time when she's let out to work the generator. In that case we'd have to do it this evening or we'd probably be too late."

"Is there any chance of springing her from the store?" asked Matthew.

"Have to ask Sion. He's the only one who's seen what goes on there," said William. They all looked at Sion, but he shook his head sadly.

"They guard her all the time," he said. "They have guns. What we do against guns?"

"Yeh, and there's only one door and no window or anything," said Matthew. "Sounds like a non-starter."

"So that leaves the generator business," said William, "but she's even more heavily guarded then, even if she isn't locked up."

"Couldn't she make a dash for it and jump off the end of the jetty?" suggested Jamie rather forlornly. "Perhaps we could slip round by boat and pick her up."

"It will not be quite dark at this time. You will be seen," said Sion.

"Still, Jamie's right about one thing," said Matthew. "However we do this we will need a boat at the ready to make a quick getaway."

"There must be a way of her giving them the slip," Jamie went on. "If she took them by surprise a quick dash at the right moment might do the trick. As you say, we'd have to be ready for her. How d'you get messages to her, Sion? We'd have to tell her what to do."

Sion explained how he had been slipping his messages through the gap between the wall and the roof of the store.

"That's a point," said Matthew.

"What is?" asked Jamie.

"Well, the store. Going back to the idea of getting her out of the store. It's got one heavily guarded door and no windows, but it's only got a thatched roof. Not difficult to break through, if we could do it quietly enough without being seen."

All this time Nicholas, who had been left very short of energy by his illness, had sat quietly next to John, taking no part in the conversation. His head had soon flopped onto Johns lap, and they all thought he was asleep, which seemed a good thing. A general discussion started about the practicality of cutting a hole in the roof of the store, but they all agreed that it would be necessary to cut through at least one of the sisal poles which supported the thatch to make the hole big enough. The only tool they had was John's knife. It would take time, and though the guards didn't regularly go round the side of the store to look at the roof, they would surely be seen before the job was finished.

"Sion?" squeaked Nicholas in a sleepy voice.

"Just a minute, Nicholas," said William.

"But I want to ask Sion something," Nicholas insisted, sitting up. "I've got an idea."

"You have all spoken. Let him speak too," said John.

"Yes, sometimes Nicholas does have bright ideas," Jamie agreed.

"No, I just wanted to know if everybody goes with Helen down to the generator,"

"How d'you mean?" asked Matthew.

"Well, do any of the guards stay behind up at the store or by the swimming pool?" They all looked at Sion, aware that Nicholas might have come up with the seeds of a plan.

"No, I don't think so. No, I think they all go with her, and I see these men who guard her prison. They were with her at the jetty."

"But have you seen the swimming pool area while this was going on?" asked William.

"Ndiyo, one time I take message. Nobody was there."

"Do they lock the door of the store while she is out?" Nicholas went on, pushing his idea one stage further. Sion shrugged.

"I don't think so. Why they lock an empty store?"

"Brilliant, Nicholas," said William. "I think you've got it. This is what I suggest we do."

The details of the plan were knocked into shape. Nothing could be done till that evening, except to try and deliver a message to warn Helen what they were going to do. They were all worried that they had nothing to write on, but Sion produced his bar chits pad and pencil from the pocket of his shorts. They were wringing wet because he had swum across to Fig Tree Island. But as Matthew pointed out an hour in the sun would make them usable again.

"Can I take it to her?" asked William.

"Best leave it to Sion," said Matthew wisely. "He knows how to slip round here unseen. If they discover we're around her chances are nil."

"O.K. You're right," William agreed, and sat back against a tree. "Once that's done we'd do well to get some sleep," he said wearily. "We'll need to be wide awake tonight."

"Hey! Wake up now, William, man!" Matthew whispered in William's ear, making him come to with a start. The sun was glinting through the trees overhead and the air was very hot and still and buzzing with insects. His watch confirmed that it was past midday.

"I've been asleep for hours," he groaned. "What's happening?"

"Yeh, we've all slept a bit," Matthew told him, "but Sion's going now with the note for Helen. We wanted you to read it

THE TIN BOAT

first." William stood up and brushed the sand off his hands before taking the note from Sion. He read it and handed it back.

"That's fine," he said. "Good idea to tell her to take her time down at the generator. It might buy us a few more precious minutes. Good luck, Sion. Sure you don't want someone to go with you?"

"I think it is best if I go alone," Sion confirmed. "I have done this before. Maybe they see me and they think 'He is just Njemps boy. He will not bother us.'"

"I wouldn't count on it," said William.

"He is right," John agreed. "Now, kwenda Sion. I come to watch you till you are safely across the water."

John returned half an hour later having followed Sion's progress, swimming across the narrow channel to the north of Fig Tree Island and picking his way from shadow to shadow until he reached his cave. After that there was nothing to do but wait. Nerves were on edge now and sleep was out of the question.

William was very silent. He didn't seem to want to talk to anybody. Nicholas wouldn't leave John's side.

"You can come and help me with something," John said to him. "Come this way." He took John's hand and they went off along the shore.

Jamie and Matthew were deep in a serious conversation.

"Why's William so determined to do this himself?" asked Matthew. "I mean, she's my sister, not his, and he's already run more risks for her than any of us."

"Well, he's the oldest," said Jamie. "I s'pose it should be him, unless John does it."

"Yeh, I'd thought of that. He'd do it, too. You know what he's like. That's why I don't want to ask him. It's my sister and my problem."

"Anyway, John's much more valuable operating the boat. That part of the plan is just as important as the other," said Jamie.

"True," said Matthew. "Why William and not me, then?"

"Don't you trust William then?" asked Jamie, coming to his cousin's defense. "He's done pretty well so far. Amazingly well, really, even he has made one or two blunders."

"Oh, it's not that. He's been fantastic," Matthew agreed. "It's just that I get this creepy feeling that he doesn't mind what happens to him as long as Helen's O.K. He really likes her, doesn't he?"

"Yeh, well, she's been really nice to him, hasn't she? She's made sure he's joined in everything. I've never known him enjoy himself so much."

"Well, he sure was a bundle of misery to start with. Man, what a drag!"

"Not really his fault," said Jamie protectively. "Anyway, he's completely different now."

"Certainly is," Matthew agreed.

John and Nicholas returned struggling under the weight of a powerful looking outboard motor which was covered in sandy soil. Nicholas was looking very pleased with himself.

"Hey! Where did you get that from?" demanded Jamie.

"It's the big engine off the speedboat," said Nicholas, grinning all over his face. "John buried it here to hide it after the speedboat sank. If we can make it work it will give us a faster getaway boat." John laughed at Nicholas's enthusiasm.

"It can be a spare engine if one of them does not work," he said.

"Can't we put it on the tin boat? It used to be a water-skiing boat, didn't it Matthew?"

"Yeh, that's right," said Matthew. "Not sure it ever had quite such a big engine, did it, John?" John shook his head.

"Maybe it is too powerful for that boat. I think we use Blue Banana tonight. If her engine does not work, now we have a spare one. Now we must clean it up." John had no real intention of using the speedboat engine for the rescue. His purpose was to give them all an occupation while they were waiting. Already the appearance of the engine had broken the mounting tension, so he was well pleased with his idea.

THE TIN BOAT

"C'mon, William," said Matthew. "You coming to help clean this thing up?"

"Yeh, sure," said William as if returning to them from a great distance. John produced a few tools from Blue Banana. They couldn't strip the engine down completely, but they managed to get into it well enough to clean it reasonably thoroughly.

The work occupied them for several hours. They all became engrossed in what they were doing under John's supervision. At times they even managed to forget the perils they faced that night and Helen's desperate situation. Certainly they hadn't noticed that Sion had been gone for a very long time. They even forgot from time to time how close they were to the rebels in the camp, and John had to remind them frequently to work quietly. Still, he could see that the work had lifted their moral and that made him happy.

By the time the engine was reassembled and they went down to the water to wash the oil off their hands the sun had lost a good deal of its brightness, and the cliff face of Gibraltar half way across the lake had taken on a clear pink colour. Evening was not far away. William felt the grip of fear in his stomach, but he was determined to appear calm to the other boys.

"Let's try the engine now," suggested Nicholas cheerfully. The others almost jumped on him.

"You idiot!" said Jamie. "You can hear the sound of a boat engine from miles away."

"Oh, yes, sorry," said Nicholas, chastened and disappointed. At that moment Sion appeared through the trees. His gloomy face told them immediately that all was not well.

"God, you look pretty miserable," said Matthew anxiously. "What's up?" Sion opened his hand and showed them the soggy, crumpled piece of paper."I sorry. I could not take it to her," he said, not daring to look any of them in the face. He explained how he had hung about all afternoon in a hiding place close to Helen's prison waiting for a chance to drop the note under the eaves to her. Unfortunately two of the rebels had chosen a shady spot beside the store to go to sleep, and he hadn't dared approach it for fear of disturbing them. "Sorry sana," he said miserably. "Maybe I could have done it, but I scared if they wake they see me."

"No, you were right," William reassured him. "The plan doesn't totally depend on her knowing about it in advance, and it would have been a disaster if you'd been caught."

Sion was only slightly cheered by what William had said, so Matthew took him aside and spoke to him in Swahili. He told him what a great job he had done, and asked him if he had had enough, offering to take his place and go with William. At this Sion pulled himself together and reacted quite sharply.

"I go," he insisted. "Soon be a moran. I am not a coward," and without waiting for any more argument he turned to William and said, "I think we must go now. Nearly generator time." William rose to his feet.

"Got the knife?" asked Jamie.

"It is here," said John, handing William the long-bladed sheath knife which he had used to carve the goat meat. William was too nervous to speak.

"Good luck!" said Matthew. "We'll be ready for you with the boat." Nicholas and John also wished William luck, and he accepted with a silent nod of his head before turning to follow Sion.

He felt better once they were on their way. A week before he would have been terrified of swimming through reeds where there might be a hippo or even a crocodile, but he had already crossed the channel between the islands twice in the past twenty-four hours, and the dangers seemed minimal compared to what he was about to face. Besides that Sion knew the lake and its creatures so well that William was totally confident in following him.

He took off his shorts to make the short swim, holding them above his head with his flip-flops and swimming with one hand. He reckoned that little comforts like having dry shorts might be very welcome in the anxious hours ahead. Once on dry land again he and Sion made a dash for the shadow of the cliff, where he put his shorts on again. During the pause he said something to Sion which he had not wanted to say in front of the others.

"When we get there, keep watch if you can but don't be seen. If anything goes wrong get back to Fig Tree Island and warn the others. I'm not coming out again without Helen, whatever happens."

"I not leave without you," Sion insisted.

"Yes, you must," said William. "You are the only person who can tell the others what is happening. And besides, you've risked enough for us already. Don't let them catch you."

"But...."

"I mean it. Please. Promise me."

"O.K., then. O.K. I promise," said Sion and they smiled and shook hands.

The hiding place which Sion had occupied all afternoon, and to which he now returned with William, was just inside the boundary fence of the camp, behind the store where Helen was locked up. It gave them a view along the north wall of the store towards the swimming pool. It was extremely uncomfortable for two of them, crouched on sharp stones behind a rock, with thorn branches so low over them that they couldn't move without being scratched.

They watched for an hour or more. The two men who had been sleeping there had gone, but the guards were being unusually restless, pacing endlessly up and down along the front and side of the store, so that it was still impossible to approach and drop a message in.

Eventually a third man came hurrying round the swimming pool and said something urgently to the two guards in Swahili. William looked at Sion.

"They say the sergeant come, now! Now!" whispered Sion, and sure enough the agitated leader came storming across, followed by his henchman, and stopped in front of the door of Helen's prison, out of sight of William and Sion. Even so, they

THE TIN BOAT

could hear what the men were saying. The sergeant was speaking in English.

"You lie! You LIE!" he screamed. "These engines. None of them WORK!" This was no surprise to William, but the way the sergeant spoke made his heart stop. "I warned you," he went on. "If this boat does not work, you DIE."

There was a terrible silence. William felt that all must be lost. He wanted to make a desperate bid to try and save her there and them.

"No. Wait," whispered Sion, seeing the panic in his face. At least they heard Helen's weak little voice.

"What about the boat itself? Does it float?" She seemed to be trying to humour them, playing for time again. Indeed the sergeant did sound a little calmer when he replied.

"It is not ready yet. They try soon. But what use is it? No engine. NO ENGINE!"

"You could tow it behind Islander, no trouble at all," said Helen.

'She must have known this was coming,' thought William. 'She seems to have had that answer all worked out beforehand.' Once again he was amazed at her courage and ingenuity. So it seemed was the sergeant.

"O.K. You have akili mingi, I say that," he said after a pause. "You come now. Work the light engine. We need light to finish the boat. So you keep your life a little longer. But if this boat sink, that is the end. Finish."

"God! It's now or never," said William when they'd all gone. "That boat will never float, will it Sion?" Sion shook his head.

"That old boat. It is bure kabisa," he said.

Helen was hardly conscious of walking down to the back jetty that evening. She had struggled all that time to keep her head clear and think positively, because she knew her life depended on it. She knew now that her scope for playing for time had just about come to an end. Once the rebels heaved the old wooden boat into the water she knew for sure what would happen. The boat had been lying there drying out in the sun, its timbers warping, for more than two years. There must be dozens of places where the water could seep in between the planks, and that would be the end for her.

Her head was reeling as they pushed her forwards down the steep path. Waves of panic overcame her and she thought she would faint. Once in the generator house she pulled herself together for long enough to do what she had to do, but she wasn't thinking and she switched on the fuel in full view of the sergeant, showing him quite clearly how easy it was.

She realized her mistake immediately. She went white, expecting her life to be snuffed out that instant. Then without warning she made a sudden dash for the jetty. It was a hopeless gesture, and she didn't get far. A forest of strong black arms grabbed her, and hauled her back to face their leader.

"Now, now, mzungu, LIAR! Nakwenda wapi, eh?" She looked at him in utter helplessness. No flash of inspiration came to her this time, for her brain had almost ceased to work. She was on the very edge of consciousness. "I would like to kill you now, but you may still have your uses. Let us see what happens to this boat. Take her back!"

One man grabbed each of her arms and pulled her towards the path, but overcome by shock she felt her legs give way and she fainted.

"Carry her!" roared the sergeant. "Lock her up quick! She must not do that again. She is all we have to bargain with."

She had come round by the time they reached the swimming pool, and although she felt very weak she managed to walk the last few yards to her prison, still with the vice-like grip of the two guards on her arms. They opened the door, pushed her in, and slammed it, locking her in as quickly as they could. In the circumstances they were not surprised to hear her scream. They must have thought she had stumbled and fallen as they pushed her.

THE TIN BOAT

"Don't make a sound," William's voice whispered to her. She knew at once that it was him, and she clung to him sobbing and covered his face with her tears.

CHAPTER 29

The night was unbearably still. The evening lake wind seemed to have failed them when they most needed it. Even the frogs were silent, and apart from the distant voices of the men still working on the boat the only sound came from the scratching of the crickets. It was not enough to drown even a whisper between them from the hearing of the guards outside the door. They dared not make any move which might betray William's presence there.

Helen lay in silence with her head on his shoulder, still sobbing from time to time, but calmer now that she was not alone. She dared not ask, nor he explain to her, why he had chosen to share her captivity, or whether he could see any way out for them.

'Damn this wind! Why won't it blow?' he thought. Above all he wished he had had time to finish whittling through the one sisal roofing pole which he had to break to make a big enough gap for their escape. Cutting a hole in the thatch had been no problem. He had replaced the reeds so that the hole was no longer visible, but when the time came a single push would remove them again. He really needed a saw or at least a serrated knife to cut the pole. John's knife had just jammed in the wood, so he had been forced to start the laborious task of whittling slices out of it to weaken it. He wasn't far from completing the job, but Helen's unexpectedly sudden return had stopped him just too soon. The pole might even break now, but not without making a noise. The wind had to start blowing.

After a while her sobbing ceased. Although in the silence they dared not even whisper to each other, he knew now that she had put her trust in him. 'Good,' he thought. 'All we can do is wait. I can keep watch and listen for the wind.' His own mind was clear. He felt surprisingly calm. His whole effort had been directed towards reaching Helen. Though in theory the plan for rescuing her was clear in his mind, his imagination had not taken him beyond the point of being reunited with her, and sharing whatever ordeal she was going through. His fear had been of failing to reach her. Now that he was there with her, and she could unload her own momentous struggle to save herself onto his shoulders, he was no longer afraid.

Perhaps it was because he was still dressed only in his shorts that he was so sensitive to the first stirrings of the breeze. He had no idea how much time had passed, but suddenly a distinct drop in temperature made him sit up. Sure enough he could hear the rustle of a light wind in the thatch over his head.

Either his movement or the sound of the wind woke Helen too. She groaned and struggled as if she needed to break free of him, but realising who he was she came closer to him again and whispered to him.

"William! It's really you!"

"Ssh! They don't know I'm here," he told her. "Keep your voice very low. I think there's enough wind to stop them hearing."

THE TIN BOAT

"But why are you here? It just makes two of us they'll kill. They're threatening to kill me if that old boat doesn't float, and they can't get off the island tonight. And it won't float. No chance. I'm amazed they haven't come for me already."

He held her tight and tried to comfort her by saying,

"They could just be trying to frighten you. They may still want to try and bargain your life for their freedom. That's why they took you, we know that. But whatever happens you won't be alone." They were quiet for a while. Then he whispered, "They're not going to get you. I won't let them. Now listen. I've cut a hole in the thatch roof up the far end on this side." He pointed to where he had been at work on the roof. "As you can see, I haven't quite finished cutting through the pole. You arrived back too soon. But even that might give with a push. The trouble is it will make a hell of a noise. Still, if anything happens, make a dash for it and try and get out through there,"

"It's incredible," whispered Helen excitedly. "Why didn't I trust you? I even saw you hiding in the boat this morning, but I never believed you would have been doing all this."

"Sion tried to get a message to you, but that didn't work out. I'm sorry," William explained. "Anyway, he's hiding down by the boundary fence. He will lead you back to Fig Tree Island where John, Matthew, Jamie and Nicholas will be waiting with the boat."

"Good grief, man!" She gasped, almost too loud. "You've all come and risked your lives for me."

'Is it that surprising?' thought William. "So that's the plan," he said. "When I say go, you go. No hesitating. O.K.? You feeling strong enough?"

"You bet!" she laughed, and squeezed his hand hard to prove it.

"Ow!" he squealed.

"Ssh!" she whispered. Luckily the wind was increasing, because they were both giggling from the joy of being together, and of talking about escape and freedom. They calmed down, and Helen said, "Where will you be? You haven't told me that."

THE TIN BOAT

"Oh, right behind you," he assured her. "It's just that if we do get separated you must keep going. If only I had finished cutting that pole we might have been able to make a dash for it right now."

All this time, because the wind was from the west, they could hear the men repairing the boat down at the back jetty. Whatever William thought, Helen knew that what was happening down there would finally force the issue and dictate the moment at which they must try and break out.

Suddenly the voices started up the familiar rhythmic chorus.

"HaramBEE! HaramBEE!"

"My God! This is it. They're launching the wretched boat," groaned Helen. The guards outside had also heard the sound and knew what it meant.

"Eh! The boat!" said one of them. "Now we get out of this place."

"If it work. I go see," said the other.

"I come too," said the first.

"You must stay here," ordered the second.

"But I want to see this," the first insisted. Helen and William could hear them clattering around with their rifles. Then they seemed to move off. There was silence outside. Helen got up and pressed her ear to the door.

"Quick!" she whispered. "I think they've both gone. Get to work with your knife."

"Are you sure?" asked William.

"Pretty well. Anyway, we've got to risk it. Any minute now the boat will sink, and that'll be it." William climbed onto the bed and worked away with his knife. After taking a few more slices out of the pole he put one hand either side of the gash he had made and pulled sharply downwards. The pole gave way with a crack. They waited in agonising silence but there was no reaction from outside the door.

"O.K. then. Swap places," William ordered, taking control of the situation. "Put your hand against the place where I've cut the hole and be ready when I say to push it out and climb through." She obeyed without any argument.

Just then they heard a tremendous commotion from down at the jetty. They heard one of the guards cry out,

"It is sinking!"

"Oh, no! This really is it!" said Helen.

"Yeh, get that hole uncovered. Pull the stuff inwards, though, if you can. They're less likely to see you. Then be ready to go. I've got the knife. I'll stay by the door just in case they surprise us."

"Oh God! Be careful!" she pleaded. She pulled at the thatch. It came away very easily, and she soon found herself looking out at a starry sky, the wind blowing refreshingly in her face. She beckoned to William to follow her, but he waved her on, indicating that he would guard the door until she was safely out.

By climbing onto the end of the sun bed she was able to put her head out through the hole in the roof and look around. The moon had just appeared over the horizon behind her. She could see a corner of the swimming pool bar to her left. Through the open part of the bar she caught a glimpse of the two guards still leaning over the wall watching what was happening below at the jetty. There was a small lawn in front of her which sloped down to her right towards the bamboo boundary fence.

She hesitated for a moment, then seeing nobody apart from the two guards she pulled herself up until she was sitting on top of the wall of the store. It wasn't easy because her arms were weak after her ordeal, and because the gap was narrow even with part of one pole removed. To pull her legs over the wall she had to trust the thatched roof to hold when she sat on it.

William saw her legs disappear, and was about to follow her when she fell back on the bed.

"They're coming!" she gasped. "The guards are coming!"

"O.K. Don't panic," said William. "Get ready to go again. As soon as I hear them come round this side, I'll signal and you go."

The guards must have run back, for they were outside the door in no time, one of them saying,

"The sergeant is coming. This is it for the mzungu." William gave the signal. Helen climbed onto the roof once more.

Suddenly there was a flash and a deafening explosion from somewhere beyond the swimming pool. Helen instinctively flattened herself against the thatched roof, one leg still dangling down into the store. Another explosion followed even closer to them. She could see the glow of a fire starting, probably in the roof of the bar.

'My God! We're being attacked,' William thought. Through the wind he heard the sound of rifle fire. He could also hear the raised voices of the guards outside the store. To his horror the key started to rattle in the door. "Bloody hell! They're coming in!" He slipped behind the door and, clutching the knife, he waited for it to open.

One of the guards burst in. Seeing Helen's leg he raised his rifle.

"Go! Helen!" William screamed, and rushed at the man, digging the knife into his back. The guard cried out in pain and let his rifle fall. By now the second guard was in the doorway with his rifle at the hip, pointing onto the store. William kicked the door as hard as he could, knocking the rifle upwards. With a fleeting glance over his shoulder to make sure Helen had gone he pushed blindly past the second guard before he had time to recover his balance.

It all happened very quickly. For a moment William thought he had escaped, but the guard stuck out his leg and tripped him up as he started to run. His heart missed a beat as, sprawled on the floor, he heard the bolt of a rifle click behind him. Another tremendous explosion beside the swimming pool made the guard hesitate for long enough to allow William to scamper out and round the corner of the store. Terrified, he sprinted across the little lawn, not daring to look round. He was almost in the cover of the rocks and trees when the shot rang out. He felt a thud and the pain in his left arm. He grabbed it with his right hand and kept running. There was

THE TIN BOAT

another shot but he was in the shadow now, and his pursuer could only have guessed where to shoot.

"William, are you O.K.?" came Helen's anxious voice from beside him.

"You hit?" asked Sion.

"For God's sake!" screamed William. "I told you to get the hell out of it. Now run!"

"But you've been hit," said Helen. "You need help."

"I can manage! Move! I think we've got the army at us too." They followed Sion as fast as they could, taking the shortest route to the lakeside opposite Fig Tree Island.

There was a tremendous amount of gunfire behind them now, and the sky was beginning to glow from the fire sweeping through the big bar roof, fanned by the strong wind. William could feel the blood from his wound seeping through his fingers. It was throbbing desperately. He was feeling sick, and his head was starting to spin. He grew fainter and fainter and knew he wasn't going to be able to go much further. As they reached the top of the escarpment above the lake he groaned and fell.

"NO!" screamed Helen. Stooping and cradling his head on her knee, she examined the wound. She tore a strip off the kikoi round her waste, filthy though it was, and made a bandage of it to try and stop the bleeding.

"Sion!" she shouted. "Do you know where the others are?"

"Ndiyo."

"Well kwenda, man! See if you can get help." Sion stood there as if stunned, not wanting to leave them. "Please!" She said. "Go quickly! It's our only hope."

THE TIN BOAT

CHAPTER 30

"John? Couldn't we put the big engine on the tin boat?" Nicholas persisted. While Jamie and Matthew had become very edgy the moment William and Sion had departed, Nicholas had maintained an unflagging interest in the speedboat engine. He was probably too young to take in the full significance of the situation they were in. It just seemed a waste to him to have cleaned up the big engine and then not to use it. "The tin boat engine keeps going wrong," he went on. "What if it goes wrong again?"

All along John had been determined to use Blue Banana when the time came to make their getaway. The tin boat was only to be used as a standby. Still, he had to agree that there was some sense in what Nicholas was saying. The small engine was unreliable, and the larger one would give them extra speed if they needed it, though he doubted that the tin boat would remain stable if it was run flat out.

Besides that, he wanted the boys occupied again. There was a long wait ahead. William and Sion were going to try and bring Helen to them on Fig Tree, where they could embark in Blue Banana out of sight of the camp. They proposed to bring her out in the hours between darkness falling and the moon rising, when they should have the advantage of the wind to cover any noise they made. If they were not back before the rising of the moon John was to bring Blue Banana in to the shore below Sion's cave and come looking for them. If William needed help before that he would send Sion back.

"O.K. Kuja. We change these engines," John said, much to Nicholas's delight. They all set to work, and once the job was done Nicholas pleaded yet again to try it out.

"Not on your life," said Matthew. "It's so still they're bound to hear." Indeed the lack of evening breeze seemed to be a bad sign. They knew how much the usual noisy evening wind would help William. It had been so reliable the last few days. It should have started by now.

"What if we need the tin boat in a hurry and it doesn't work?" bleated Nicholas. "That engine's bound to take a bit of starting anyway."

"It's only a backup," Jamie pointed out. "We won't use it unless we get separated or Blue fails." Nicholas seemed very disappointed.

"As soon as the wind blows so they can't hear us I'm going to try it," he insisted, and refused to get out of the tin boat.

"Oh, come on Nicholas!" said Jamie. "We're all up tight enough as it is. Don't make things worse!"

"Is O.K." John said. "I go and sit with him." He climbed into the tin boat and sat on the thwart next to Nicholas and put a comforting arm round his shoulder. And so the four of them settled down and waited for darkness.

"What the hell d'you think's happening?" said Matthew. "I want to go and see."

"Yeh, they may need help," said Jamie.

"Hapana. We stick to our plan," John insisted. "Sion come if they need us."

"O.K. So what d'you think's going on?" Matthew was too nervous to stay still.

THE TIN BOAT

"William say he wait till the wind blow. I think that is the trouble," said John. Matthew thought he was probably right, but he wouldn't settle, and wandered off through the bush towards the middle of the little island.

"Where's he gone now?" asked Jamie.

"Oh, he is all right," said John. "He is worried but he is not stupid."

"I'm worried too," said Jamie. "I've never been so nervous in my life." John comforted him with an arm round his shoulder. Before long Matthew reappeared.

"Well, at least the generator's on," he told them. "I can see some lights." It didn't mean much, but it was a sign that Helen was still alive and in action. For a while nobody spoke but the silence played on their nerves again. Matthew leapt up.

"COME ON WIND! BLOW!" His voice came out as a throttled scream of frustration. "Why didn't I go instead of William. I can't bear this waiting around, not knowing."

"Hey," said Jamie. "Do you feel just a very slight breeze blowing?"

"Yeh, I think you're right, and we're very sheltered here. It could be starting to blow properly up the top there."

"Something might happen at last. I can't stand much more waiting around either," admitted Jamie.

"I feel quite sick with nerves," Matthew agreed. The minutes ticked by, but still nothing happened. The first glow of the moon appeared in the east.

"The moon is nearly here," said John. "Get ready now. We wait ten minutes more, then we go."

Then came the first great flash and the bang.

"God Almighty," exclaimed Matthew.

"What the hell...." Another flash and explosion followed. They rushed through the bush to the centre of the island from where they could see the flames rising from the bar roof.

"We'll be seen," said Matthew, aware of the amount of light being given off by the flames, and they hurried back to John.

THE TIN BOAT

"What is it?" Matthew asked. "Any idea?"

"Army," said John. "You see where this peoples are shooting from over there?" He pointed to the spit of land on the far side of the bay opposite them. They were just in time to see a small flash and hear the thud before the next big explosion in the camp behind them.

"Mortars," said Jamie. "They're firing over our heads at the camp."

"They must have landed very quietly in the dark," said Matthew. "Hell, they'll kill them! John! We've got to stop them. They won't know where Helen and William and Sion are, and they won't have any idea we're here, either. C'mon, let's go!"

"I go," said John. "You boys wait here."

"Oh, no. No more waiting for me," said Matthew. "I'm coming too. If the army see me they'll believe we're here. And anyway, it's best to stick in pairs if we do split up, so that one of us can go back to warn the others if there's trouble."

"O.K." said John. "Into Blue Banana. Jamie and Nicholas, you wait here till we get back." Nicholas had woken up.

"What's going on?" he asked.

"Jamie'll tell you. We're off," said Matthew.

"Good luck!" shouted Jamie, as he helped push the boat out. He heard the engine start and they were gone. Just then rifle fire broke out in the camp.

"See!" said Nicholas when Jamie had explained the new situation to him. "We're bound to need the tin boat now. Come on, let's get it working." There was no argument from Jamie this time. He was desperate to do something. He pushed the tin boat out, with Nicholas on board, until he was wading up to his waist. He held it steady by the bows, with the stern pointing out into the lake to give Nicholas enough water to start the engine. Nicholas fiddled around briefly, Jamie watching his silhouette against the rising moon, before he made his first attempt to pull the starter chord. Nothing happened. He tried unsuccessfully a dozen times,

THE TIN BOAT

occasionally pumping fuel or adjusting the choke. At last he came forward to Jamie.

"You have a go," he said. "It's trying but I'm just not strong enough. It needs just a little bit quicker pull."

"Is there a paddle in there?" Jamie asked.

"Yes," said Nicholas.

"O.K., let's both get in and paddle into deeper water." And so they did. Jamie had the engine started in a couple of pulls. He put it into forward gear and the boat lurched forward so violently that they both fell into the bottom.

"Steady, Jamie, honestly!" Nicholas squealed. "It's a huge engine for this boat. We've got to go slowly." Jamie restored the engine to neutral.

"O.K., it works then," he said. "We'd better get back in case the others come." They switched off the engine and paddled back to the shore. Flames and smoke were being driven across the water from the bar. More rifle fire startled them. It seemed to be coming from rather closer this time.

"Oh, no! That came from the swimming pool," said Jamie, with a terrible foreboding of disaster. "Let's see if we can get any idea of what's going on." They climbed to the top of the little island once more, being careful to stay hidden in the trees. From there they could see the fire clearly, and in its light people running away from the camp past the swimming pool. Yet more rifle fire seemed to be coming from the southern point of the camp.

"The army must have landed there too," said Jamie.

"Look!" said Nicholas, pointing to the lake immediately below them. "Someone's in the water. He's swimming this way."

"Could be Sion," said Jamie. "Let's go down and see, but keep out of sight just in case." They clambered down and hid in the reeds until they saw Sion climb out of the water and were sure it was him. Then they called out to him.

"Quick," he shouted back. "Get John with the boat. Where have you been? They escape, but William, he is shot in the arm. He cannot go on. Helen, she stay with him. I come for help." He spoke breathlessly. By the time he had finished he had reached the two boys.

"Where?" said Jamie. "Where are they?" Sion pointed up the escarpment towards his cave.

"Up there. Not far," he said. "Wapi John?"

"They've gone," said Jamie. "He and Matthew went to stop the army shelling you."

"Oh, no! We need the boat now!" wailed Sion.

"C'mon. The tin boat!" said Nicholas. They ran back over the top, scratching themselves in their haste, cursing but letting nothing stop then. Jamie took command.

"Right! I'll start the engine," he said breathlessly. "Nicholas, you drive. Sion, you sit up front. It should be steadier like that." They pushed the boat out. Mercifully it started with no problem. When Sion was settled in the bows and Jamie on the thwart Nicholas eased it into gear. It swayed around a bit but he soon brought it under control. As they came round the north end of Fig Tree Island they were aware of being all too visible in the light of the fire, and this made them nervous. They were even more worried when they saw the difficulties of taking the tin boat quickly in and out to the shore through the tangle of reeds. Yet if they didn't take the boat in close, they would be faced with trying to carry William through the water.

Nicholas drew the boat up alongside a dead tree which stuck out of the water at the edge of the reeds. He put the engine into neutral and Jamie made the bow painter fast to the tree.

"It'd be much better if you stayed out here, so you can keep the engine running," he said to Nicholas.

"But you'll never be able to carry William out here," Nicholas protested. "You'll have to swim yourselves. What we need is an ambach."

"Yeh," said Jamie. They both looked at Sion.

"Nataka ngadich?" he asked.

"Ndiyo," said Jamie.

"O.K. I find ngadich," said Sion confidently,

"But where? Is it near? We've not got much time."

"Very near. I fetch it," Sion promised.

"O.K. Great. Where are William and Helen?" Sion pointed up the escarpment straight above them. There was a fall of rocks which would provide a difficult but manageable assent.

"Right. I'll go up," said Jamie to Sion. "You get the ambach. Bring it here then come and help me. Nicholas, you keep the engine running. The tin boat must be READY TO GO!"

As he slipped over the side with Sion another burst of rifle fire told them that the battle was moving towards them, and that the danger to William and Helen was now very great.

CHAPTER 31

John and Matthew hadn't even reached the shore when they came under fire from the army, in fact from the very people they had come to talk to. John had been forced to swerve away, but Matthew shouted,

"No! Go on! We must stop them!" He stood up in the boat, thrusting both arms up in the air. John slowed the engine down and approached the shore once more. Suddenly the bright light of a torch was shining in their faces. A voice called out,

"Put up your hands! Up! And this other man! Up!" John cut out the engine and raised his hands too. "Now leave the boat and come here!" They climbed out, taking the chance to pull the boat onto the rocks far enough to stop it floating away. They were barely on dry land when John felt a rifle barrel in his ribs. "Now, who are you?"

"My name's Matthew, and my Dad owns the Pelican Camp," piped up Matthew. "My sister is up there. They are holding her as a hostage. If you keep firing those mortars you will kill her."

"Who is this man?"

"He is my friend. His name is John. He is a young mzee of the Njemps tribe and a boat driver for Pelican Camp." Matthew spelt out the facts slowly and deliberately, determined that what he said should sound convincing.

"O.K.," said the soldier with the torch. "You go and talk to the lieutenant. This soldier take you. This man stay here."

"Right. I'll be back," said Matthew as cheerfully as he could to John. He was led across the rocky shore onto some slightly higher ground. There he could make out a group of six or seven soldiers, as well as the mortar which was now silent. His escort saluted one of the men, pointing Matthew out to him and explaining who he was. The lieutenant greeted him pleasantly enough.

"So you want to save your sister?" he said.

"Of course I do," said Matthew angrily.

"Yes, of course. We would like this too. But we must also stop these people escaping. That is my orders."

"But my friend William, he's fourteen like my sister, he went up there to rescue her with a young Njemps boy who is also my friend. They might be on their way out right now. Please call a ceasefire just for a while until we know."

"I wish I could do what you ask," the lieutenant said in a sympathetic voice. "But you see how it is. We make initial bombardment from here. Now another force has landed at the camp jetty. They drive these rebels this way. More of my men are in position to cut off their escape."

Matthew could see that the engagement was now centred round the area just above the escarpment. The army must have already overrun the camp.

"They'll have got her by now if she hasn't escaped," he said. "As far as we know she was being held in the nearest of those buildings on top of the hill. We were hoping they'd come out just down here." He pointed down the beach south of where they had landed. "They still haven't arrived. Can't we try and find them? Please?"

"No," said the lieutenant. "You cannot go that way. When these rebels see that they are cut off they may come this way. We are ready for them. There will be more shooting here."

"Oh, no!" cried Matthew. "We've left two more wazungu children on the little island there. They might all be caught up in it. Please! There's going to be a terrible disaster."

"O.K. But this is against my orders," said the officer. Matthew almost fainted with relief. "We try moving up the beach towards the camp. We see if we can see them. You know this place well?"

"Absolutely," said Matthew. "So does John. We can both help you. Please stop that man pointing a gun at him. He's a friend. I promise."

"O.K.," said the lieutenant, and gave the necessary order. "Now come with me."

Nicholas wasn't going to hang around doing nothing. From the tin boat he had watched where Sion had left the ambach boat before going up the escarpment to help Jamie. It was in the very shallow water between the shore and the reeds. Nicholas was trying to work out the quickest way of getting the ambach through the narrow gap in the reeds when the time came.

The water-skiing rope, which had provided them all with so many hours of pleasure only a few days before, was still attached to the stern and coiled up underneath the thwart. It was too good an opportunity to miss. Although Jamie had told him that he was to stay with the boat, he decided to take his own initiative.

Leaving the boat tied to the tree with the engine idling, he took the handle end of the rope and swam through the reeds with it to the ambach. It was just long enough to make the distance. He knew that the frail bow of the little boat would be too weak to take the strain of the rope with any sort of load on board, so he threaded the handle between two of the logs low down on the waterline where the ambach wood was thicker. Even then he was not satisfied, and he wove the rope in and out between the logs until he was sure that the load was as evenly distributed as possible.

He swam back to the tin boat. Pulling himself aboard was far more difficult than he had imagined, with nobody to help him or counterbalance the boat. He nearly destroyed all their chances by tipping it over. Once again his technical ingenuity came to his rescue. He tied the bow hard up to the tree with no slack in the rope at all, and climbed in over the stern past the warm purring engine. 'Whew! I nearly mucked that up,' he thought, 'but now I'm ready for a quick getaway.'

Unfortunately while splashing around in the water he had been spotted from the top of the escarpment.

"Eh! I see a boat! Quick! Get the sergeant! Maybe we three get away!"

The voice coming suddenly from so close above her head made Helen jump out of her skin. William was still unconscious and she hadn't dared to try and move him since she had sent Sion for help. 'Now I've got no choice,' she thought. 'They'll come over the top any minute.'

She heaved William up into a sitting position, winding his good arm round her neck, and tried to raise him to his feet. It was no use. She hadn't much strength left and he was too heavy for her. She tried to drag him down backwards, her arms hooked under his shoulders. It was very slow going, but she felt that every foot of progress brought them further from their enemies and deeper into the shadows of the overhanging trees. She struggled on as far as she could, but she was soon exhausted. She slumped over William's body and began to cry.

"We've had it," she sobbed. "I can't go on."

Suddenly she heard Jamie's voice calling from not far below her.

"Helen! Where the hell are you?"

"Here! Right above you! Quick! They're coming down this

THE TIN BOAT

way."

"We're right with you!" said Jamie, and a moment later he appeared with Sion, puffing and blowing but very businesslike. He didn't waste time on greetings. "You take his shoulders, Sion," he said. "I'll get his feet."

"What shall I do?" queried Helen. Jamie could see that she was at the end of her tether.

"Go on down," he said. "This is easier with two. You'll see an ambach down there. Nicholas is waiting in the tin boat out behind the reeds opposite it. Try and swim out to him. It's not far. Leave the ambach for us to put William in."

"Where's Matthew, then?" asked Helen.

"He's O.K. He went with John Boat to stop the army firing mortars at you."

"Nice of him," quipped Helen.

"Go on! Quick! And make sure Nicholas doesn't try any clever tricks." They had already started moving William slowly down the rock fall as Jamie spoke. It was extremely difficult for them to keep their footing under his weight.

"Watch your backs! They're not far behind you," Helen warned them as she left.

They were only half way down the rocks by the time Helen was scampering across the beach in the moonlight below them.

"There! It is the girl!" came a shout from above them. "She's going to take the boat. Shoot, or we'll lose it!" A shot rang out but she kept going.

Moving round the shore in the direction of the camp, Matthew and John and their new found army friends heard the shot.

"What they shooting?" said the lieutenant.

"It might be them. God! If only the moon was a bit higher we could see!" said Matthew. Looking over his shoulder the lieutenant shouted,

"FLARE! That way!" The firework shot into the sky with a trail of smoke. Soon the whole bay and escarpment were flooded with light. Now, if only for a moment, they could see the whole situation - the tin boat out beyond the reeds, and Nicholas trying with all his strength to help Helen aboard - Jamie and Sion struggling down the rock face under the weight of William's body, and three men armed with rifles coming over the top of the escarpment above them.

"Oh, no!" gasped Matthew. "William's wounded or dead or something. I'm going to help."

John grabbed him as he tried to make a run for it, for he would almost certainly have been caught in the crossfire. For now the attention of the soldiers was concentrated on the three rebels. There could be no doubt that the shot had come from them. The soldiers returned fire briefly, and before the flare died they saw the rebels' heads go down.

"Good! Keep up sporadic firing at that target," ordered the lieutenant. "Try to keep them pinned down. Two men go inland. Take them from the rear. But all of you. Watch out for our friends. Don't aim low!"

'God! I hope those guys know what they're doing,' thought Matthew.

It may have been the sound of the shots or the light of the flare, but something brought William briefly back to consciousness, to the enormous relief of Jamie and Sion. It was almost impossible terrain to move around on carrying somebody heavier than either of them.

"He's coming round," said Jamie. "C'mon now, William. Try and help us, just over this little bit."

William groaned. He managed to stand with one of them on either side supporting him. He shrieked when Jamie tried to hold him by his bad arm, and nearly passed out again with the pain, but the shots from the army down to their left startled him back to life again. He forced his legs to work enough to help them shift him down from rock to rock until they were on the level shore, where faintness overtook him once more. Jamie and Sion found themselves temporarily blinded once the light of the flare had died, so they were forced to pause until their eyes became accustomed to the dim light again. There was enough moonlight to see by, though the glow from the fire in the bar had subsided. It must have almost burnt itself out.

As they dragged William across the beach they could hear their pursuers coming swiftly down the rocks behind them. From time to time shots rang out from the army, the bullets whistling off the rocks way above them.

Jamie felt that he was in the last stages of exhaustion. Sweat was pouring from every part of his body, and his mouth was so dry that he couldn't swallow. Every muscle was crying out in agony, but above all it was his feet which were taking the brunt of the ordeal. He only worried about his pursuers when he could actually see or hear them. The unevenness of the ground, the stubbing of toes and twisting of ankles were a far greater enemy, although he was fully aware that the rebels were gaining on them. He wondered if Sion was as near collapse as he was.

"Nzuri, Sion?" he croaked.

"Nzuri tu, ndiyo. Na choka kabisa."

'Yes,' thought Jamie, 'choka kabisa is right. Worn out.'

"Nearly there. Keep going," he gasped.

"Those men. They nearly here too," said Sion.

"Try not to think about them," said Jamie. "Just push on."

"Sah! Those rebels, sah. I think they going down the rocks after the wazungu children. I scared we hit the totos, sah. I cannot see them now, sah," one of the soldiers reported to the lieutenant.

"O.K. One more flare!" the lieutenant ordered. By the time the second flare went up Jamie and Sion had reached the ambach.

"What the hell has Nicholas done here?" croaked Jamie.

"You're attached to the tin boat," Nicholas shouted to them. "Get William into the ambach and we'll help pull."

'Typical Nicholas!' thought Jamie. 'Still, fair enough.' He scooped up a quick handfull of water to drink before they heaved William onto the little craft. It was wonderful to be relieved of the weight.

The whole beach was suddenly flooded with light again. Looking back they could see that the three rebels had reached the shore. The army must have seen them too, because there was a tremendous burst of gunfire which made it impossible for Nicholas to hear what Jamie was saying.

"Bloody hell!" screamed Jamie. "Quick, Sion! Swim and get into the boat. Tell Nicholas to start pulling. I'll guide it through the reeds." Sion obeyed.

The flare hung in the sky. Jamie swung round once more to see the rebels half way across the beach. They were almost upon him. More shots were fired. One of the men fell, but the others didn't pause for a moment to help him.

"Get him! Grab him!" one of them bellowed. "We must have that boat." Jamie pushed the ambach from behind and started to swim, but he was too exhausted and he had the nightmarish feeling of not moving forward at all. Already the men were splashing into the water behind him.

"PULL!" he screamed. At last he felt a tug and started to be dragged forward. He clung to the stern of the ambach with both hands and tried to guide it between the reeds, but it was all happening too slowly. The men were almost on top of him. He knew the army wouldn't dare shoot now.

He felt a hand touch his ankle. He kicked violently and pulled himself up so that his chest was over the stern of the ambach, resting on William's feet. Gripping the sides of the little boat as hard as he could he yelled,

"GO! GO! GO!"

Nicholas understood. Helen had already untied the bow. He slammed the motor into gear and revved up. The ambach lurched forward and sped out through the reeds, towed by the boat. Jamie held on like grim death, using his feet as rudders. He didn't dare look behind him. If he had he would have seen the rebels take up their rifles and aim them at him. By this time though the flare had died, and they too were temporarily blinded. They had no idea where they were shooting.

Once out past the reeds Jamie could forget about steering. He hung on until they were beyond Fig Tree Island, where his strength

THE TIN BOAT

finally gave out.

"Help! I'm going!" he called out, and let go.

"It's O.K. We're safe now," said Helen. Nicholas slowed the engine right down and turned in as tight a circle as he dared, while Sion and Helen pulled in the ambach. They had churned up the water so much that they couldn't see Jamie straight away.

"Where are you?" shouted Nicholas.

"I'm over here."

"Keep shouting then!" In that way they homed in on him until they saw his head bobbing up and down in the moonlight. By that time they had brought the ambach alongside the boat. They eased up close to Jamie and hauled him aboard.

"You guys are incredible," said Helen. "I never saw such an effort as that in my life."

Jamie lay in the boat with his head over the side, gasping and spluttering and feeling that he might be sick. The others were helping William on board. They were delighted to find that the spray had once again revived him, so that he wasn't a completely dead weight to lift into the boat.

"Ugh! Thank God that's over," gasped Jamie. "Brilliant driving, Nicholas, but I reckon let's go slowly now." At last they were all able to laugh.

Matthew hadn't dared watch after the second flare went up and he could see how great was the danger to his friends. He crouched down behind John until it was all over. At last he felt John's hand on his shoulder. He looked up to see John's face bending over him.

"Tell me, John. Are they O.K.?" he whispered.

"I think so. Ndiyo. Yote nzuri," said John. The lieutenant, who had been standing on higher ground, was much more positive. He came over to them.

"Good! Good! They have done well, your rafikis," he said with a smile. "Now, young Bwana Matthew and your friend John, back to your boat. We close in now. Maybe minge shooting. Stay out on the water until it is over. I think you have had enough war."

"Asante sana," said. Matthew. "You have saved their lives. C'mon John, we've got to see if William's O.K."

They ran back along the shore and hurriedly launched Blue Banana. They passed behind Fig Tree Island to keep away from the shooting. Already the battle had flared up again behind them. As they passed the south end of the little island they could see the embers of the bar roof which were reflected brightly in the water of the lake. Silhouetted against the reflection was the shape of the tin boat. Matthew instantly picked out Helen, whom he had thought he might never see again, and his eyes were filled with tears of joy.

"Hey! Kill the engine, John!" he said, choking with emotion. John slowed it right down but kept it ticking over. At the same time a third flare burst into light above them.

"HI! HELEN! ALL YOU GUYS! WE'RE HERE!" Matthew shouted. A great cheer went up from the children in the tin boat. Arms were waved in the air and Helen almost tipped the boat over by trying to stand up. "WE'RE COMING ALONGSIDE!" he shouted.

"William? You O.K., man?" asked Matthew. He was greatly relieved to see William trying to sit up, though he looked pretty weak. "Is he all right?"

"He was hit in the arm," said Helen. "He's lost quite a bit of blood, but I think he'll be O.K. I wish there was enough light to see properly. Perhaps we can go ashore to the camp now."

"No. That army guy asked us not to until the shooting stops."

"Fair enough," said Helen. "Will you be O.K., William?"

"Yes, I think so," said William.

"I'm sure it's just a flesh wound," Helen went on. "He can move his fingers and so on."

"Stupid, isn't it?" said William. "I don't know why I conked out like that."

"Probably shock, and loss of blood," said Helen.

"Still, no excuse for leaving you to struggle with me like that. You must have thought me pretty pathetic."

"Do you really think that?" she said with the sweetest of smiles.

THE TIN BOAT

All the children slept through the dark hours before the dawn. The wind had dropped and the water lapped idly against the sides of the two boats. Only John stayed awake, sitting in the stern of Blue Banana watching over them. Helen had fallen asleep after changing the blood-soaked dressing on William's arm. She lay with her head on his shoulder in the tin boat. Matthew had made himself comfortable in the bows of Blue Banana, and Jamie lay next to him with his head on the thwart. Nicholas lay curled up in the arms of Sion, who had rocked him to sleep.

Only the occasional shot could be heard from somewhere in the central hills of the island. John had thought of taking the children ashore, but seeing that they were all asleep he decided to let them be. The two boats were lashed together. He had turned off the engines, and in the total calm which had descended on the lake he was able to hold their position with the occasional stroke of the paddle.

'Sleep on, watoto, my fine children. One day you will be like other wazungu, all business and worries, and will you still be my friends then?' His thoughts turned to his new young wife, and how tomorrow he would be with her again. 'Give me children,' he thought, 'children to love like these.'

CHAPTER 32

They were greeted at the main Pelican Camp jetty that morning by no less a personage than the general himself.

"Well, well! I am so very glad to see you safe," he said as they stepped ashore, and he shook each one of them by the hand. "You have caused me much worry."

"Is the war over?" asked Matthew seriously. The general laughed.

"Certainly for you the war is over," he said, "and I think soon for my men too. There is very little resistance now. Your lovely Pelican Camp, I am afraid it has suffered great damage. I was once here as a guest, many years ago. I hope one day it will be as it was."

"I hope so too," said Helen, "but let's not think about that now. Where's Dad? Is he here? And these boys' parents. Can we see them?"

"I'm afraid they are not here yet," said the general. "You must understand you have been caught up in quite a battle here. Your families are safe, I promise you. They are in Marigat now, not far away, and as soon as I have allowed the roadblocks to be cleared, they will be brought here."

"How soon will that be?" asked Jamie.

"Oh, not long," he assured them. "You see your families by the end of the day."

"Well, that's great," said Helen, "only they'll be worried stiff about us."

"Ah!" said the general. "That you yourselves can remedy. They are at the police station which is my headquarters. I have installed a radio in the office here. Come with me. We will make contact with Marigat. You can speak to them. That will make them happy."

"Here that, Nicholas?" said Jamie. "We can talk to Mum and Dad on their radio." Nicholas didn't show the sort of enthusiasm which might have been expected. His eyes were glazed. He was clearly suffering from some sort of reaction to the extraordinary experiences he had been through. He took John's hand.

"Will you come with me?" he said.

"Yes, Nicholas. I come. I come," said John. The general was looking at William's damaged arm. Helen had found a bandage in the first-aid box in Blue Banana, which was at least cleaner than the strips of kikoi which she had originally used as dressings.

"You show this to my medical officer," he said. "We have dawas and field dressings. He should look at that other boy's head too. Now, let us go up to the office."

"Hello! Dad! Yes, it's me! Over..., Yes, no I'm fine, really I am. Over..,. No, he's here too. He's fine. Well, bit of a cut on the head which they've had a look at. Nothing serious. Over.... Yes, they're all right here. Over.... No, no, we're at Pelican Camp. Over.. Not good, Dad. Listen, I can't tell you all about it now. William's wounded. Not bad, luckily, but he got a bullet in his arm. Over.... Well, he'll probably have to. The M.O.'s dealing with it right now. Over.... No, really it's nasty but it's not too serious. You owe him your daughter's life, you know.... What?.... Yes, Dad, I promise you I'm O.K. Listen, see you tonight. Over.... Matthew, put these things on and speak to Dad."

"Dad, hi.... what.... I'm fine....How d'you work this thing.... Hello...."

275

THE TIN BOAT

William was listening to all this while the medical officer was dressing his wound. If the process of cleaning out the wound was painful, it was easier to bear than the hurt of being the only one with no parents around to celebrate his survival. Of course he would have a chance to speak to Sue or Pam, but it wasn't the same. Even Helen's father had obviously been more interested in his daughter's welfare than in the fact, which she had tried to tell him, that it had been he who had saved her.

Matthew was finishing his conversation with his father.

".... Yes. Over.... Yes, too right. Some fishing trip, eh? Over.... No, Dad. Sorry. No fish. Over.... What? Who? Over.... Sue. Oh. yeh. Jamie, your Mum's on. Come and talk to her."

"Ow!" said William as the M.O. disinfected the deepest part of the wound.

"Is it paining?" asked the Asian M.O.

"S'O.K.," said William bravely.

"Well, I have altogether finished cleaning it now. I will dress it for you, then you must keep it clean and you will be absolutely fine. Take it easy, though. After a shock like this you must not be all the time running around. I will give you some more dressing for today. Tomorrow perhaps you should show it to a doctor once more, but for the moment I expect your girlfriend can look after it. She seems to have done a good job in the circumstances."

"Who? Oh, you mean Helen. Yes, I think she knows what she's doing," William agreed. The M.O. applied the bandage as they talked. The wound was stinging a bit but not throbbing as it had been, and once it was firmly supported by the bandage and his arm was tied up in a sling it felt much more comfortable.

"Nicholas, come and talk to Mum," Jamie called out. Nicholas was sitting with John and Sion on the steps down to the garden. He seemed to be uninterested in speaking to his parents on the radio.

"Kuja," said John, taking him by the hand over to the radio. "Your Mummy will want to hear your voice."

"Stay with me, though," said Nicholas anxiously, as Jamie helped him put on the headset.

"Press this when you want to speak, and let it go when you're listening," he explained.

"Yes, yes, I know," said Nicholas. "Hello," he started in his high-pitched telephone voice. "It's Nicholas.... O.K. Over.... Yes, yes,... Do you want to talk to William? Over.... Yes, he's here. Over.... No, it's got a bandage on. Over.... Hang on. Where's William? He's gone off somewhere. Over.... Yes. O.K. This evening." He took off the headphones and laid them on the table, and took John once more by the hand.

"Have they gone?" asked Jamie. "I'm sure William would have liked to speak to them."

"Mum said they'd see us all this evening," said Nicholas.

"You could have got them to hang on while we found him," said Jamie, but Nicholas paid no attention. "He's in a strange mood, my brother," he said to Helen. "He's totally switched off and he won't leave John's side for a moment. I'm a bit bothered about him."

"Yeh, I've been watching him too," said Helen. "You know he's very little and I think it's only just hit him that what we were all caught up in was for real, and that it could all have gone terribly wrong. He was incredible with that boat last night, but I'm not sure he saw it as much more than a game. Now the whole thing has come home to him with a bang and knocked him for six. John seems to be his lifeline. I don't think a voice on a crackly radio is enough for him to cling to, even your Mum's. Do you see what I'm getting at? I wouldn't worry. He'll be fine once they all arrive back tonight."

"Yes, I think I see what you mean," said Jamie. "Gosh, we'd all have been in a hell of a mess without John, and Sion too, wouldn't we?"

"Too right," said Helen. "But listen, I think we must let them go back to their families now. They'll be just as anxious as our families were. Stay close to Nicholas. He'll need you when they go." The general came to join them.

"We still have unfinished business in the north," he explained. "I could offer to have you taken to the mainland, but I think you would be safer here for today. Are you able too look after yourselves till this evening? I will leave some rations for you, so you will not be hungry."

"Thanks," said Helen. "Thanks for everything. Don't worry about us. We'll be fine."

"Kwaheri then, and good luck. You are brave children. Your families will be proud of you. Your two friends from the Njemps people, they too have brought much honour to their tribe."

"I know. We have everything to thank them for. Kwaheri," said Helen, and Matthew and Jamie too bid the general farewell.

"Anyone know where William went?" asked Helen, but they all shrugged their shoulders.

"No idea," said Jamie.

"I'll go and have a look for him," she said.

She found him rummaging around in the deep freezes in the food store.

"What on earth are you doing?" she asked. "We needn't worry about all that now. They've left some rations for us."

"I was just seeing what was left," said William. "All the fresh and tinned stuff's gone of course, and look at the mess they've made. But they haven't touched the stuff in the freezes. Probably thought it was useless to them like this. I've had to chuck some of it, but if we got the generator going we could save a lot of it."

"You're an extraordinary guy," she said affectionately. "We'll get John to help us with the generator before he goes. Come on. Come and join the others. Leave that now." William seemed reluctant to move.

"Oh, William, you're not feeling left out again are you?" she said, penetrating to the very heart of his feelings, but in such a sympathetic way that he could not possibly resent her. "I know what it must feel like, being the only one with no parents here to greet you. Well, I'm not going to let you be left out." She took his hand in both of hers and squeezed it gently. "You're the hero of the hour. Well much more than that. What you did was wonderful. I owe you my life. I've just told Dad that. Come on now, we must let John and Sion go home. We'll get the generator started, and then we'll go down to the jetty to see them off."

She helped him repack the deep freezes. Then she took him by the hand and led him back to join the others at the house.

"John, I promise, we're fine," Helen insisted as they stood on the jetty to say goodbye to him and Sion. "The army's left food for us and William's discovered all that stuff in the freeze. We'll give the house a bit of a clean and it'll be quite usable. Go to your family. They will want to see you safe and well. Take Blue Banana. The dear old tin boat will be all we need. We won't be going on any fishing trips today, I don't think."

"O.K. I go now," said John. "You come and find me if you need help. Sion, you coming?"

"Couldn't Sion stay with us?" asked Nicholas. He looked very miserable at the idea of their little group splitting up.

"Sion's family will want to see him too," said Helen, "but he'll come back soon, won't you Sion?" Sion nodded. He probably wouldn't have taken much persuading to stay, but they all knew it was right that he should go. He went round sadly saying kwaheri to each of them.

"Wish you could come to England one day, so we could show you our home," Jamie said to him. Sion's eyes lit up.

"That's a brilliant idea," said Helen. "I'm sure our families would get together to pay your fare. You've deserved all that and more. Would you like that, Sion?" Their young Njemps friend was speechless with excitement. "We'll work on it then."

"I owe you money," John said to Matthew.

"Oh, rubbish, man! What on earth for?" said Matthew.

"What's all this about?" Helen broke in.

"Money for my bride price. Matthew lend it to me. I not forget, but now, no Pelican Camp. No wages."

"You never told me about this," said Helen to her brother. He looked rather embarrassed.

"That was when John found the tin boat for us," he explained.

"Anyway, you owe me nothing. It is all of us who owe you. Perhaps, though, you could help us sometime by thinking of a good way of saying thank you to Lemeriai and his family. You are all very kind people."

After that John embraced each one of them, last of all Nicholas, who clung to him and wouldn't let him go.

"I'm coming with you," he said. "I've got to come with you."

"Oh, Nicholas!" said John with his wonderful smile. "Your Mummy and Daddy come today. Not long to wait. You stay now. I come and see you. I promise. Very soon."

"Come on," said Jamie. "Let John go now. He is very tired, and his wife and his mother are waiting for him."

So John and Sion departed across the lake. The children stood silently on the jetty and watched the boat until it vanished beyond Teddy Bear Island. The noise of the engine could be heard no more. The still air was filled instead with the call of the fish eagles, the piping of the kingfishers, and the busy chattering of the weaver birds. The sound of gunfire in that peaceful place seemed so remote a possibility as to be unimaginable.

"I wonder if those bastards have left me any olives," said Matthew.

The kitchen was a shambles, and anyway all the gas had been used up, so they lit a fire on the beach in the shade of a tree and made some sort of a meal out of the rations they had been given. They were all too tired to be hungry, and most of the food ended up on the bird table, where it was pounced on hungrily by the weavers.

"The only satisfied customers we'll have around here for a while," said Matthew gloomily. "Let's go round and see how bad the damage is."

It was a depressing little trip. The bar was completely destroyed, though miraculously the other thatched buildings had escaped the fire. However several of the tents to the east of the bar had been burnt, probably because the sparks had been blown that way. The mess was appalling. There were broken glasses and bottles

THE TIN BOAT

everywhere.

Wandering up towards the swimming pool area they found a crater beside the path made by one of the mortar shells. Helen squeezed William's hand.

"I don't want to go back up there yet," she said. "It sounds silly but I can't face it."

"Don't blame you," said William. "C'mon, let's go back to the house."

"Yeh, siesta time, I reckon," agreed Matthew.

William woke at about four because his arm was in pain. He found Helen wandering around looking rather miserable.

"What is it?" he said. "Can't sleep?"

"Oh, I did for a while, but I had such nightmares." She clung to him and said, "I was so frightened."

"Do you want to talk about it?" He wondered how best to help her.

"One day I'll tell you all about it, but not now," she said. "For the moment I just want to forget it, though I'll never forget what you and the others did."

They were standing in the burnt out bar, looking up through the few remaining charred timbers at the sky.

"Will it ever be the same again, d'you reckon?" he asked her.

"My Dad and his partners built it all from scratch in the first place," said Helen. "I'm sure it can be done again if he wants to do it. Oh, let's leave this miserable sight. I can't bear to look at it. Let's take the tin boat out to the raft."

"It's possible my Dad won't want to go on with the Camp after what's happened," Helen speculated, as they sat together on the raft, with the tin boat tied to the ladder beside them, watching the sky loose its glare and the colours become richer and clearer. "He may think people won't want to come any more."

"Why on earth shouldn't they?" asked William.

"Oh, you know. Tourists are easily scared off by a bit of bad publicity in their papers back home. They'll think it's all too dangerous."

"And you?"

"Me what?"

"Do you think it's all too dangerous after what you've been through?"

Low over the water two pelicans flew from north to south, using the minimum of effort and gliding with the occasional beat of their wings. Further on a line of white-faced tree ducks were heading with more rapid wing beats in the same direction. There was no wind, and the only clouds were piled over the hills way beyond the western shore of the lake.

"It's my home," said Helen. "Look at it. Would you want to leave it, even after a thing like this?"

"No I wouldn't, and I don't," said William.

"It's agony, isn't it, thinking that this might be the end of it. Perhaps it's easier never to have had a taste of anything as wonderful as this, easier than knowing it's here and having to say goodbye to it."

"Easier," said William, "but not better. Do you think I'd prefer never to have seen and enjoyed all this, even if I know I've got to go back to my dreary life at home. No, no. Live for the moment. I've learnt that much out here. You've taught me that. So have these Njemps people. They understand that." He looked her in the eye. "But as your brother might say, it's going to be hard to say kwaheri, man!"

"They're coming! They're coming!" shouted the three boys across the water as they ran down the path towards the jetty.

"Look! We can see the boat!"

"Can you see it?" asked Helen, standing up beside William.

"Yeh, there it is, just passing Teddy Bear. Looks like Krumas."

"Hey! Helen! Can't we take the tin boat and go and meet them?" called Matthew from the jetty. William looked at Helen.

"What d'you reckon? Good idea?" he asked.

"Yeh, great. Let's go!" she said enthusiastically. They jumped

THE TIN BOAT

into the boat and went back to collect the boys. Everybody agreed that Helen should drive, but they pleaded with her not to go flat out because they were still using the big engine.

They were no more than a hundred metres from Krumas, and everybody in both boats had started cheering and waving, when the big engine spluttered and died.

"Oh, no!" groaned all the children. Helen tried to restart it, and so did Jamie, but it was no use.

"Fuel?" suggested Nicholas. "I bet we're out of fuel." He took the cap off the red fuel tank and looked inside. "Not a drop," he declared.

"I don't believe it," said Helen. "Where are the paddles?"

"We didn't bring any paddles," said Jamie.

Matthew took off his shirt and waved it in the air, and shouted.

"HELP! RESCUE! THE TIN BOAT'S OUT OF PETROL! RESCUE! RESCUE!"

THE END

SWAHILI GLOSSARY

akili	*intelligence*
asante	*thank you*
askari	*guard, night watchman*
boma	*kraal*
bure	*broken*
bwana	*sir, boss*
choka	*exhausted*
chunga	*take care of*
hakuna	*no, none*
hapa	*here*
hapana	*no, not*
jambo	*hello*
kabisa	*completely*
kidogo	*small*
kijana	*youth*
kikoi	*wrap-around cloth*
kuja	*come*
dawa	*medicine*
duka	*shop*
fundi	*expert*
kwaheri	*goodbye*
kwenda	*go*
maji	*water*
mamba	*crocodile*
mbaya	*bad*
meli	*boat*
memsahib	*madam, boss*
mimi	*I, me*
mneno	*row, disturbance*
moran	*young warrior*
mtoto	*child*
mzee	*old man, chief*
mzungu	*white person*
nataka	*want, need*

ndiyo	*yes*
ngini	*more, again, another*
panga	*large cutting tool*
posho	*maize meal*
rafiki	*friend*
samaki	*fish*
sana	*very*
sasa	*now*
shuka	*cloak*
suferia	*cooking pot*
tayari	*ready*
toto	*child*
Uhuru	*Kenyan Independence*
wageni	*guests*
wapi	*where*
wazee	*old men, chiefs*
wazungu	*white people*

SWAHILI PHRASES

Ch 1	p 2	Jambo, John. Habari Yaku?
		Hello, John. How are you?
Ch 1	p 4	Eh! Askari! Kuja!
		Eh! Nightwatchman! Come!
Ch 1	p 7	Hapa pesa yaku
		Here's your pay
Ch 2	p 12	Wapi driver ya meli ya Pelican Camp?
		Where's the boat driver for Pelican Camp?
		Wapi mutu ya Pelican Camp?
		Where's the man from Pelican Camp?
		Ndyio. Iku hapa.
		Yes. He's here.
Ch 2	p 13	Habari yaku? Habari Yote?
		How are you? How are you all?
		Wewe kbwa sasa!
		He's big now!
Ch 2	p 13	Huyu kijana naitwa William.
		This young man is William.
Ch 3	p 17	Mbaya sana
		Very bad
Ch 4	p 22	Pole, pole kidogo
		A bit slower
Ch 4	p 23	Chunga howa sana
		watch this carefully
Ch 4	p 24	Ngoja hapa kidogo
		Wait here for a little while
Ch 5	p 31	Nataka nini?
		What do you want?
Ch 5	p 32	Wengi wageni
		Many guests
Ch 5	p 33	wengi samaki
		many fish
Ch 8	p 58	Helen nakuja. Nzuri.
		Helen's come. That's good.

		Helen yupo hapa
		Helen is here
Ch 9	p 63	Wengi ngombe
		Many cows
Ch 9	p 64	pande ile
		that way
		Kwaheru yote. Asante sana.
		Goodbye everybody. Thank you very much.
Ch 9	p 68	Moja! Mbili! Moja! Mbili!
		One! Two! One! Two!
		Moja! Mbili! Tatu! Nne!
		One! Two! Three! Four!
Ch 9	p 70	John na sema asante sana. Yeye na sema hapana ngoja. Yeye hapana kuja sasa
		John says many thanks. He says don't wait. He cannot come now.
Ch 9	p 72	Mtu moja na kwenda,
		Na kwenda lima shamba.
		Mutu moja na mbwa yake
		Na kwenda lima shamba.
		Watu wawili na kwenda
		Na kwenda lima shamba.
		Watu wawili
		Mutu moja na mbwa yake
		Na kwenda lima shamba.
		One man went to mow
		Went to mow a meadow.
		One man and his dog
		Went to mow a meadow.
		Two men went to mow
		Went to mow a meadow
		Two men, one man and his dog
		Went to mow a meadow.
Ch 11	p 85	Wanwakuja sasa
		They are coming now

Ch 15	p 115	Hapana nzuri	
		not good	
Ch 15	p 116	choka kabisa	
		absolutely exhausted	
Ch 16	p 120	Mneno nakwisha	
		The trouble is over	
Ch 16	p 127	JOHN! KUJA! WATU YA MELI YOTE! KUJA! HARAKA! HARAKA!	
		JOHN! COME! ALL BOAT DRIVERS! COME! HURRY! HURRY!	
Ch 17	p140	Mimi na kuja	
		I'm coming	
Ch 18	p143	Wapi Helen? Helem iku hapa. Watoto wote wapo hapa. Nzuri sana, Neecola.	
		Where's Helen? Helen is here. All the children are here. Everything's fine, Nicholas.	
Ch 18	p 146	Ye nakuja! John nakuja!	
		He's come! John's come!	
Ch 18	p 147	Iku mneno mgubwa sana.	
		There's big trouble	
Ch 18	p 148	Nataka chukula?	
		Would you like some food?	
Ch 18	p 149	Kwaheri, Neecolas. Lala salama	
		Good night Nicholas. Sleep well.	
Ch 20	p 165	Iku generator hapa	
		Here's the generator	
Ch 21	p 174	Chukula tayari! Kuja hapa yote!	
		The meal is ready! Come here everyone.	
Ch 22	p 184	Chunga sana!	
		Watch out!	
Ch 22	p 187	Saidia mimi!	
		Help me!	
		Mimi Nakuja!	
		I'm coming!	
Ch 23	p 194	Kwenda! Sasa!	
		Come! Now!	

Ch 24 p 200 Wapi rafiki yaku?
              Where are your friends?
              Ambia mimi!
              Speak to me!
Ch 24 p 203 Wapi kijana mzungu William.
              Where's the white boy William?
Ch 25 p 209 Nataka maji
              We need water
Ch 26 p 216 Yeye na wesa wakisha taa
              She knows how to work it
Ch 26 p 217 SIYO MNENO!
              NO TROUBLE!
Ch 26 p 218 Bure kabisa
              Completely useless
Ch 27 p 231 Ngoja! Nataka meli ngini.
              Wait! We need another boat.
Ch 28 p 246 akili mingi
              plenty of brains
Ch 28 p 247 bure kabisa
              completely useless
              Nakwenda wapi?
              Where are you going?
Ch 29 p 252 HaramBEE! HaramBEE!
              Heave! Heave!
Ch 31 p 269 Nzuri tu, ndio. Na choka kabisa
              I'm OK, yes, but I'm totally exhausted

Acknowledgements

I am grateful to Gillian Littlewood and Ruth Fison, without whom I would never have had the chance to experience the life of Lake Baringo. They also helped me with my very limited Swahili. I also have to thank the Leakey family, Jonny, Julia and Nigel, who provided the opportunities at Baringo for myself and my family out of which so much of the novel grew. I'd also like to thank my sons Jamie and Nicholas, as well as Paul Mitchell, whose adventures gave me the idea for this novel. My sons have also been very helpful as readers and critics. My wife Caroline has been a huge support since I decided to dig out my old manuscript and rewrite something which grew out of a previous life before I met her. She has given me invaluable advice as a reader from the perspective of somebody who doesn't know Baringo.

Printed in Great Britain
by Amazon.co.uk, Ltd.,
Marston Gate.